I0684681

John Boncoddo was hanging by his neck from the fire sprinkler mounted over the bed. He wasn't very tall and his feet didn't reach the mattress. His arms hung limply at his sides. He looked skinnier than I remembered, but we all become somewhat diminished when we die. And he was very much dead. I used the little penlight on my keychain and shined it into his face. His eyes were open and unblinking. The light wasn't strong enough for me to tell if he was showing the discoloration of asphyxia, but I didn't think he'd died by hanging. The hilt of some sort of edged weapon protruding from his chest seemed a far likelier explanation, although I couldn't for the life of me imagine why the killer would have hanged him afterward.

MANAGANSETT PRESS

Don D'Ammassa is the author of:

Horror
Blood Beast
Servant of Chaos*
Caverns of Chaos*
Wings over Manhattan
The Gargoyle
That Way Madness Lies*
Little Evils*
Passing Death*
Date with the Dark*
The Devil Is in the Details*
Living Things*
Shadows Over R'Lyeh*

Science Fiction
Scarab*
Haven*
Narcissus*
Translation Station
The Sinking Island*
Alien & Otherwise*
Wormdance*
Sandcastles*
Carbon Copies*

Mysteries
Murder in Silverplate*
Dead of Winter*
Death at the Art Gallery*
Death on the Mountain*
Death on Black Island*

Fantasy
The Kaleidoscope*
Elaborate Lies*
The Maltese Gargoyle*
Perilous Pursuits*
Multiplicity*

Nonfiction
The Encyclopedia of Science
Fiction
The Encyclopedia of Fantasy and
Horror
The Encyclopedia of Adventure
Fiction
Masters of Detection Vol I*
Masters of Detection Vol II*
Masters of Detection Vol III*
Architects of Tomorrow Vol I*

*published by Managansett Press

DEATH IN BLACK AND WHITE

Don D'Ammassa

This book is a work of fiction. Names, places, and events are not based on real people or places. Any resemblance is purely coincidental.

Copyright ©2015 by Don D'Ammassa. All rights reserved. If you would like to use material from this book other than brief excerpts for review purposes, prior written permission must be received by contacting the author at dondammassa@cox.net.

Managansett Press Edition 2015

DEATH IN BLACK AND WHITE

CHAPTER ONE

I finished stacking the last of a dozen large cardboard cartons in one corner of the attic and watched as Dusty swept up the remnants of her model of the Fukushima nuclear plant and its surroundings. Whenever Dusty was working on a book, she fashioned some sort of physical model to help her visualize what was taking place. Her editor had been quite happy with the latest spy novel and Dusty was in that unsettling period between projects when she often felt guilty about not having a book underway. Although she and her father had been at odds since her early teens, she had absorbed many of his Calvinist attitudes about idle hands. I, on the other hand, was much more inclined toward a sedentary and unproductive life style. No, that's not quite true. I could probably have sold Birch Investigations to one of my competitors for enough to live in reasonable comfort without working another day in my life, but I'd be bored within weeks.

"So much for Japan. What's next? How about a story in which two young children are kept prisoner in an unfurnished attic?" I spread my arms to indicate our surrounding. "All you'd need would be a couple of dolls to represent the characters."

"It's been done." We'd gone through this routine more than once in the past, so I suppose it had become a tradition.

"I thought you said everything had already been done."

"There are degrees of done." She emptied the dust pan into a trash bag. "I don't know what I want to do next. Maybe a children's book. Maybe a detective story. Maybe a romance novel or even a western."

"I've lost any lingering fondness I might have had for murder mysteries." Someone had killed one of my employees two months earlier, and Dusty and I had both been shot at in the aftermath. "A romantic comedy is more my style. And the public really likes fluff in its reading material. You could produce a real tear jerker and I'll invest in tissue manufacturers. We'll make a fortune."

"You have the heart of an accountant."

"And the investment portfolio of one as well. Don't mock the not quite rich guy."

Dusty tied off the trash bag and handed it to me. "Maybe a horror novel. How do you feel about having bats in our belfry?"

"'As long as I'm the only one who gets to bite your neck."

"No vampires though. I know they're popular but they've become just another cliché."

"How about erotica? A passionate novel about the love affair between a succubus and a zombie?"

"The research might be fun." She kissed me.

We might have made some preliminary notes that afternoon, but the phone started to ring before we made it to the bedroom. I was tempted to ignore it, but I was hoping for a positive report from some surveillance we were conducting. It wasn't the call I was waiting for. Steve, my secretary slash administrative assistant had some questions about a contract proposal I had hastily drawn up so that I could take Friday off. Apparently I'd been a bit too hasty and had left out a few things which, if Steve hadn't caught them, would have turned a profitable job into a disaster. I answered his questions, thanked him warmly, and then I was on my way to the bedroom, where Dusty was hopefully waiting patiently for my arrival.

But the call had lasted just long enough to disrupt things. I had left my cell phone on the kitchen table because, frankly, I hated being so easy to reach and it beeped at just the right moment to catch my attention as I walked past the archway. I almost kept going, but it was possible that my surveillance crew had tried the land line, found it busy, and called my cell instead. But it wasn't a call. It was a text.

"Just arrived. Room 416, Driscoll Hotel. Dinner tonight? My treat. Meet at my room at 6. Pick up package at desk on your way." The message was from John Boncoddo, who thought he had been my best friend during our high school years. He wasn't a bad guy but he lacked social skills and at the time I'd been virtuously tolerant and perhaps mildly flattered by his puppy like admiration. He was, however, too tangled up in his own internal world to properly understand the mutual obligations of friendship.

I glanced at my watch. It was a little after four o'clock. I sighed and finally made it to the bedroom. "I have news."

"Good or bad?"

"A little of both. We have to go to Providence."

"And that would be why?"

"An old friend is in town for the film festival. He wants to take us to supper."

"Which old friend?" Her voice was wary.

My shoulders slumped and my head dropped. "John Boncoddo," I said quietly

"Oh boy!" Dusty gave an exaggerated sigh. "Can't you tell him I'm about to undergo heart surgery or something?"

"I'm not a good liar."

"Yes, you are, actually."

"I've never lied to you."

"No, because I'd see right through you, but you're pretty devious when you want to be."

"Is that a compliment or an insult?"

"Probably both. So when do we have to show up?"

"He says six."

She sighed. "I hope you appreciate the sacrifices I make for you. I'll get dressed."

Banter aside, I think Dusty was secretly pleased. The Vintage Film Festival was an annual event that rotated from the west coast to either the Midwest or South to the East Coast each year, at least theoretically. Every once in a while circumstances disrupted the schedule. It was the brainchild of Daryl Plimpton, a self proclaimed film enthusiast who was actually just a particularly rapacious entrepreneur who had found a profitable niche to exploit. That wasn't entire fair because leaving aside his personality flaws, Daryl was very good at what he did and while I might have reservations about his motivation and sometimes his methods, the fact was that he invariably orchestrated a well organized convention that delivered ample value to the people who attended. The fact that Daryl made a reasonably comfortable living doing it might offend purists but it was hard to quarrel with the results. The first festival had less than a hundred participants; this year's would draw close to two thousand.

The VFF was being held in Providence this year and Dusty and I had actually been looking forward to it for months even though we were less than enthused about Daryl. Competent he might be, but Daryl was a human leech who exploited the vulnerable. He had the ethics of a flatworm. That said, the advertising for this year's convention included promised screenings of movies and television programs some of whcih had never been released on DVD or VHS, and weren't available on the internet or only in fuzzy unwatchable copies. Dusty and I also had a special connection since we'd met at one of Daryl's conventions in Cleveland three years earlier.

John Boncoddo had introduced us.

I'd lived in or around Rhode Island all my life except for my college years. John had gone to the University of Rhode Island briefly, dropped out, and moved to the West Coast where I'd lost track of him for about five years. He now owned a small company that did special effects for low budget movies – mostly CGI – and occasionally did restorations of old prints. He had come to the very first VFF back in 1998, but I didn't run into him until I attended the third, two years later, in Syracuse, New York. I'd like to say that the years had mellowed him but he was still the same awkward, socially inept irritant that I remembered. He had an opinion on everything, frequently uninformed, and expressed himself loudly and sometimes without waiting his turn. If someone remonstrated with him, he'd sulk for a few minutes, then revert to his usual behavior mode.

We'd kept in touch via intermittent email, which was much more tolerable since he was a poor typist and rarely wrote anything lengthy. He attended every VFF as well as several other festivals and I sometimes wondered who ran his business while he was away so often. I didn't actually see him again until 2006 because I was putting together what was now the reasonably successful Birch Investigations. That year the VFF was in Boston. It was the first time Dusty attended, although we didn't meet until 2010 in Chicago. She had known John for a couple of years by then and was dating a good looking but rather untalented minor actor at the time. The four of us had somehow ended up going to dinner as a group and I'd been captivated. Fortunately, so was Dusty, and when we ran into each other the following morning at one of the showings – a Boston Blackie movie – we were in deep like if not love.

So we were both in John's debt.

I parked in the lot behind the Biltmore, which was theoretically hosting the convention, although the attendees were spread among at least four more hotels and the screenings were being held at various locations including the Rhode Island School of Design campus. The city of Providence has made a big deal out of promoting the arts and attracting just this sort of convention, so they had provided a good deal of support. We had almost an hour to kill before we needed to be at the Driscoll, which was only four blocks away, so we registered and received our badges and program schedules. We had planned to show up first thing Saturday morning, but the line was quite short and we decided to get it over with. Dusty insisted on pinning my badge to my lapel because she says I always get it crooked when I do it myself. I usually riposted that the only people interested in talking to me knew me by sight anyway, but it was one of those arguments that disguised mutual affection.

The bored looking woman who handed us our packets asked if we wanted to attend one of the showings of *At the Mountains of Madness*. "Saturday night and Sunday only. There's an extra charge."

I should probably explain about this. Horror writer H.P. Lovecraft wrote a short novel with this title back around 1930, but it was too long for his usual markets and it didn't appear in print until 1936. I never really saw the attraction but it's a very atmospheric account of an expedition to Antarctica that finds the ruins of an alien civilization. Anyway, three years later a small group of amateur movie enthusiasts raised some money and set out to create a film version. They spent two years on the project but it remained unreleased at the outbreak of the war. The three major players in the production were all dead a year later, two in the Pacific, one in North Africa. They were young men, all three died intestate, and the last of their estates wasn't settled until 1948, by which time no trace was found of their movie except for a few brief but tantalizing bits that had been edited out of their working cut. The bizarre landscapes they had created as backdrops were surprisingly advanced give the era and their limited budget. There were energetic efforts to locate surviving copies during the 1950s and then again in the 1980s, but it was generally believed that all copies had been destroyed or lost.

10

Two other cast members, Adele Leslie and Ernest Gilles, had disappeared and were never tracked down. Gilles may have gotten married and Gilles had told family members that he was going to work on a freighter and see Asia.

That had been the situation until last year when Daryl Plimpton announced that he had located a nearly finished version missing only credits and probably a final edit. It had never been copyrighted so a few distant descendents of the original filmmakers failed to wrest it away from him. Everyone expected that Daryl would sell distribution rights, and he probably would at some point, but for the time being he restricted it to limited live screenings for which he charged all the traffic would bear.

"How much?"

"Twenty-five dollars."

"For the two of us?"

"Each."

I thought about it. "We'll think about it."

"Let's wait for the DVD," said Dusty as we walked away.

We took a quick walk through the convention area, which was mostly on the top three floors of the hotel. Lash Larue, dressed in black, was cracking his whip in one of the viewing rooms while a pack of outlaws tried to tackle him. Sidney Toler was pretending to be Chinese in a Charlie Chan movie next door and in a third we saw Cary Grant struggling through the desert. A large open area was crowded with dealer's tables selling a variety of movie memorabilia including lobby cards, black and white stills, books about specific films or genres or actors, DVDs – some of which were of dubious provenance, and various other items including action figures and copies of screenplays. I passed a display of Chewbacca and Han Solo figures and frowned.

"I thought this was supposed to be limited to vintage movies."

Dusty punched my arm. "You're showing your age. Vintage is defined by Daryl as no less than thirty years old. *Star Wars* was 1977."

I did some mental subtraction. "Time sure does fly."

One table had an array of DVDs adorned with cartoonish drawings and a sign that said "Public Domain Movies". A computer monitor faced outward and we paused a second to watch Victor Mature embrace Hedy Lamarr. "*Demetrios and the Gladiators*," I suggested.

Dusty shook her head. "No, *Samson and Delilah*, I think. It was Susan Hayward who played Messalina."

"Any old excuse for Victor to bare his chest."

Dusty looked thoughtful. "I'm getting an idea."

"I hope it involves my bare chest rather than his."

"No, I mean for my next book. I think maybe I'll do something historical. The fall of Constantinople or something like that."

"So long as you don't burn down the attic."

"Don't worry. The city didn't burn."

"I won't ask what actually did happen." I glanced at my watch. "We need to get going or we'll be late."

It felt like an endless wait for an elevator but eventually we made it down to the lobby. There were small clumps of people scattered about and a few familiar faces, but none I could put a name to until we were just about to leave. The door opened in front of us and in walked someone I had no trouble identifying. Sasha Bullard did not strike me as the kind of person who would be interested in vintage movies so I assumed she was here on official business. She was a homicide detective in Providence who spent a lot of time working with the state police. Two uniformed officers came in behind her, looking grim.

She nodded politely and even managed a skimpy smile for Dusty. "I should have known you'd be mixed up in this."

"Mixed up in what?" I think my voice dripped innocence, and justly so. "We just got here."

"Text message or phone call?"

"Text. What are we talking about?"

She looked around to make sure we couldn't be overheard. "Someone called in anonymously and said there'd been a murder at the film festival." She glanced around. "I don't suppose you've stumbled across any bodies?"

"No dead ones," said Dusty. "We haven't seen any signs of a disturbance. Are you sure it isn't a prank?"

"I'm actually hoping it is. This is supposed to be my weekend off." She looked around. "Is there anyone in authority I could talk to?"

I told her how to find Registration. "One of them should be able to reach the man in charge. His name is Daryl Plimpton. I imagine he has people helping him but he's a control freak. If anything happened, he'll know about it."

"Are you here on a case?"

I shook my head. "Definitely not. We came to watch movies and talk to some old friends."

"Don't let any of them get killed, okay? I have reservations for a week at a nice bed and breakfast in Vermont."

The threesome moved away and five minutes later Dusty and I were outside the Biltmore and headed toward the Driscoll. There were lots of people on the streets. Small shops and restaurants had returned to the downtown and I reflected happily that the day of the shopping mall had declined if not entirely passed. We walked along Westminster Street until we reached Pearlman, then turned left. The Driscoll's dark blue awning covered the sidewalk ahead and to our right.

The lobby was small for a hotel, rather cluttered, but almost unpopulated. A uniformed attendant was emptying ashtrays. Behind the desk, a similarly dressed young woman appeared bored but she smiled warmly when we approached. "Checking in?"

"No, we're here to see one of your guests. He asked us to pick up a package at the front desk."

She frowned and shuffled papers. "I don't recall…wait, here's one. I wonder how that got there. What's the name?"

"Birch."

Her frown turned into a smile and she handled it over. It was very small, the length and width of a credit card and not much thicker, wrapped in plain gray paper and tied with white string. My last name was printed on one side.

"What do you suppose that is?" asked Dusty.

I shrugged. "John likes to play games." First it had been pushing tiny pieces of cardboard across a field of hexes, then Dungeons & Dragons. Then he started inventing his own.

"Are you going to open it?"

"No, not yet. Let's go talk to him first."

The elevators were set at an odd angle and it took a few seconds before we located them. They were old enough to have those creaky double doors, one solid, one a metallic lattice that closed and opened in succession. There was an audible shudder as we started to rise and Dusty and I exchanged glances.

"It's like stepping back into the past," I said.

"As long as it's not falling back into the past."

It took forever to reach the fourth floor. People on the eighth and highest would be wise to pack a snack before embarking. The doors opened on a dingy, poorly lit elevator lobby beyond which were even dingier, darker corridors extending to left and right. The carpet was worn, the wall paper wasn't peeling but its original pattern had almost completely faded, and there was a faintly musty odor that made my nose wrinkle. I'd never been in the Driscoll before and I made a resolution to avoid it in the future. That was to prove more difficult than I realized.

Room 416 was the last door on the left, facing 415 and with a door to the stairwell between them. We had neither seen nor heard any signs of life since we'd exited from the elevator. A sheet of hotel stationery was taped to the door, a short message printed in large Times New Roman characters in all caps.

PAUL. OPEN THE PACKAGE AND COME ON IN. WILL EXPLAIN INSIDE.

Dusty and I looked at each other. "So I guess we open it?"

"This is odd, even for John."

"Remember the scavenger hunt in Hartford?"

"Okay, maybe not so odd." I still held the small package in my hand. The string was knotted tight but I worked it over one corner and pulled it free. 'Hold this." I handed the string to Dusty and started stripping off the paper. Inside was a cardboard box emblazoned with a King of Spades and the word "Hoyle". Playing cards? It didn't feel heavy enough. I opened the flap and shook out a single plastic card that had "Hotel Driscoll" printed at one end with a stylized arrow pointing down the length of the card.

"It's a room key," I said unnecessarily.

"Hence his invitation to come in."

"Why can't he open the door himself?" I turned and knocked impatiently. There was no answer.

"Maybe he's not there. That would explain why he left the key at the desk."

"But then why did he tell us to come up to his room? He could have left a message to meet him somewhere else."

"John doesn't always do things the logical way. He must have had some reason for going to all this trouble."

I turned the key card back and forth in my hand. "I don't like this. It feels like breaking and entering."

"We could go back to the lobby and call his room on the house phone."

"If he's not answering the door, then he's not likely to pick up the phone." I drew a deep breath. "All right. Let's stop wasting time." I slipped the card key into its slot, grabbed the handle, and pushed. The door opened.

It was dark inside the room. There were no lights on and the curtains were drawn. I could hear a faucet dripping but no other sound. "Johnny? Are you in there?"

No one answered. There was nothing overt, or at least nothing that I consciously noticed, but I felt a distinct uneasiness. Dusty started to push past me but I held her back. "No. Wait here. Something's wrong." I groped around and found the light switch, flipped it. Nothing changed. I tried again, knowing as I did so that it would make no difference.

"What is it?" asked Dusty, but her voice was uncertain now.

"Let me check this out." I stepped forward tentatively. It was like dragging my leg through molasses. I think I knew what I was going to find, at least in general terms, but I couldn't act on that knowledge until I was sure. Two more steps seemed to drain the energy out of me but by then I was far enough into the room to see around the corner of the bathroom. I sighed and my shoulders slumped.

"Dusty, I need you to go downstairs to the front desk. Have them track down Detective Bullard if she's still in the hotel, otherwise, have them call the police. When they find her, bring her upstairs. Don't tell the desk clerk anything unless you have to."

I heard the catch in her voice. "All right. Are you staying here?"

"I'll be right by the door. Hurry."

I heard her footsteps recede behind me. I hadn't quite told a fib. I was going to be right by the door when she came back. But first I had to take a closer look.

CHAPTER TWO

John Boncoddo was hanging by his neck from the fire sprinkler mounted over the bed. He wasn't very tall and his feet didn't reach the mattress. His arms hung limply at his sides. He looked skinnier than I remembered, but we all become somewhat diminished when we die. And he was very much dead. I used the little penlight on my keychain and shined it into his face. His eyes were open and unblinking. The light wasn't strong enough for me to tell if he was showing the discoloration of asphyxia, but I didn't think he'd died by hanging. The hilt of some sort of edged weapon protruding from his chest seemed a far likelier explanation, although I couldn't for the life of me imagine why the killer would have hanged him afterward.

I took a quick look around the room from where I stood, directly my woefully inadequate light into the corners. One of the pillows was missing from the bed. A suitcase was on the second bed, opened. Two folded shirts were on top with hangers but there were gaps suggesting that John had begun unpacking. I didn't open any of the drawers but I took a peek into the closet. There was nothing there.

"What did you get yourself into this time, Johnny?" I hadn't meant to speak aloud and the sound of my voice seemed disproportionately strident. I retreated to the doorway and waited for the cavalry to arrive.

Objectively it took less than a quarter hour but it felt like days. During that time, I didn't see or hear another human being unless you count traffic noises from outside. The elevator passed the fourth floor several times but never stopped until it finally did, disgorging Dusty, Bullard, and the two uniforms. I wondered if Bullard would be able to recover her deposit from the bed and breakfast, because I was pretty sure she wasn't going anywhere this weekend.

"Please don't tell me what I think you're about to tell me." Bullard's expression was grim.

"Dead body, male, late thirties, hanging from the sprinkler head."

She raised an eyebrow. "Suicide?"

"Not unless he stabbed himself in the heart while he was choking to death."

Bullard shook her head disgustedly. "Touch anything?"

"The door and the light switch. The lights don't work."

"Let's take a look." She pushed past me and went into the room. I stayed where I was. A couple of minutes passed while the uniforms and I stared at each other and then she was back. "Know who he was?"

"Yep. John Boncoddo. High school friend."

"Was the door open?"

I shook my head and told her about the text message, the package we'd retrieved from the front desk, and pointed to the note on the door.

"I'm going to need your cell phone."

"It's at the house. I forgot to bring it. The packaging is in my jacket pocket," I tapped the appropriate place. "I haven't handled it since I found him."

"And the string is in my handbag," added Dusty.

Bullard turned to one of the uniforms. "Go down to the desk and call it in. We'll want the crime scene unit and the coroner. Better have a couple more bodies to keep order. Then send the manager and the chief of security up here. Tell them we have a suspicious death but nothing else." He nodded and started off.

"How well did you know the deceased?"

"We went to school together. Friends but not close. We email each other a few times a year and I occasionally run into him at film festivals. He introduced me to Dusty a while back."

"You knew him also?"

Dusty nodded. "I met him six or seven years ago in Memphis."

"I don't suppose either of you have any idea who might have wanted him dead?"

We both shook our heads and it was only then that I realized we'd been speaking barely above a whisper. The presence of the dead does that, although John was certainly well beyond being disturbed.

The elevator door opened and three people came down the corridor toward us. One was a tallish woman with bright red hair wearing a business suit. The second was the uniform Bullard had sent downstairs. The third was someone I knew, although it took a couple of seconds to recognize him.

The woman was clearly used to being in charge. She introduced herself to Bullard as Margaret Drake. Her companion, as I already knew, was Mickey Palotto. "He's our chief of security." That I hadn't known. Mickey had been two years ahead of John and I at Cumberland High School. He was a vicious bully and I wasn't particularly surprised that he'd gone into security work, but he had never shown much ambition, initiative, or even common sense. I couldn't imagine how he'd gotten into a position of authority, even at a second rate hotel. Mickey had always been heavy but he'd never been very fit, and that hadn't changed. Our eyes met and I knew he'd recognized me but he didn't say anything. The last time we'd spoken had been just after a fist fight behind the school gymnasium. I am happy to say that I won.

"There's a dead man in the room behind me," said Bullard. "I need to have this area isolated while my people work the scene."

"Has there been some kind of accident?" I could tell by her voice that Drake didn't believe that it was an accident. "Or a suicide?" This was clearly the answer she preferred, since it wouldn't reflect upon the hotel.

"We've just found the body and the coroner's office hasn't arrived yet. We'll know more once they've had a look."

"I understand. What do you need us to do?"

"'I'd like to move people out of these three rooms." She indicated rooms 413 through 415. "I'll have someone posted in the stairwell just outside this door."

Drake nodded, turned to Mickey. "Give me your radio."

Mickey unclipped a small radio from his belt and handed it to her. She spoke briefly, waited a few seconds, then thanked someone. "415 is vacant. The guests assigned to the other two haven't checked in yet and they'll be relocated." She pursed her lips. "We're fully booked so this is going to cause trouble unless we have some no-shows." Drake already had trouble and it was a lot worse than a couple of disgruntled guests.

"Fine. We'll also need some light bulbs. Someone has removed them from all the fixtures in this room."

Drake frowned. "But why?" She shrugged and spoke into the radio again. "Someone will be right up."

"I'd like to use that room," she pointed toward 415. "Can you open it up for us?"

Mickey did the honors, using his master. He turned on the lights. "I'll have to disable the lock or prop the door open unless you want a key card."

"Disable it if you would."

A bellhop arrived a moment later carrying a package of light bulbs. He looked at us all with obvious curiosity but no one enlightened him. Drake said "Thank you, Martin. Stay close, would you? You might be needed." He retreated a few steps, looking understandably curious, but didn't leave.

Mickey had finally finished tinkering with the door lock when the elevator sighed open again, this time disgorging half a dozen men and women, each carrying their kits. I didn't recognize any of them but they were obviously the crime scene unit.

Bullard spoke to Drake. "We'll be as discreet as possible, but we're going to have to ask a lot of questions. If you could assign someone knowledgeable to work with us, it would save a lot of time."

Drake turned toward Mickey but Bullard diverted her. She was a good judge of character and I suspected she'd been less than impressed. "It doesn't need to be one of your key people. Just someone who knows his or her way around and can tell us who we need to talk to."

Drake seemed uncertain, but then she remembered the bellhop hovering a few feet away. "Martin, could you help us out here?" He started forward. "Martin's our most senior employee, Detective. He knows everything there is to know about the Driscoll."

"Fine. We'll let you know if we need anything else." It was clearly a dismissal. Drake hesitated a second longer, then gestured to Mickey. They reached the elevator just as the coroner's people arrived.

Dusty and I were ushered into 415 where one of the technicians donned gloves and took the wrapping paper and key card from my pocket and the twine from Dusty's handbag. We sat together on the couch while two people set up their equipment. Everyone else had disappeared into the room across the hall except the bellhop, who sat in an armchair across from us. He was around sixty years old, solidly built, with thinning hair. Although he sat quietly with his eyes half closed, I could sense that he was excited. Life as a bellhop at the Driscoll was probably very dull.

"Life with you is never boring," said Dusty softly, apparently having read my thoughts.

"You knew him too," I protested.

"Only casually. You went to school with him and you were the one he texted."

"Were you friends of the gentleman?" The bellhop had obviously been listening to us.

"Not close, but yes." My suspicious nature asserted itself. "How did you know that it was a man?"

"I carried his bag up when he checked in. Not a very large person if I remember correctly. Not a big tipper either." He smiled thinly.

"What time was that?"

"Just after three o'clock. That's when my shift started."

"He was alone?"

"Oh yes."

"Did he seem depressed or anxious or anything like that?"

Martin - I remembered his name - shook his head. "He was a little impatient. The elevators here are pretty slow. I don't believe he said anything out of the routine while I was with him. Certainly nothing memorable."

"You showed him to his room?"

"Of course. I opened the curtains and showed him where he could plug in his computer."

"Were the lights working?"

Martin looked at me oddly. "Yes. Why wouldn't they be?"

We were asked to make statements while things were fresh in our minds. "We'll do the formal one later. If you'd just speak clearly and face the recorder." Dusty went first. Mine was longer because I'd actually gone inside the room and found the body, but otherwise there was no significant difference. I neglected to mention that I'd taken a closer look. The technician prompted us a couple of times but asked no probing questions. "Detective Bullard will want to go into this in more detail when she has time."

One of the technicians walked in carrying a very large transparent evidence bag. It contained a standard hotel pillow, but there was a dark splotch in its center. Ignoring us, she spoke to one of the others indicating that the photography and videotaping were done and that it was time to start searching for trace evidence. The evidence bag disappeared into a large case and the remaining technician gave us a look that suggested he believed we were going to steal, or at least contaminate, it as soon as he looked away.

"Was that a burn mark?" Dusty's voice, though pitched at a normal level, seemed quite loud.

I resisted the temptation to whisper. "Sort of. I'd guess that someone fired a handgun through it."

"Why would someone do that?" And then she answered her own question. "To muffle the sound, obviously. But was Johnny shot? I thought you said someone had hanged him."

"That was after the fact. He was already dead. There was no indication of cyanosis. And he'd been stabbed in the heart."

"So what killed him? A gun or a knife?"

"I have no idea." The bellhop had settled back in his chair and his eyes were closed, but I knew he was listening to every word. I certainly would have. I leaned forward. "How long have you been working here?"

His eyes opened. "Thirty-nine years last month. I started right after high school and except for a gap of about six months, I've been here ever since. I plan to retire the end of next year."

"I imagine you've seen a lot of changes."

He became more animated. "Indeed I have. The Driscoll was never going to compete with the Biltmore, of course, but it was a fashionable place to stay when in the 1970s. We had quite a few celebrities in our time. I once showed Sean Connery to his room, and I served drinks to Lena Horne in the bar downstairs, when we had a real bar downstairs."

"You weren't always a bellhop then?"

Martin shook his head. "Well, yes and no. I've been a lot of things around here at one time or another. Tended bar, delivered room service, worked in the laundry – when we had a laundry. I've done valet parking and made up rooms and worked with the maintenance crew. Helped out in the kitchen. And the last few years we've had to cut corners and reduce staff. I've even filled in on the graveyard shift at the desk. I think that's why they keep me around. They know they can put me almost anywhere and I'll do a good job." I had the feeling that Martin might turn out to be very useful over the course of the next couple of days.

Bullard appeared then, looking disgusted, or weary, or both. "I'm going to need to talk to the two of you about your late friend."

"We'll do whatever we can to help," said Dusty.

Bullard nodded and turned to Martin. "I gather you know your way around this place."

He stood up. "As well as anyone."

"I want you to take Detective Doyle for a grand tour. I'm particularly interested in entrances and exits, particularly with access to this stairwell. And we're going to have to search for the missing light bulbs so if you can think of any likely hiding places, that would be helpful as well."

Martin frowned. "If someone smashed them first, they could be almost anywhere."

"The thought had occurred to me but we have to make the effort. Doyle is waiting in the corridor. He's the one with the dark blue jacket and the sour expression."

Martin left and Bullard dropped into his chair. "So what kind of person was the late Mr. Boncoddo?"

Dusty and I looked at one another. "You first," she said.

I took a deep breath. "John and I went to school together, seventh grade through graduation. We weren't exactly close but I felt responsible for him sometimes because he had no real friends, no social skills, and the other kids made fun of him. He wouldn't fight back so he got slapped around a lot but never really badly beaten. I tried to get him to stay out of situations where he'd get into trouble, but he always went back."

"Stubborn?"

"Not really. Oblivious. He never learned anything from his social interactions."

"Was he a good student?"

I nodded. "Actually he was. John was probably a lot smarter than the rest of us, but he couldn't apply himself. No, that's wrong. He would study something once and retain it indefinitely. But he couldn't maintain his focus."

"So what happened after high school?"

"He spent a year or two at URI, but dropped out, or maybe flunked out. Then I heard that he'd moved out west some place. I didn't hear from him for a few years and then one day I got an email. He was living in California and had started his own business."

"What kind of business"

"He did special effects. Models and miniatures at first, but CGI stuff later. You know, computer generated images. He also did work restoring damaged or fading prints and even had his own DVD label for awhile, but that flopped. He didn't have the right contacts for distribution and even if he had developed some, vintage films don't command the big bucks."

"Did the two of you ever get together?"

"We corresponded on and off for the next couple of years but I didn't actually see him in the flesh until 2001. He'd been trying to get me to attend film festivals ever since we'd gotten back in touch. The Vintage Film Festival was in Albuquerque that year and as it happened I was going out to Santa Fe about the same time so I combined the trip. He was pretty much as I remembered him, both physically and behaviorally."

"Married?"

I laughed. "Not likely."

"Family?"

I had to think about that one. "No siblings that I remember. His father was gone before I met him but I don't think he'd died. Mother was a sweet old woman but not quite right. Today she'd be a conspiracy theorist. Back then she talked about UFOs and fairy rings. I have no idea if she's still alive."

"Anything significant happen since 2001?"

"Well, he introduced me to Dusty in 2010. I think that's very significant but it's probably not going to help you."

"This text you received. Was that in character?"

"It wasn't out of character. Most of our correspondence was electronic. And we did often get together when we were both in the same place. The business with the package at the desk was odd though. I don't think he sent that message."

Bullard nodded. "Neither do I. Someone wanted you to find the body. And there's no cell phone in his room that we can find."

"Can you trace it by GPS?"

"I have someone looking into it." She turned to Dusty. "So how did you know the deceased?"

"I met him in Boston in 2000. I was fifteen years old and I'd taken the bus up with another girl from my class. It was a bit of an adventure because I'd been sneaky about it. My father had very strict ideas about where young ladies should go and who they should talk to. I told him we were going shopping and he even gave me some extra money. We didn't know anyone and when John came up to us and offered to show us around, we were flattered. He was an adult and we were still kids. It was very public so we weren't worried or anything and John always seemed asexual. I've never heard anything that would suggest otherwise."

"No romantic entanglements? Jealous boyfriends?"

Dusty shook her head. "He could be really irritating some times. He liked to hear himself talk and was convinced that he understood things thoroughly even when his knowledge was superficial. He could also be quite blunt. He once asked Terry Wareham how she'd managed to get so fat so quickly. I think he was actually interested."

"How often did you see him after that?"

"Rarely. I only made it to the East Coast film festivals for the next several years, so I would have seen him in 2003, 2006, and 2009. We had lunch together at one of those but I don't remember which one. Sometimes we'd run into each other in a corridor or attend the same screening. I usually came with friends. Then I went out to Chicago in 2010 to celebrate my first novel. I didn't know a lot of people there and John did, so I sort of attached myself so that I'd get introduced around. We went out with a dinner party one night and Paul was there and ended up sitting next to me. I was living in an apartment less than a mile from his house so we had a lot in common. By the end of the evening we'd arranged to meet for breakfast."

A technician came in and told Bullard that the photographers had left. "Find the cell phone yet?"

"No sign of one. There was a length of rubber tubing under the bed. It was still damp."

"What kind of tubing?"

"Looks like it's a piece of garden hose."

"Well, bag it and keep looking." She turned back in our direction. "So how many people attending this little get together are likely to have known the victim?"

Dusty and I exchanged glances. "Depends on how you define your terms. If you're looking for relatively close friends, maybe a dozen. People who had met him at least once? I'd guess a few hundred. People who knew his face? At least half of the people attending."

Bullard had looked uncomfortable at the word "hundred". "How big is this thing anyway?"

"With walk-ins, probably two thousand people."

Her jaw didn't drop, but it quivered. "I don't have the resources to conduct a couple of hundred interviews."

"It would have to be more than that. There's no way of knowing who should be on the list unless you talk to everyone. John got around. He was pushy. He loved having an audience and, to be fair, on some subjects he really knew his stuff."

"I knew when I saw you standing in that doorway that this was going to be a headache. Any suggestions about where we should start? The two of you must know a lot of these people. Could you go through a list of attendees and pick out the likely ones?"

"There are dozens that we know by first name only," explained Dusty. "And we don't know who is actually attending this year. We'd be better off walking around for a while and noting down names." She tapped her badge, which listed her full name.

"I can have someone go down to registration and find out who checked in early enough to have killed Boncoddo and then texted you."

I shook my head. "It doesn't work that way. They don't record check in times and by now half the attendees have probably registered. Anyway, the killer could have registered later."

"If he or she is even an attendee," added Dusty. "Shot, stabbed, and hanged? Sounds like a nut to me and John might have been chosen at random."

"Then why the call to Paul?" argued Bullard.

I had an answer to that one. "That might have been random as well. The killer could have read through John's email, identified me as someone local, and made the call. Or I suppose he might have talked to John while he was still alive and gotten my name somehow. The point was to have the body found. I don't think it mattered who actually opened the door."

"Then why not just call the front desk and ask them to send someone up on some flimsy excuse?"

I shrugged. "It was more dramatic this way. And by making the appointment for dinner, the killer arranged for a couple of hours to get away, cover his tracks, whatever."

"Or her tracks," added Dusty. "John wasn't that big a guy."

"It would still take some effort to lift him high enough to get his head through the noose," said Bullard.

"Not really," said Dusty coolly. "I'd have put a chair on the bed, lifted him onto that, arranged the rope, then removed the chair. I'm pretty small but I could have managed it."

"Is that a confession?"

Dusty made a face.

A tall man with a grim expression came through the door and Bullard stood up. "We're taking the body out. I'm guessing you want some fast answers."

"Most of my suspects are only here for the weekend, Pat. Anything you can do to expedite things would be helpful."

"I'll try to have something preliminary for you in the morning. Anything before that would be a guess."

"Do you have time and cause of death yet?"

Pat, who was presumably from the coroner's office, glanced at the two of us but didn't object to our presence. "Unofficially I'd say he died early to mid-afternoon."

"COD?"

"Well, that's the interesting part. He was hanged after the fact. And stabbed in the heart."

"I didn't see much blood."

"No, that was post mortem as well. The victim was shot in the right ear with a handgun, probably a .38. It was almost certainly from close range but there are no powder burns."

"The shot was fired through the pillow."

Pat nodded. "Again, probably. The bullet is still somewhere inside his skull."

"But why the knife then?"

There was a twinkle in Pat's eye and I thought his lips twitched slightly toward a smile. "Why the gunshot for that matter? He was already dead when it was fired."

I blinked. I think we all blinked.

"Then what was the cause of death?" asked Bullard. She sounded annoyed now. I didn't blame her.

But Pat just shrugged. "I have no idea. I'll need to open him up and take a look around first. But whoever did this either really hated this guy or has a bizarre sense of humor. At least I think you can safely say this was premeditated."

Bullard agreed. "No one routinely carries around a gun, a dagger, and a heavy rope. Not in a downtown hotel." She had forgotten the length of garden hose.

Pat left a few seconds later. Bullard stood staring at the empty doorway for at least a full minute before turning back to us. "I could really use some unofficial help here. Can you make me that list of people I should talk to? You know this crowd. Tell me anything that looks off to you."

"You might start with Daryl Plimpton," I said. "He's been running these festivals from the start. I think it's how he supports himself. He did everything himself at first but they're too big for that now so he has a small staff, mostly volunteer. There's always a lot of tension there. Daryl likes to control everything even when it's impractical and he has a short temper."

"Was your late friend working for him?"

"Not that I know of." I glanced at Dusty and she shook her head in confirmation. "John wasn't very organized. He'd cause more problems than he fixed."

28

"But you said he has his own business."

"Yeah, I don't know how that works. He must have found a niche where people put up with him because they don't have good alternatives."

Dusty put a hand on my knee. "I don't think he actually runs things on a day to day basis," she said. "I'm pretty sure he has a manager who probably does the real work. I know John travels...traveled a lot."

"Do you have a name?"

"No, I don't even remember what the company is called." She looked at me but I had no idea.

"I'll be calling the West Coast for background anyway," said Bullard. "But anything you can remember about it might be helpful."

Bullard walked across the corridor and disappeared into 416. I stood up. "I suppose we should walk around and start taking names."

Dusty fumbled in her bag and pulled out a small notepad and pen. "I'm ready when you are."

The remaining technician ignored us when we left.

CHAPTER THREE

The lobby still wasn't crowded but there were several people standing around. I spotted Martin, the bellhop, with a jowly man who was apparently Bullard's latest partner. They disappeared around a corner. Half a dozen people were waiting to check in but none of them looked familiar to me. A uniformed police office stood to one side attempting, unsuccessfully, to look casual.

It was dark now and I glanced at my watch. We'd been inside the Driscoll for just over two hours. "We ought to eat something," suggested Dusty, and my stomach immediately rumbled its agreement.

We ate at one of the trendy little cafes that came and went in this area and Dusty got to write down two names in her notebook. Muriel Bates was sitting two tables away with a younger woman we didn't know. It didn't appear that she had seen us; the two of them were talking intently and were oblivious to their surroundings. It might have been adversarial, but they kept their voices down. Muriel and John had never been a couple exactly but they were often seen in one another's company so she would be high on our list. Dusty also saw Jimmy Gonsalves walk past on the street. Neither of us knew very much about Jimmy because he rarely said much, but he'd been in the dinner party the night Dusty and I had met, and I was quite sure I'd seen him talking to John on more than one occasion.

We spent about an hour wandering through the convention area at the Biltmore. I recognized a few people but none of them had more than superficial links to John. Dusty added Fred Hastings – she had to sneak a look at his nametag – because she'd once seem him arguing with John at a panel discussion. She also added Jo Parkin, whom we both knew fairly well, and our research was delayed for a while when we ran into her so that we could catch up. Jo wore a red bordered name tag that identified her as part of the staff. "I'm sort of a troubleshooter."

"How's Daryl?" I asked.

She rolled her eyes. "He's being Daryl. Enough said."

We made the usual vague and not entirely sincere promises to get together later in the weekend and went our separate ways. By ten o'clock, we had added Ray Riccello, Romeo Bolduc, and Helen Viele to the list, and we had a half dozen names with even more remote connections to John Boncoddo. John really didn't have intimates of either sex. He had a kind of social ineptness forcefield that made it virtually impossible to get close to him.

"I don't think this is going to be very helpful to Sasha," said Dusty as we made our way back to the Driscoll to deliver our list. "None of these people knew John very well as far as I can see and I can't imagine why any of them would wish him harm, other than maybe laryngitis."

"One of them might know something that could help. Some of them have probably seen John more often than we did."

"And it might not have had anything to do with the film festival crowd. He did have a private life."

"In California," I pointed out.

"But he was brought up here in Rhode Island. It might have been a long standing grudge."

"Or he might have been chosen at random."

"But why would a random killer have been so brutal? He was hanged, stabbed, and shot."

The elevator stopped and we got out on the fourth floor. "All of that happened after he was dead. There must have been another reason for the overkill."

Bullard wasn't around so we turned over our list to one of the technicians. They seemed to be mostly done as well. "Find anything?" I asked, not expecting an answer.

"Someone dropped a wrench into the back of the toilet." He sounded weary. "It's like investigating a game of Clue." His eyes narrowed. "I shouldn't have told you that. Keep it to yourself, would you?"

"Our lips are sealed. Tell Bullard that we'll be back in the morning. She has Dusty's cell number."

Neither of us said much on the drive home, which was interrupted when I stopped and bought a disposable cell phone to use while the police were playing with mine. Now that I wasn't spending my time trying to recall names and faces and recognize

31

people in crowds, I actually started to think about the death of John Boncoddo simply as a death and not just as a bizarre crime. It would be overstating things wildly to claim that I was heartbroken. Even when we were in high school together, I thought of him as more of an obligation than a friend. His focus was so tightly restricted to his own concerns that there wasn't room for anyone else. I had fought with my fists in his defense at least once but I don't recall that he even thanked me afterward. It wasn't that he was unkind or disloyal or mean or even stupid. He was just disengaged.

That said, I had felt a kind of duty to watch out for him, and some affection as well. It had dulled to an ember over the years and I felt a twinge of regret that I had left him on his own, even though he was the one who had left, moving to California without even telling me he was going. He might have left a forwarding address but his mother moved away right afterward and I had no way of locating him until he finally sent me an email year later. It was probably for the best because if I had been forced to interact with him on a regular basis, I might have been the one who murdered him. I couldn't imagine how he managed to run a company. His turnover rate must have been horrendous.

"You're feeling guilty, aren't you?" Dusty patted my shoulder.

"Just a twinge. Have you been reading my mind again?"

"Reading your mood. I'm getting good at it. I used to think you were cool and self contained, but you're surprisingly demonstrative once I learned to pick up the cues."

"Old habits die hard. I used to look out for him."

"Does that mean you're going to be doing a little detecting of your own?"

I shook my head. "Not a chance. Bullard is good at her job and I like being on her good side. She'd be peeved if I stuck my nose in."

"She might ask."

"I doubt it. I don't have a stake in this game, or maybe I anted up but I folded my hand a long time ago."

She didn't say anything else until we got home. I'm not sure if she believed me. I'm not even sure that I believed me.

The murder was mentioned on the late night local news, but only briefly. A guest at the Driscoll Hotel had been found dead in his room under suspicious circumstances. The Providence Police were investigating. The victim's name would not be released until next of kin were notified. The reporter hinted that it might be suicide, suggesting that Bullard's security precautions were holding, at least for the moment. Not that it would fool the killer. I checked the Providence Journal website but there was no mention of the incident. Dusty brewed some Irish coffee for the two of us and after that we went to bed. I didn't sleep well.

Morning came as it habitually does and I let the shower wash the sleep away. Dusty was waiting for her turn when I emerged so I had pancakes cooking when she came downstairs. "What time are we going to Providence?"

"I hadn't thought about it. Have you looked at the schedule? Found any movies you absolutely have to see?"

"You know perfectly well that neither of us is going to be able to sit still long enough to watch a movie until we know what happened to John."

I didn't have a good answer for that so I flipped the pancakes and brooded.

We left the house at 9:00 and parked at the Biltmore garage thirty minutes later. The lobby was mobbed and there was a long line at registration. Some people were just arriving, many more had checked in during the evening after registration had closed for the day. I saw Jo Parkin rushing from somewhere to somewhere else and I thought I caught a glimpse of Daryl Plimpton, but by the time it occurred to me to go over and talk to him, he'd vanished, if it had been him that I'd seen in the first place.

We did a quick pass through the convention area to gather more names and I spotted Tanya Gregory and Dusty noticed Bob Strossi, whom I had only met once or twice and briefly on both occasions. Tanya had been involved in a screaming match with John at the Denver festival, which I hadn't attended, but it had been a topic of conversation for at least two years following. Bob Strossi had reportedly worked for John's film company for a few months. Rumor had it that his departure had been rancorous. There were a couple of others we added with question marks. They knew John but neither of us had ever seen them interact on anything but the most casual level.

The Driscoll lobby was crowded. Most of the people were obviously tourists in town for the festival. One of them I recognized as a reporter and a couple more I suspected. When we got off on the fourth floor, there was a uniformed officer sitting there. "I need to see your key card before you can go any further."

"We're not guests. We're here to see Detective Bullard," I explained.

"She's kind of busy right now. What's the nature of your business?" He sounded bored, skeptical, and annoyed all at once.

"She asked us to make up a list of suspects. We have some names to add to her list."

"You can leave that with me. I'll see that she gets it."

Now I was irritated. "It's not that simple."

Dusty spoke up quickly. "She said she wanted to ask us some more questions and that we should come by during the morning." She didn't bat her eyes or anything so obvious, but I could see the muscles in his face relaxing slightly. He picked up his radio from a small table and spoke into it, listened briefly, then put it back.

"I guess you can go through. They're in 416."

I forced a friendly smile and we started down the hall to the murder scene.

Room 416 looked a lot different in the daylight with the curtains open and the lamps on. It was still worn out and dingy and there was a faint smell of cigarette smoke, but everything was spotless. This was not a credit to the hotel necessarily. I assumed the technicians had vacuumed and dusted everything looking for trace evidence. There were only two of them remaining, one doing something arcane in a corner, the other out of sight in the bathroom.

Bullard was standing beside the bed talking into her cell phone. She must have gone home at some point because she was wearing a fresh set of clothing, but she looked as though she hadn't slept much, if at all. She sketched a wave when we came in but it was not an enthusiastic effort. Neither of us sat down. It didn't seem appropriate somehow.

She finished her call and Dusty handed her the new names we'd come up with. Bullard barely glanced at the sheet before slipping it into a notebook that lay on the bed. The covers and pillows were gone; it was just a bare mattress now.

"Any progress?" I asked.

She made a disgusted sound. "That was the coroner's office. They're doing the autopsy now. It appears that someone hit the late Mr. Boncoddo on the head with the proverbial blunt object."

"Was that the cause of death then?"

She laughed but it was strained. "Of course not. That would mean we had an answer to at least one question. The blow was serious enough to have caused unconsciousness and possibly a concussion. It was not likely to be life threatening. On the other hand, the blow was struck while he was still alive, which is more than we can say for the knife, the noose, or the gun, all of which were postmortem embellishments."

"Someone's playing a game," suggested Dusty.

"You think?" Bullard shook her head. "Why does every case you get involved with have to be so complicated, Birch? Couldn't you just stumble on a mugging or a domestic dispute or something?"

"My failings are many," I admitted. "Did you find the gun?"

"No, but I think we have the blunt object. There was a bloody wrench in the back of the toilet. That had to be a joke too. If the killer wanted to hide it, why would he put it in such an obvious place? If he wanted us to find it, why not just leave it in plain sight?"

"Like I said," Dusty answered. "He – or she – is playing a game."

"Poker is a game. Chess is a game. Murder is not a game."

"A gun, a knife, a blunt object, a rope. Have you ever played Clue, Sasha?"

"No, I was strictly a Monopoly enthusiast. Even as a child I knew the only way to live well was to get rich. But one of the technicians explained it to me this morning. He suggested we start looking for Colonel Mustard."

"I don't think he came to the festival this year," I replied with as straight a face as I could manage. "And there's no conservatory in the hotel."

"Don't start."

"What about John's phone?"

"It's here in the hotel somewhere. We tried calling but no one answered. I've got people looking for it."

"Have you talked to Daryl Plimpton yet?"

She sighed and sat down on the bed so Dusty and I drifted over to the settee. "Yes, I interviewed him just before midnight. He is not happy that we are wasting his time. He is not happy that security is so lax that such a thing could happen at his event. He is certain that this was a random killing with no connection to the film festival. He has an alibi, insisted upon that even before we told him the approximate time of death. He knows the mayor and the governor personally and will have something to say to both of them about all of this. He's a pretty important person and his time is valuable. He knows his rights and doesn't understand why a more experienced – presumably male – detective has not been assigned to the case."

"That sounds like Daryl," said Dusty.

"He came around eventually." Bullard smiled. "I told him that I might have to shut down some of his function areas in order to search for clues. He took the hint."

"Daryl is reasonably bright," I observed. "But he holds grudges."

"So do I."

I was in the process of handing her my cell phone so that she could see the text message when the one already in her pocket beeped. She held it to her ear, listened a while, said "Okay," and returned it to her pocket. "Our killer has been in touch."

"Oh?" I could tell she was trying to decide whether or not to explain further. She decided in our favor.

"He called in and sent a letter. Both say exactly the same thing. 'Room 416 was the first.' No signature."

"So maybe John was chosen randomly after all."

"Which just makes my job that much harder."

I reminded myself that this was not my job. I sympathized with Bullard but I wasn't planning to share her pain. "I'll bet the lab guys don't find anything helpful. The killer is too organized to make a silly mistake."

She nodded. "The individual words were cut out of a newspaper and glued in place. Same for the address on the envelope. No prints, of course. I'd have been suspicious if there had been."

"How about the phone call? Anything there?"

"It was a recording, about ten seconds long. Each word was spoken in a different voice. I'd guess it had been recorded from television or DVDs or something."

"Male or female voices?" Dusty asked.

"Both."

I handed her my cell. "I don't think you're going to find anything helpful when you locate John's phone. The killer probably just tossed it when he was done. I'm surprised he didn't remove the battery."

Bullard nodded. "It's just another part of the game, but we still have to find it. Are you two sticking around?"

"We paid for memberships. We're hoping to visit with a couple of old friends."

"I'd like to be able to get in touch with you if something comes up. I still think this has something to do with this convention."

I wasn't unhappy at the prospect of having an inside track despite my resolve to stay away from the investigation. "Any reason in particular?"

"Your friend was killed about an hour after he checked in. It's almost as though someone was lying in wait for him. And the elaborate death scene doesn't feel like a random serial killer. It was personal. But now I wonder if it's still just stage setting."

I frowned, then realized what she was getting at. "Maybe John wasn't the real target. He was just camouflage."

"It's an unhappy possibility."

"Still could be random."

"Yeah. Life sucks." And her phone rang again.

It took longer this time. Bullard paced back and forth, mostly listening, occasionally asking generic questions which didn't tell us much about whatever the subject of the conversation was. I was wondering if it was time to go but when Dusty and I stood up, Bullard waved for us to stay where we were. We did, but we didn't sit back down.

At last she put the cell away and stared at a blank wall for a few seconds. Bullard is as sharp as they come. Her unsuccessful cases almost always came because her superiors decided she'd spent too much time on them and that she would be more useful elsewhere. She was no Sherlock Holmes – who was? – but she was observant, organized, analytical, and determined. She was also very pragmatic.

"If I tell you two something, will you keep it to yourselves?" She knew the answer. The question was ritual. We reassured her. "The autopsy still isn't technically over but the coroner found a couple of interesting things already. One of them I'd half expected. The victim's stomach was full of poison – arsenic – enough to wipe out everyone in the hotel."

I had one of my rare moments of almost clairvoyant clarity. "The rubber hose."

Bullard raised her eyebrows appreciatively. "Private eye hits home run."

Dusty had no idea what we were talking about and I realized she hadn't heard about the length of rubber hose found under the bed. I explained and she was ahead of me half way through. "Someone forced the tube down his throat and poured in the arsenic."

"There was bruising in his trachea and esophagus," confirmed Bullard. The arsenic was in solution. The coroner suggests that after the hose was full of the fluid, the killer used some kind of plunger to force it all into the stomach."

"Wouldn't he have vomited it up?" asked Dusty.

"Ordinarily, yes. But he was already dead when the poison was administered."

"So we still don't have a cause of death?" I confess that this struck me as rather funny at the time, but possibly I was in shock.

"Oh, yes we do. John Boncoddo drowned." She looked back and forth between us. "And he drowned in salt water. His lungs were full of it."

My friends will tell you that I'm rarely at a loss for words, though I often keep them to myself. They'd be right. On this occasion, it was as though my thought processes had simultaneously begun to race uncontrollably and frozen solidly in place. Dusty's expression suggested that she was similarly dazzled, but she recovered more quickly.

"Are you seriously trying to tell us that John was dragged down to the Bay, drowned, and then carried back to his room? Or was he already dead and zombified when he checked in?"

That nudged me a little. "Do we know for sure that it was John who checked in and whom the bellhop led upstairs? If John was already dead, maybe it was the killer impersonating him, who somehow brought the body up later?"

Bullard shook her head. "The time frame doesn't work and the bellhop identified the body as the man he had spoken to earlier in the day. Besides, we know he wasn't drowned in Narragansett Bay. The water in his lungs was full of salt, all right, but it was table salt."

"You're kidding me."

Bullard shook her head. "Actually, I find that a bit reassuring. I was really beginning to think I was stuck in a board game."

Dusty shook her head. "Not unless there's a candlestick and a lead pipe you're not telling us about." Neither Bullard nor I responded. "Those are the other two weapons in Clue," she explained.

"Which makes this no less bizarre." Bullard sighed. "Off the record I could use your help on this one." She was speaking to me but she turned her head to include Dusty. "I can't tell two thousand people not to leave the city until I complete my investigation. If Boncoddo was targeted specifically, you know people who might have some ideas but who wouldn't talk to me about it. If it's a random crazy, he'll probably strike again."

"You think the messages were genuine?"

"They mentioned the room number. As far as I know, that hasn't leaked yet." She sounded weary.

"Doesn't mean it hasn't. I know the security man who was up here. He's not the discreet type." Mickey Palotto had been a sneak and a bully. He'd been caught vandalizing cars at least twice and narrowly avoided jail time for shoplifting. The only reason they caught him for the last was because he bragged about it once too often.

"Have you talked to any of the people we suggested?" asked Dusty.

"Just Plimpton. But he's supposed to have someone locating the others for us. Both hotels are loaning us the use of an office for interviews." She looked around. "There's not much else we can do here but we're holding this room for another couple of days just in case."

"Whoever the killer was, he or she walked in here with some kind of bag or other large container."

Bullard blinked. "How do you figure that?"

"They were carrying a piece of hose, a gun, a dagger, a container of arsenic and another of table salt, a good sized length of rope, and a wrench. That adds up to considerable volume."

"Good point. After all," she added sarcastically. "How many people in a hotel are likely to have a suitcase with them?"

CHAPTER THREE

Dusty and I returned to the Biltmore. There actually was a movie about to start that I wanted to see, a 1944 comedy starring Chester Morris called *Double Exposure*, but I knew that I would be unable to sit still even for its relatively short screening time. We went up to the main dealers' room – there were a few satellite areas scattered around – and pretended to be browsing the merchandise when we were actually browsing the crowd. It didn't take long to spot someone we wanted to talk to. Bob Strossi was dickering with a bearded man hawking lobby cards and other memorabilia. Dusty barely knew him so we separated and I walked over, pretending to be interested in some black and white stills of Dorothy Provine.

I acted as though I hadn't noticed Bob until the dealer excused himself to talk to another customer. "Bob! I haven't seen you since Cleveland. What was that, four years ago?"

For a second I thought he'd failed to recognize me. We were acquaintances, not friends. But then I remembered that his face rarely gave anything away and that he always seemed to be rehearsing his words before he spoke.

"I haven't been to a festival in a while. Money has been tight."

When we'd last met, Bob had just parted ways with John's company. "What've you been up to?"

"Film development. Assisting the producers. Some location scouting. Nothing you'd have heard of. Direct to video stuff. It's crap but it pays and the work is steady."

"Did you see the papers this morning?"

"No. Should I have?"

"John Boncoddo died yesterday." Actually, I hadn't seen the morning paper either, but the story was on the internet and someone had released John's name.

Bob made a sound somewhere between a snort and a grunt. "What'd he do? Stick his dick into an electric outlet?"

"Oh, that's right. I forgot you used to work for him," I lied. "How'd that work out?"

"It didn't. So how did he die? Painfully, I hope."

"It's not clear. The paper said the police hadn't determined whether it was suicide or an accident or what."

The dealer came back but Bob shook his head and stepped away from the table. "Nice seeing you, Birch." He walked off into the crowd.

Not the most productive interview I've ever conducted. It turned out that Dusty was having much better luck.

I found her talking to Muriel Bates and the younger woman I had seen with her at the restaurant. Muriel had been a skinny teenager when she first started showing up a film festivals. John took her under his wing at some point and they spent a lot of time together, although I don't know if there ever had any contact away from film fandom. She was originally from Nebraska or Kansas or some place around there, and she'd struck me as almost unrealistically naïve on the few occasions when I'd spoken to her. I doubt they had a physical relationship – John had never expressed any interest in sex or romance or anything else outside the world of movies and, occasionally, television shows, although he always insisted they were an inferior form.

Eventually the fledgling left the nest. I don't think there was any overt breakup, just a winnowing away as she grew more confident and developed other friends. She'd filled out a little and although she'd never pose on the cover of *Cosmopolitan*, she was not unattractive. Her voice was a problem though. It was high pitched, almost squeaky, and she almost always talked just above a whisper because she was so self conscious about it.

Dusty waved for me to join them. "Muriel and I were just talking about what happened to John. She was supposed to get together with him later this weekend. This is her sister, Angela."

I shook hands with Angela, who looked as though she was terrified, and habitually so. I'm surprised that I didn't notice the resemblance because she looked a lot like Muriel had a few years earlier.

"They're going to get a late breakfast and I thought we might join them." Dusty had always found Muriel to be annoyingly passive so I was a bit surprised until I realized what was going on. Dusty was detecting. This was not one of her more endearing qualities and on one occasion it had nearly gotten the two of us killed. If I'd been forewarned, I would have given her The Lecture, but that opportunity was past now.

"Sure. I could use some coffee and a bagel. Where to?"

There was a bagel shop about a block away. It was filled with people wearing convention membership badges, but they all seemed to be getting their food to go so we had no trouble finding a tiny table in the rear where we could sit. Angela had hot chocolate, Muriel drank tea, while Dusty and I over caffeinated ourselves.

"So how have you been?" I asked, hoping to disrupt whatever verbal strategy Dusty might be developing. Yes, we were supposedly going to help Bullard if we could, but I planned to do so passively, ears and eyes open, mouth shut. My little gambit with Strossi had been an aberration, I told myself.

"Oh, you know, about the same as ever. I'm back living in a tiny apartment in Chicago."

"But not much longer," said Angela, who dropped her eyes when Muriel looked in her direction. I thought I saw a hint of anger, which looked so inappropriate on meek little Muriel that it startled me.

"Didn't you move to Michigan for a while?" asked Dusty, whom I was quite sure had made the same observation.

Muriel nodded. "I spent a couple of months there as a kind of research assistant for a west coast company. But that was just a temporary thing."

"What kind of research?" I wondered aloud.

Muriel shrugged but her eyes were wary. "I had to sign a confidentiality agreement and I'm not supposed to talk about it. It was boring anyway." Her voice changed tone slightly, or maybe I just imagined it because I was on edge.

I decided to change the subject. "Terrible thing about John." This wasn't fishing, exactly. We all knew John and it would be more peculiar if we didn't talk about it.

Muriel nodded energetically. "Horrible. I hadn't seen him in almost a year, but we kept in touch. He was really looking forward to this year's festival. We both were."

"Are you on the committee this year?" asked Dusty.

"No, not really. I helped out with the programming committee a little, but it was unofficial. Daryl and I don't work together well."

"Daryl doesn't work well with anyone, so that's not much of a distinction." Dusty had volunteered to be on the convention committee once and had vowed never to do so again. She took a sip of her coffee and I could almost hear the gears working inside her head as she chose her next question. "Has John been acting any different lately?"

"Not really. I mean, it's hard to tell from emails and I think we've only talked on the phone once this year. I know he had some money problems for a while, but he was pretty sure he was going to get that all cleared up before the end of the year."

Now she had me hooked. The question came out before I realized I was going to say anything. "What kind of money problems?"

Muriel hesitated. "Something to do with his business. I guess they lost a couple of their best clients. There was a real flurry of work when DVDs of vintage films started going on the market, but the most commercial ones are available now and the streaming services don't require the same degree of quality so the restoration business mostly dried up. He had to mortgage his house and stuff, but it wasn't like millions of dollars or anything like that. And he was expecting some money he was due so he wasn't really worried."

"Do you know where the money was coming from?" I asked.

"John didn't tell me his private business." It was obvious to me that Muriel either did know or had a strong suspicion but wasn't about to tell us. I saw that Dusty had come to the same conclusion, but I shook my head slightly to indicate she should back off. Muriel could get very stubborn when she didn't want to do something that was being urged upon her.

"I see Bob Strossi is here." Despite my irritation that Dusty had gotten me into this conversation, I found that I was caught up in it now. "Didn't he use to work for John?"

"For about five minutes. I knew that wouldn't work. John was a purist; Bob is all for enhancement." This was an old argument in the film community. Should classic movies be simply restored to their original state, or should modern technology make "improvements" to appeal to contemporary tastes. Colorization was the biggest bone of contention, but there were others.

"Did he quit or was he fired?"

Muriel seemed more at ease now but Angela was squirming uncomfortably. "I think it was a little of both. What is usually called a mutual agreement to go their separate ways." She glanced at her sister. "Do you know any of the gory details?" She glanced back and forth between Dusty and I quickly. "Angela and Bob dated for a while."

Angela, who was blushing, spoke barely above a whisper. "We went out twice. Once at last year's festival, and then a few weeks ago he was in Cleveland on business and we went out to dinner. It really wasn't a date."

Muriel smiled. "I bet he thought it was." Angela, although rather too thin and far too self effacing as far as I was concerned, radiated a vulnerable simplicity that some men found appealing. I didn't know Strossi well. He was a big man, solid and tall, with craggy features and a booming voice. They were both socially inept, although in very different ways.

"Is he working again?"

"Oh yes. John gave him a glowing recommendation. He scouts locations for movies and does odd jobs, but he's looking for something more permanent. That's why he was in Cleveland. He likes travelling so the job was perfect for him." There was a hint of animation in her voice and I suspected that despite her disavowal, she had thought of their evening together as a date.

Dusty turned toward Angela. "So what kinds of movies do you like, Angela? Romantic comedies? Noir?"

The glimmer of self assertion of a moment before promptly went out. "Oh, nothing in particular. I just came along to keep Muriel company."

That was a fib. But Angela's business was Angela's business and I suspected that it had something to do with Bob Strossi. We finished our food and tossed the trash into a receptacle, then walked toward the hotel. Back at the Biltmore, we made vague plans about having lunch together which we all knew were not going to happen and the Bates sisters wandered off in the direction of screening room one.

"What do you think you're doing, Dusty?" I tried to make my voice sound mature and chiding at the same time.

"Just catching up with an old friend." Her smile was dazzling and disingenuous.

"We're supposed to gather names and observe. This isn't our investigation. Detective Bullard is going to be very unhappy if we say or do anything that infringes on her duties."

"And rightly so. But we won't do that. We're going to ask perfectly innocent questions of people we know, questions I might add that we would probably have asked them anyway. If we turn up anything interesting, we'll pass it on to her at the first opportunity. And I noticed you couldn't resist a hint of the third degree."

I was about to escalate my warning when we were interrupted. Terry Wareham and Jimmy Gonsalves had appeared out of the crowd and spotted us. Terry was an odd duck. She had cofounded the VFF with Daryl – although she was only credited as being an assistant - and the two of them had lived together for several years, until they had a very public breakup at the festival in Albuquerque. She still attended every year and was on the board of trustees, but she rarely had any direct involvement in administering the festivals. As far as I knew, she and Daryl hadn't spoken since the day she had found out he was also seeing Helen Viele, which had proved to be an even shorter association. Helen had an exaggerated need for novelty in her bed partners. Terry had started to work on her weight problem in recent years and was considerably slimmer than I remembered, though still a bit pudgy.

Jimmy I didn't know very well at all, even though he was a regular. Jimmy was almost unnaturally quiet and he tended to blend into the scenery. He'd been part of dinner parties I'd attended but I don't remember him ever saying very much and he always seemed to be alone. Terry was a few years older than he and had been living with a plumber in Milwaukee who refused to watch black and white movies. She had recently relocated to Albany, which was where Jimmy was from, but it was because she'd had a very welcome job offer. I doubted very much that she and Jimmy were a couple but they were obviously together for some purpose at the moment.

"We missed you last year," said Terry after we'd exchanged the usual greetings.

"Both of us were busy. I needed space for more offices at work so we had construction going and Dusty was facing a deadline."

"I enjoyed your last," Terry informed Dusty, and unlike most people she actually meant it. She was an enthusiastic if somewhat undiscriminating reader. "Jimmy has some good news we're trying to spread around."

Like I said, I didn't know much about Jimmy. He was my age or a bit older and just slightly overweight. It showed mostly in his face. I thought someone had told me he was a computer programmer or something similar, but I couldn't remember any details. I doubt we had exchanged fifty words in our lives, which is a little unusual since I'm one of those people who feels guilty if anyone is left out of a conversation and I usually make an effort to draw people out. Dusty says it's an aspect of my insatiable curiosity and I suppose she's right.

Jimmy seemed content to let Terry do the talking but she clearly wanted him to explain himself. He cleared his throat and wouldn't quite meet anyone's eyes, but his voice was level and confident. "I bought a movie theater."

I don't know about Dusty but I thought I'd misheard him. "It's in Albany," said Terry. "I used to live in the same neighborhood when I was a kid and I remember the Saturday matinees. It closed down a long time ago. They couldn't afford to convert to stadium seating and replace all the projection equipment with digital. And there was no handicap access."

Jimmy gathered himself together. "They sold it as a tear down, but I had it checked out. It needs a new fire suppression system and some repairs here and there, but the wheelchair ramp won't be difficult and since I'm keeping the old projectors and seating, it won't cost a whole lot to reopen."

"That sounds great," I said guardedly. Actually, it sounded like a good way to lose a lot of money really fast. "But how are you going to compete with the big cinema chains?"

"I won't. I'm only going to show vintage movies. Cheap rental so I can sell cheap tickets. Make my money on the refreshments like everyone else."

Terry looked almost flushed with enthusiasm. "Tell them about Saturdays."

"Special matinee every Saturday. Three movies, three cartoons, previews, newsreel, and a cliff hanger serial. *Zorro, the Whispering Shadow, Congo Bill*, stuff like that. A lot of it is public domain. I'll need a digital system eventually, I suppose, but I'll wait until I can get a used one without any frills. Two bucks for adults, one buck for kids."

I wondered if Jimmy had talked to an accountant. At those rates – even with popcorn and soda thrown in – he'd never even cover his overhead – maintenance, insurance, employee wages and benefits. There were a lot of expenses running a business that weren't obvious. I should know. My agency only turned a profit in its third year.

"What's the property tax like?" I asked.

"Not a problem. The city arts council will subsidize that since it's going to be a non-profit."

"Non-profit?" Dusty and I spoke in unison.

"Sure. You don't think I could make any real money this way, do you? I'll be lucky to break even. But people will get to see all these movies again the way they were meant to be seen."

I appreciated his enthusiasm, if not his financial acumen. "You're taking a lot of risk there. You could lose your entire investment, you know."

"That's all right. It was a kind of windfall anyway. I never really felt like I was entitled to it."

There was a slight pause and Dusty changed the subject quickly. "Wasn't it horrible about John Boncoddo?"

Jimmy nodded vaguely and Terry allowed herself to look sad, though only for a moment. I remembered that she had never been able to tolerate John. His boisterous nature and conviction that he was welcome to join any conversation that appealed to him had not set well with her.

"They didn't say much about it on the news. I suppose it was suicide. John was always the nervous type."

I felt the urge to defend my friend, even though she was technically correct. "His intentions were always good. He was just so enthusiastic about everything and he always wanted to share. And no, it wasn't suicide." I probably shouldn't have said

48

the last, since the police had been characteristically vague about the circumstances of his death. That wouldn't last though, since they were presumably already questioning people at the festival.

"Do you know something the rest of us don't?" asked Terry. She was aware that I ran a detective agency.

"I know that John was not the kind of person to take his own life."

Terry's face cycled through a list of reactions before she could choose one. "I could see why someone might want to punch him in the mouth, but he wasn't annoying enough for someone to kill him."

I didn't respond. I had already said too much. Dusty came to the rescue. "There are a lot of crazy people in the world. Maybe someone just picked him at random."

"Yeah, I can see that."

We were interrupted at that point by Jo Parkin, who was looking rather harried. "There you are! I've been looking all over for you."

She was obviously speaking to me but I had no idea why. "What can I do for you, Jo?"

"Daryl asked me to find you. He needs to talk to you about something." She looked around hastily as though afraid the wrong person might be listening in. Terry gave a little understanding wave and she and Jimmy drifted away.

"What does he want to talk to me about?" I really didn't care for Daryl at all. I don't think I had realized how much I disliked him until that very minute. It wouldn't be long before I had an even better excuse.

"I'm not supposed to say anything about it where I might be overheard." She glanced around at the completely uncaring throng and lowered her voice. "It's about the murder."

"If Daryl knows anything about John's death, he needs to talk to the police, not me."

"Oh, he's already spoken to them. He was really concerned when he heard."

I'd bet the rent that he hadn't shed a tear, not even metaphorically. "So what has that got to do with me?"

Something in my tone must have gotten through because Jo was instantly defensive, and perhaps slightly irritated. She wasn't

49

exactly a Daryl groupie, but I know they'd spent a few nights together at previous festivals. "He said he thought you might be able to help."

I sighed. "Daryl has been watching too many Boston Blackie movies. The police neither require nor desire the help of private investigators. They consider us poachers at best, active impediments at worst. I happen to know the detective assigned to this case," which I probably shouldn't have mentioned, "and she's very good at her job."

Jo nodded but I thought it signified acknowledgment rather than agreement. "I'm sure that's true. Look, why don't you just talk to Daryl and find out what he wants. You can always turn him down."

I was ready to get stubborn but Dusty put her hand on my arm. "Why don't we talk to him, Paul? It couldn't hurt." She gave me a meaningful look. Unfortunately, the meaning was that we were on the case and Daryl was potentially an important witness. I felt a very uncharacteristic urge to pick her up and shake her, but instead I nodded.

"I suppose you're right. Let's go."

Jo took out her cell phone and called to find out where Daryl was. "He'll meet us in operations, down past the green room."

The crowd had become much heavier during the last few minutes and it took us longer than usual to make our way through it, Jo leading. We climbed the stairs to the second level, passing a couple dressed to look like the leads from *The Thin Man*. The guy doing William Powell looked a lot like him, but his partner was more Kim Kardashian than Myrna Loy.

The green room was packed as well with people who were appearing on the various panel discussions standing in line to draw cups of bad coffee from large urns mounted on a table. We passed without stopping. The next room was even bigger. There were almost a dozen computers set up, most of them manned or womanned. Stacks of paper – time schedules, hotel maps, and attendance lists – were scattered about. No one looked up when we entered and I didn't see Daryl.

"He's this way. Private office."

At the rear of the room was another door that indeed led to a private space that barely accommodated a small table with a laptop and printer. Daryl was sitting behind the desk and he did glance up, but his eyes went immediately back to the screen, which we couldn't see. I suspected it was blank and that he was just trying to point out subliminally that his time was more valuable than ours. He played that kind of game a lot. There was one folding chair in front of the desk. I gestured for Dusty to sit and she did. Jo retreated into one corner.

Daryl looked pretty much the same as always. He was older, obviously, but he had always seemed to me prematurely aged. He was gray haired when I first met him, but it was a bit lighter now. He wore a sports coat and a white shirt, no tie, and his hair was so neat it looked fake. I noticed that his moustache was thinner than it used to be and I thought I saw a few lines that were new, but when he leaned back and looked at me directly, I felt my usual antagonism.

"Nice to see you again, Birch." He glanced at Dusty. "And you as well, Rhodes. I gather the two of you are still together." Before we could answer, he turned to Jo. "I won't need you for this, Jo."

I didn't turn to see how she took this dismissal, but the door closed behind me almost immediately. "What can we do for you, Daryl?"

"I assume you've heard about yesterday's incident."

"If you mean John Boncoddo's murder, I'd call it rather more than an incident."

He dismissed my annoyance with a wave. "Whatever. John was a friend of mine too, you realize."

Actually, I didn't think that was true. Daryl did not have any friends. He had hundreds of acquaintances and dozens of admirers, some of whom were devoted in some degree to making his life easier, but I doubt that Daryl had ever returned the favor unless it was the preliminary to requesting an even bigger sacrifice. "It doesn't seem to have scared away your customers." That was designed to irritate him, I confess. Daryl preferred to be thought of as a philanthropist supporting the arts and providing access to classic films for people who might not otherwise have the opportunity to see them. I admit that he was providing a service, and a welcome one, but his motives were primarily pecuniary. The festivals and a few minor events that he arranged during the intervals between them were his main source of income, and he did not lead a particularly ascetic life.

"This will be out largest attendance since New York City." Daryl could never resist a chance to boast. "And I don't want anything to go wrong."

"I'm sure John is sorry that his death put your plans in jeopardy." I was being petty but I didn't like being summoned and I was pretty sure I wasn't going to like what Daryl wanted from me either.

He pretended not to be offended, but I'm sure he filed my remark away. Daryl had a long memory for affronts, intentional or otherwise, and was always watching for a chance to avenge them. For a split second I wondered if Daryl had killed John, but no, that wouldn't be his style. He would have chosen something more public.

"The police interviewed me this morning."

"I imagine they'll be talking to a number of people. John had a lot of friends here."

"I asked them to minimize the disruption. Local police are generally willing to be cooperative at events like this. They don't want to risk losing the out of state money."

I couldn't imagine Detective Bullard pulling any punches just because it might offend a tourist, but I didn't say anything.

"Personally I think someone just chose John at random. He'd just checked in. Someone must have followed him up to his room, got inside somehow, and that was that. It probably had nothing to do with the festival at all."

"That's certainly possible," I conceded.

"The police seem to feel otherwise. The detective in charge – an unpleasant woman – suggests that the circumstances surrounding John's death indicate that whoever did it was acting out of extreme and very personal hatred. If she's right, John had made a very bad enemy."

I doubted that Bullard had told Daryl the specifics of John's death, so I didn't enlighten him. "Which turns the spotlight back on the festival."

"So it seems."

"What do you want me to do about it?" I was pretty sure I knew approximately what he was going to say next, and it turned out that I was absolutely right.

"You're a professional, Birch. And you know how to be discreet. It would help the festival immensely if you could find out what really happened and this was all cleared up without unnecessary publicity."

"Are you trying to hire my services, Daryl?"

He looked uncomfortable. "Our budget is really tight this year. I thought you might look around a little, in the interests of the community. And out of courtesy to John's memory, of course."

"You do some lecturing around the country, don't t you?"

The change of subject obviously puzzled him. "Yes, actually I do quite a bit. A lot of colleges have film clubs and things like that."

"Do you charge them a fee or do you donate your time?"

"Well, I have expenses, you realize, and..." He stopped, realizing where this was heading. "It's not the same thing at all. This is how I make my living and I barely get by as it is. You have a successful business."

It wasn't worth arguing. Dusty wasn't going to let me get away with not looking into John's death anyway, and if Daryl was cooperative, it would be easier in the long run. "All right, I'll keep my eyes open. No promises."

"That's all I ask." But not as much as he hoped for, obviously.

"How much did the police tell you?"

Daryl provided a concise summary. Bullard had said only that John had died under suspicious circumstances; Daryl had correctly interpolated that it was murder. Daryl was not a stupid man. She had mentioned that John had died less than an hour after checking in but she did not mention the circumstances of his death, nor had she mentioned that Dusty and I were involved. The questions she had asked had been predictable. Who were John's closest friends? "I mentioned the two of you, I'm afraid." Did he have any enemies? "I told them John had a tendency to irritate people but that I didn't know of anyone who actively hated him. I did mention Bob Strossi, since they would have found out about him anyway." They had asked about John's business in California and Daryl had told them quite a lot. "I used him for a couple of restoration projects. He was really good at that sort of thing."

"Whose names did you give them besides ours?"

Daryl pushed some paper around his desk and handed me a printout. There were about twenty names on the list. There were some that Dusty and I had not thought of, and others that we had thought of whom Daryl had not included. "These are the people registered at the convention. I told her that it wasn't necessarily one of our members."

"Is there anything else I need to know?"

Daryl hesitated, then shook his head, and I knew that he was lying. Dusty got up and we started to go but Daryl called out just as I opened the door. "Before I forget, you should come to the main ball room at 9:00 tomorrow night if you're not attending the banquet. I have something very important to announce."

"We'll try," I said insincerely. Daryl's definition of what was important was closely associated with what was good for Daryl and might well be of little interest to anyone else.

CHAPTER FOUR

I made a completely futile effort to dampen Dusty's enthusiasm. "Sasha Bullard runs a tight ship. She won't appreciate if we start making waves. Or even ripples."

"Don't be silly. She asked for our help, remember?"

"She asked for a list of names. She didn't swear us in as deputies."

"Don't be such a spoil sport." She pretended to pout. "We're just going to talk to people like we would have done anyway. We'll just be a little more focused about what we want to talk about."

"Thereby tipping off the killer that we're hot on his or her trail. That usually doesn't come out well, remember?"

She put her hands on her hips and cocked her head slightly to one side. "Do you really think that any of the people on our list could kill anyone? This is about as passive a crowd as you can get, if we don't count Daryl."

"Killers don't always look the part, as we have reason to know. And someone did kill John."

That struck home, at least a little. "All right, I grant your point. But look, we'd be talking about John's death anyway. It would be stranger if we avoided the subject."

"Yeah, I guess. But keep in mind that we're not supposed to know any more than anyone else. Bullard hasn't told the press that we found the body."

"Okay, but the thing about that is, the killer already knows that we did, because the killer arranged it so that we would."

She was right. I hadn't thought about that. "I'm not convinced that proves the killer was one of our crowd. They had John's cell; they could have chosen me at random, or skimmed the messages until they found someone local."

"It wasn't a spur of the moment thing. Someone put a lot of planning into this."

"Yes, but John could still have been chosen randomly. An unaccompanied male, particularly a little guy who could be overpowered without too much difficulty. The killer could have staked out the hotel until a likely victim showed up. Remember,

John was killed less than an hour after he arrived. Most people wouldn't even know that he had arrived."

We were back on the balcony overlooking the main lobby. The crowd seethed below us and there were lines at the elevators. I spotted a discarded program someone had dropped on a chair and picked it up.

"What are you looking for?" Dusty tried to read by leaning her head against my arm.

Most of the screenings were in the Biltmore and the Marriott, as were the main program events. There was a special shuttle to move attendees from one location to the next. There were two dealers' rooms, one in the Driscoll, the other a sprawling affair in the function rooms at the top of the Biltmore. The panels were similarly distributed. I found Romeo Bolduc's name listed for a panel that should be ending in about twenty minutes. It was at the Driscoll. Romeo and John had exchanged insults publicly on a couple of occasions, although I had no idea what their disagreements were about. As far as I know there had never been anything physical between them.

"Let's take a walk."

"Are you going to tell me what we're doing?"

I smiled secretively. "Eventually."

It was a ten minute walk to the Driscoll and since it took another five to find the right room, we didn't have long to wait. The doors opened and a fairly large crowd began to head for the restrooms or another program item or just milled around talking to one another or reading their program guides. The topic of the panel had been "Bad Casting: Which Actors Played the Most Inappropriate Parts."

Romeo appeared like a whale breaching. He was even more enormous than I remembered. It wouldn't be long before he had to attend festivals in a motorized cart. His hair was unruly and he hadn't shaved that morning, or perhaps for a couple of mornings. It was hard to tell because the whiskers were buried in multiple chins. I was about ready to cross him off my mental list of suspects just based on his physical condition, but when I thought about it, I had to admit that there was no element of John's murder that he could not have physically accomplished if he was motivated enough. I couldn't see him planning the elaborate murder scene, but he was intelligent enough, just unfocused, lazy, and unimaginative.

"Romeo!" I called.

He swiveled his head in our direction and raised his eyebrows in acknowledgment. When we'd both been younger, and he was a hundred pounds or so lighter, we'd had dinner together a few times and drinks a few more. He could be very entertaining when he was talking about something he cared about and knew well. Unfortunately, there were only a couple of things that fell into that category, which rather limited our conversation. Back when Jimmy Carter was President, Romeo admitted that he had no idea who the Vice-President was, and he only bought a computer to download film clips and read websites devoted to vintage movies.

The crowd made way for him and he smiled when he spotted Dusty. I always suspected Romeo was a frustrated Romeo. "Paul, Dusty, how are you both? It's been a while. I missed last year's festival. Broke an ankle."

"We missed it too. I saw your name on the program and we wanted to make sure we at least said hello this time."

Romeo spotted an open couch – there were no chairs that could accommodate his girth – and gravitated toward it, pulling us in his wake. On panels, he always used two chairs set side by side. He collapsed onto it with an audible sigh, and the couch gave an audible groan of protest.

We caught up a little – Romeo's life never changed so that part was short, and he had no interest in my agency or Dusty's books, so our half was about the same. "I assume you've heard about John."

His face fell a little. "Terrible thing. John and I weren't on the best of terms you know, and I feel kind of bad about it now."

"I thought the two of you were friends. Didn't you work on some projects together?" Dusty spoke up before I could, but the question was pretty much what I had planned to ask.

"When we were a lot younger, we did some stuff, yeah. After John started his business he didn't have much time for stuff that wouldn't pay, but he did a couple of things for me as favors, and I did some research he needed in return. I know he tended to get on people's nerves because he had so much nervous energy, but it never bothered me. I like working with enthusiastic people."

"So what did you guys argue about?" I had to admit the question felt less intrusive from Dusty than it probably would have been for me.

"It was silly really, now that I think back on it. I wrote this article for *Periodpics*, you know, the film collectors' magazine. It was about famous lost films like *London After Midnight* and the first Charlie Chan movie and stuff like that. I mentioned *At the Mountains of Madness* a couple of times and said it was almost certainly lost forever. When I sent John an advance copy of the article, he told me I should take those references out. I asked him if he knew something that I didn't know and he wouldn't say anything, and I was a little miffed when he wouldn't explain. Then six months later, Daryl announces that he's found a print and debuts it at that year's festival. I was still a little pissed and when I saw John I asked him why he hadn't told me the whole story. He knew I would have kept my mouth shut if he'd asked. But he denied ever having said anything in the first place, insisted he hadn't known a thing about Daryl's discovery, and he was so obviously lying that I guess I raised my voice and he raised his and we both have pretty loud voices. It was mostly my fault though because John was never the kind to hold a grudge, but I was having some health problems at the time and I was feeling sorry for myself and probably looking for someone else to blame. I'm pretty sure that John helped restore the film though. I have no idea why he didn't want anyone to know about it."

"Does anyone know the details about how Daryl came up with a copy?"

Romeo shrugged. "I imagine someone does, but he wouldn't tell me when I asked. I was going to write an article about it. I would have given him credit and some free publicity, but he said it was nobody's business but his. Wouldn't say a thing."

Dusty had subsided, her face thoughtful, but I had a couple of more things I wanted to ask. "Do you know if John was on bad terms with anyone else?"

As I said, Romeo wasn't dumb. "Someone killed him, didn't they? The newspaper story was noncommittal and I never thought he was the kind to commit suicide."

"The police haven't said anything either way."

"They never do. That's one thing the movies get right, mostly. And no, I don't know anyone who'd be that mad at John. Bob Strossi was pretty steamed when he got canned, but he picked up a nice gig in its place and I don't think he held much of a grudge. Daryl complained a couple of times that John would hog all the time on a panel, or ask too many questions from the audience, but there's a couple of other people that do the same thing, and at least one of them is much worse than John ever was. I think sometimes that people would stand in line to murder Gene Mallett."

"Is he here?" asked Dusty.

"No, thank God. Broke his leg riding a dirt bike."

"Can you think of anyone else?"

Romeo scratched his head theatrically. "If John was killed, I don't think it was anyone from our group. We all sit around and let things unfold on the screen. We don't really do much ourselves – present company excepted, of course."

And I had to admit that he had a point. But then we talked to Tanya Gregory.

Ray Riccello had once directed a movie called *Return to Dragstrip Hollow*. It wasn't a very good movie and it had national distribution for about five minutes before going straight to VHS and later DVD. It was a slasher style horror movie, underlit, poorly acted, unimaginatively scripted, and with lots of fake blood and screaming. The person who had done most of the screaming was Tanya Gregory, a petite blonde who couldn't act but looked gorgeous in a tight top and cutoff jeans. It would be fair to say that she was the only reason it was still available. Tanya went on to star in *Swamp Monster, The Cancun Bikini Massacre*, and *The Vomitorium*, but her screen career ended at that point because she refused to go topless, let alone do full nudity.

I doubt that Ray made much money from his stint as director because the producers were notorious for screwing the help. But he did get to call himself a director, and that bestowed a certain degree of respect, deserved or not. He appeared on panels regularly, sometimes had his room comped by a convention committee, signed autographs, even wrote his memoirs, available from Amazon only. The biggest advantage of that one time gig was that he ended up with Tanya Gregory, who drank like a fish, swore like a longshoreman, and dressed like a prostitute, but who was entirely loyal to her man. She and Ray were inseparable and had been together for better than ten years now, although they had never married. The nature of their relationship was a frequent subject of speculation.

Dusty and I had spotted Ray in a crowd while we were making up our list, but he'd been alone. Dusty has spotted Tanya a little while later. Although she could be very outspoken when she was alone, she always deferred to Ray, and since we almost always saw her in his company, that was the persona that stuck in our minds. She was almost a non-entity, but probably by choice. The characters she portrayed on screen were always brazen, self confident, and outgoing; in person, she was relatively quiet and deferred to Ray. She worked in an office somewhere.

They were together in the lobby of the Driscoll, surrounded by a group of mostly young males. Tanya had donned her movie star persona and wore a kind of sarong except that it was slit up the sides almost to her waist to show her legs when she walked. She was holding onto Ray's arm while he answered questions. Although she downplayed her intelligence publicly, I knew that Tanya had originally planned to take over her parents' business, a very profitable bed and breakfast. Ray and John had not been speaking on terms for a long time. I had no idea why and until now had been uninterested in finding out. Death changes things.

I guided Dusty to a position where I knew Ray could see us and when I caught his eye I made a brief beckoning gesture to indicate I wanted to talk. Ray gave a half nod and apparently summed up whatever he was saying. His audience began to drift away as the two of them came toward us.

"Hey, Paul! Long time no see." He stuck out a hand and I shook it while Tanya eyed us suspiciously. Or at least eyed Dusty suspiciously. As far as I know she had never had a reason to suspect Ray had wandering eyes, let alone hands, but she always seemed to feel that other women would be irresistibly drawn to him. To be fair, quite a few were. Even aside from his reputation, he was good looking. He was as tall as I am, though a bit on the thin side, with a faintly olive complexion and wavy dark hair that I suspect he colored to cover up the gray. Ray was in his early forties, though he looked younger. Tanya somehow managed to look the same as she had ten years earlier, until you looked into her eyes.

I asked how he was doing. "I'm getting by." Was he working? "I have some projects under consideration." We did small talk for a couple of minutes before Dusty asked if they'd heard about John.

"Yeah. Terrible thing. A big loss to the community." It all came out as a kind of extended word and I suspected that he'd come up with this as his standard answer to the question. All of the regular attendees would be talking about it by now, of course.

And that's when Tanya surprised me.

Tanya was less shy about speaking her mind when she was away from Ray, but she inevitably deferred to him in his presence. I sometimes wondered if her relationship with Ray was a part that she had decided to play and that she was quite literally acting as the devoted lover. They occasionally attended parties separately and it was quite a different Tanya who made coarse jokes, argued heatedly, even shouted down people who annoyed her. So I was quite taken aback when she spoke up sharply while Ray was standing right there.

"Well I for one won't miss the sniveling bastard." Her voice was loud and carried through the room and several conversations around us came to a brief halt, then resumed hesitantly.

Ray gave her an admonishing look and she dropped her eyes, and thankfully her voice. "Well, it's true. My cousin sold him some movie memorabilia and it was worth a lot more than he paid. She was going to talk to a lawyer about it but then she decided it wasn't worth the effort, so he got away with it."

"When was this?" I asked, trying to sound casual.

"I don't know. About three years ago, I think. She had a bunch of posters and stuff that her mom collected. When I found out how little John paid her for the first batch, I told her not to sell him anything else."

That didn't sound promising. "Didn't her family pursue it?"

Tanya shook her head. "Her mom was already dead and she hadn't spoken to her father in years. Someone convinced her it was just junk and she should be thankful she got anything at all for it."

"I can't believe John would commit suicide though," said Ray. "I thought he led a pretty pathetic life, frankly, but he seemed happy and busy. I guess you just can't tell with some people."

"The police haven't said it was suicide," said Dusty. "That usually means there are suspicious circumstances."

"You think someone killed him?" Ray's face was twisted in exaggerated disbelief. "Who would do that? He was a nebbish."

Tanya's eyes flashed but she didn't say anything. "We don't know enough about the circumstances to venture a guess," I admitted. "But if he was killed, it might have been someone we know that did it."

"That's creepy." Ray looked distressed. Tanya looked interested.

"I imagine we'll know more pretty soon." Dusty touched my arm. "Shouldn't we be going over to the Biltmore? Sasha might be looking for us."

I had extracted all that I was likely to learn from this conversation already so I followed her lead. "We'll have to get together for lunch or something."

Ray nodded automatically. "Sure thing. Let's plan on it."

"Did you pick up something I missed?" I asked as soon as we were outside.

"Not really. Tanya really didn't like John, though. Her body language was shouting at us."

"I never realized that. And apparently it's not something new. His name never came up when I've talked to her in the past I guess. Why were you in such a hurry to get away?"

"Maybe I just wanted to get you out of Tanya's clutches."

I shook my head. "Tanya is a one-man woman. And I'm a one-woman man."

"You'd better be." Her voice became more serious. "I thought we should check in with Sasha." It occurred to me to wonder how Dusty got away with calling Bullard by her first name after only having met her effectively once. If I ventured to do the same thing, I suspected that she'd incinerate me with one of her disapproving glares.

I paused in mid-step. "Aren't we going the wrong way then? The situation room is back at the Driscoll."

"I know. But she's also doing interviews in the Biltmore, remember? I saw her in the lobby when we were leaving."

I hadn't remembered. We walked back, both lost in our thoughts. The lobby looked the same as when we left, except different. It was like having a jar of marbles and shaking them up once in a while. I was struck by how normal everything was, how familiar, as if no one was aware that murder was so near. But then again, most of these people hadn't known John and it wasn't even officially a murder yet, and even if it was, there were more important things to think about – like getting a good seat to watch *Seven Keys to Baldpate*.

The desk clerk gave us directions to the room Bullard was using in a hushed voice and the same tone he would probably use to direct a traveling businessman to a brothel. It was on the first floor, but way in the back where the hotel offices were pretty much hidden from public view. The door was closed and a uniformed officer was stationed outside. We identified ourselves and he spoke into his radio.

"You can go on in," he said. "There's no one in with her."

Actually, there was a technician, a young man I'd seen at the Driscoll, but he left almost immediately. The office was furnished with a desk, four chairs, and an empty bookshelf. There was no nameplate on the door. Bullard looked tired.

"Anything turn up?" I asked as we sat down facing her.

"Nothing worth shouting about." Not that she would have felt obligated to tell us even if she had a signed confession and a half dozen witnesses, unless she thought we'd have something to give her in exchange.

"We have a couple more names for you," I told her.

Bullard groaned. "We haven't tracked down everyone on your first list yet, and those we have didn't see or hear anything, don't know anything, and are all very shocked to hear that Boncoddo might have been murdered because he didn't have any enemy in the world. One of them has an alibi – he was running a projector all afternoon – but that's the only progress we've made."

"Fred Hastings," I guessed. Fred worked as a movie projectionist in Madison, Wisconsin.

"That's him. I thought he was going to pass out when I started asking questions." Fred was shy to the point of phobia.

"We found a couple of people who didn't like John," said Dusty, and we cooperatively provided a very comprehensive summary of our morning's conversations. "But I can't see any real motive," she concluded.

I nodded to indicate I agreed.

"I talked to the guy who used to work for him," Bullard consulted her notes although I was sure she didn't need them. "Strossi. He admitted that he detested your friend and would have put the screws on him if the opportunity had presented itself. Insists he didn't hate him enough to kill him though. He sounded convincing but I'm pretty sure he was holding something back. On the other hand, he suggested that I take a closer look at Daryl Plimpton."

"Daryl might kill somebody, but only if there was money to be made. I don't think he's capable of any emotional response that isn't connected to his financial status." Jo Parkin slept with Daryl a few times and lived with him for a few months. She fled rather than left, appalled at his single mindedness and egocentricity.

"Strossi says the two of them did business together."

I nodded. "More than once, I believe. John restored old prints, converted from one format to another, things like that. Daryl sometimes bought old movies and distributed them himself. He made a great find a year or two back, a lost movie called *At the Mountains of Madness*. I wouldn't be surprised if John was the one who cleaned it up for him."

"Worth a lot of money?"

"Depends on what you consider a lot of money. Daryl hasn't released it commercially yet but he gets twenty-five a head when he shows it at festivals. If it went to DVD, I imagine he could pull in fifty thousand or so, maybe twice that. There's limited interest for the old black and white movies, but this particular one would be unusually popular."

"Why is that?"

"It was never actually released. A bunch of semi-amateurs filmed it back in the 1930s and then they got caught up in the war and most of them were killed. No one really knows what happened to it, but they'd done a couple of private showings and a few people wrote about it. We haven't seen it yet and I don't imagine it lives up to its reputation, but then again, few things do."

Bullard has clearly lost interest in the subject. "I don't suppose you spotted this Helen Viele person? No one seems to have seen her since she checked in."

We both shook our heads. "We saw her in the crowd last yesterday, but didn't talk to her."

"Was she with someone? We've left messages and the maid says she didn't sleep in her room last night, but that her bags are still there."

Helen was a bit of a groupie. Well, more than a bit. She slept around a lot, and not just with men either from what I had heard. She was young and attractive, though I found her face a bit hard, and totally uninhibited. There was a brief sensation when she was busted for drugs at the Syracuse festival, but it was a first offense and she came from money, hired a good lawyer, and got off with a slapped wrist. She had insisted that they weren't her drugs, that she was holding them for someone else.

"Helen likes to have a good time," I said. "And she doesn't like to be alone."

"I gathered that much already." Bullard referred to her notes again. "Apparently she and the deceased didn't get along."

"That's news to me." I couldn't imagine the two of them together sexually. John wouldn't have been interested and Helen would have been bored. "They were never a couple as far as I know. And not likely to be."

"She physically assaulted him a year ago."

That would have been the festival Dusty and I had missed. "This is the first I've ever heard of it. Assaulted him how?"

"Slapped his face in front of a few dozen witnesses. Told him to keep his nose out of her business. Said, and I quote, 'I could kill you', and then threw a coffee in his face."

Dusty and I exchanged looks. "I can't imagine what that would have been about."

"John wasn't the romantic type," added Dusty. "But sometimes he didn't realize when he was offending someone. He might have said something rude without realizing what it was, and Helen isn't shy about expressing her anger."

Or expressing anything else, I added silently.

"Maybe so, but I'd sure like to talk to her about it. And I still haven't talked to Romeo Bolduc and Gene Mallett. I sent someone to grab Bolduc after a panel he was on but the jackass went to the wrong room and missed him."

"Mallett's not here. Laid up with a broken leg. Dusty and I just talked to Romeo over at the Driscoll about an hour ago."

"No one else on your list knows anything or can help in any way." Bullard grimaced. "Or at least they're not volunteering."

"What are the chances that John was chosen at random?" asked Dusty.

"I can't dismiss the possibility, but it doesn't feel that way. There was a lot of pre-planning involved. This wasn't done on impulse. And I got the impression that whoever killed your friend really, really didn't like him. Hated him so much, in fact, that he had to be killed more than once."

I shook my head. "It's hard to think of John generating that much venom in someone. He was pretty much an innocuous nerd."

Bullard didn't blink. "Sometimes it doesn't take much."

CHAPTER FIVE

My stomach had started grumbling by the time we left Bullard and I suggested lunch. There was a fairly nice restaurant a block away but when we went inside we saw that it was very crowded, spillover from the festival no doubt. We were about to leave and try elsewhere when someone called my name.

It was Helen Viele. She was standing beside a table just around the corner from us. "Come sit with us. There's room." I glanced at the concierge and he just shrugged and waved us through.

Helen wasn't alone. Bob Strossi was sitting across from her, and I don't think he was as enthusiastic about seeing us as Helen appeared to be. Dusty and I sat down and a harried looking waitress put menus in front of us.

"Bob's just been telling me that someone killed John Boncoddo."

"They found him dead in his hotel room last night, but I don't think they've announced the cause of death yet," I said tactfully.

"But the police are investigating. They're talking to everyone, I gather."

"Well, not everyone," I replied. "Just the people who knew John particularly well. We just left them in fact. They're looking for you, Helen."

She nodded. "I know. They left a message on the phone in my room."

"It's probably not a good idea to ignore it," said Dusty, who was not a member of the Helen Viele fan club. Helen had once made a pass at me while Dusty was standing right there with us. And apparently on another occasion she had made an even more obvious pass at Dusty.

"Oh, I wasn't going to ignore it, but I had some things to do and then it was lunchtime and I didn't want to go through the third degree on an empty stomach. So I snagged Bob in the lobby and dragged him over here to eat lunch with me and tell me what was going on."

"I don't really know what's going on," Bob protested. "I hadn't spoken to John for a long time and I have no idea if he was into something dangerous."

"He might have stumbled into something without knowing it, you know, like *North by Northwest*. He was always sticking his nose where it didn't belong."

"Didn't I hear that you had a run in with him a while back, Helen?" I tried to make the question sound casual.

"I sure did. I told him off about it too. I wanted pull out his tongue and cut it off." She seemed to realize what she was saying wasn't very politic at the moment and visibly caught herself. "It wasn't actually that big a deal. We were at a party last year and I was staying with," she hesitated, "with a friend because I didn't get my reservation in on time to book a room at the main hotel. Anyway, this friend and I go way back and we've been more than friends off and on, if you know what I mean, and last year we were really connecting. But she's pretty shy and likes her privacy and we were being careful, but John somehow figured out what was going on and he started talking about it like everyone knew. She was standing right there and I could see her face drop so I started in on him like crazy. I wasn't really all that mad at first but I figured if I made a scene and he backed off, it would be better than letting him keep shooting his mouth off. I didn't really care who knew myself, but she was really upset. Wouldn't let me touch her for the rest of the festival either. And that really pissed me off so I looked him up later on and really laid into him some more. I wanted to scare the shit out of him so that he'd never do anything like that again."

So there was someone else who had a good reason to dislike John. The motive didn't seem strong enough to me, but people are funny. "Who was it?" I asked, not really expecting a name, and I didn't get one.

"That would be telling, wouldn't it?"

"The police are going to want to know," said Dusty.

"Life is full of disappointments, even for policemen."

"It's a woman who's investigating," I said.

"Then maybe she'll understand why I can't tell her. Anyway, she hasn't been to a festival since then. I think she got married. The cops won't be interested."

I figured that was a forlorn hope, because Bullard was very thorough and I didn't think she'd been willing to accept anything less than an actual name.

Strossi looked sullen. I guessed he'd been trying to hook up with Helen for the evening and resented our presence, although it turned out I was wrong. Ordinarily I might have sympathized with him but there were overriding concerns today. The waitress took our drink order, mumbled the specials, and went away.

"They talked to me this morning," Bob said quietly. "Someone told them I used to work for John."

"It's not a secret," said Helen before I could speak. "And they've talked to a lot of people already. No one thinks you had anything to do with it."

I remembered suddenly that Bob had a reputation for mild paranoia. "They would have contacted the company and found out anyway. Everything has to be checked out. I wouldn't worry about it."

He stirred uncomfortably. "The thing of it is, John and I had a big fight and that's why I left. Everyone there knew about it. It was a little bit physical."

"How little?" asked Dusty.

"I knocked him down. I didn't hit him but I pushed him pretty hard. He wasn't the most graceful guy. He banged his head on the corner of his desk and scalp wounds bleed like crazy. It looked a lot worse than it was and one of the secretaries fainted." He sighed. "John had stitches but he refused to file a police report. I couldn't work there after that, but I was more frustrated than angry and he gave me a good reference."

"Did you tell the police all of that?" I asked.

"Yeah, but the detective has a poker face. I don't know if she believed me or not."

The drinks came and we placed our orders. Fish and chips for me; a fancy salad for Dusty. Strossi seemed to have shrunken into himself and our efforts to include him in the subsequent trivial conversation failed completely. Helen felt obligated to tell us everything that had happened at the previous year's festival, or at least everything from her point of view. She had apparently spent four nights with four different partners. "It was the best festival I've ever attended."

I finally managed to switch the subject back to John's death but Helen had nothing more to add. "He just led such a dull, monotonous life, I can't imagine why anyone would bother."

Strossi then surprised me by leaning forward. "There was one thing out of the ordinary. He had a special project that he worked on all by himself. Wouldn't let anyone else know what it was. I have my suspicions, but I can't prove it."

"What do you think it was?" asked Helen, not very interested.

"If I had to guess, I'd say that John restored the print of *At the Mountains of Madness* that Daryl has been showing. I've seen it and someone obviously cleaned it up from the original. There are a couple of other people Daryl might have used, but they're both big outfits and it would have been hard to keep it all a secret for so long. As it is, no one that I know of suspected anything until he had the special showing in Los Angeles."

So I wasn't the only one who suspected that John had been involved. "Daryl and John weren't bosom bodies, but you might well be right. John wasn't good about keeping secrets though. I think he would have let something slip."

"He wasn't good about keeping other people's secrets," said Helen caustically. "He could keep his own just fine."

We finished eating and I made one more effort to convince Helen that she should go to the police right away.

"I suppose I should get it over with. Nothing I can say is going to help them. I'm just wasting their time and my own." She and Bob put their heads together and whispered and I assumed they were planning to get together later. It was none of my business.

"Who haven't we spoken to yet?" I asked.

Dusty pulled out our list and glanced at it. "We didn't really talk to Jo Parkin. Gene Mallett isn't here, so he's off the list. And I haven't even seen Fred Hastings. There were a few more names but they really didn't know John very well and I think we'd be wasting our time."

I had never been able to convey to Dusty that both detective work consisted of boring trivia that turned out to be a waste of time. The problem is that it was impossible to tell in advance which piece of boring trivia was going to prove to be important. "Jo is working as a gopher, isn't she?"

"That's what she said."

"Then she shouldn't be that hard to find." And she wasn't. She was sitting at the information table when we arrived there.

I had always liked Jo. I thought she made a habit of letting other people take advantage of her, but she never complained, was almost always cheerful. She had been good company whenever we'd gone out to eat in a group, and I knew that a lot of things had gone wrong in her life outside the festival world and that this was her escape from her personal problems. I told her we needed to talk to her and she glanced at her watch.

"My shift here ends in about ten minutes. How about we meet in the bar downstairs?"

The only table we could find in the bar was one of those very high ones with tall stools around it. I hate them passionately but the only alternative was to stand at the bar and I didn't want our conversation to become a public performance. Jo came in about fifteen minutes later and Dusty and I were nursing our drinks. She waved and went over to the bar and we had to wait another few minutes until she was served and joined us.

"I really need this." She took a sip of something tall, pink, and full of fruit. "You have no idea how stupid people are until you sit at an information desk. One woman wanted to know why we were showing so many movies with the color turned off. Another wanted to know if Humphrey Bogart was attending the festival. And some guy came by to suggest that we show newer movies because the older ones are boring." She took another sip. "So what's up?"

"We're trying to figure out what happened to John," said Dusty.

"Unofficially," I added hastily. "We don't want to interfere with the police investigation, but it would be better for all of us if this business is cleared up quickly."

"I heard the news a little while ago." Her expression was serious and perhaps a little bit frightened. "They're saying murder now. I can't believe it. And John was such a..." she sought for words. "He just wasn't the type who gets murdered.

He dies of a stroke in his house and no one finds him for weeks, and his cats stay alive by eating him."

"Did John have cats?" Dusty is sometimes easily distracted. Jo, on the other hand, watches too many horror movies.

"We don't know if it was personal or if John was chosen at random." I had to struggle to get the image of squirming cats out of my head. "You know the festival people better than we do, better than anyone." That was flattery but it was also probably true. Jo had worked for the festival in one capacity or another every year since I'd been attending. She tended to stay in the background, and sometimes people talked about private matters in front of her almost as if she had blended into the woodwork. Daryl, on the other hand, would be so uninterested in things that didn't affect him directly that fascinating conversations might have taken place in his presence without his noticing any of them. "We wondered if you'd heard about anything unusual in John's life recently."

She frowned, thinking. "I can't remember anything in particular. He was supposed to have a private meeting with Daryl today – I made up Daryl's schedule and he had me include a half hour for John – but obvious that's not going to happen now. I heard that his business was going through a bad patch but someone else said he was bringing in a new partner or something, someone with capital. He was feuding with Romeo, but that wasn't much more than a simmer, and Romeo wouldn't hurt a fly. Oh, and there was a fight with Helen Viele a while back. I actually saw that one. She really laid into him. I thought he was going to cry."

"Do you know what it was about?" I knew what Helen had told me, but I didn't know if she was telling the truth.

"I guess he embarrassed some friend of hers. She went on and on about invasion of privacy and not being considerate of other people's feelings. I thought she was wasting her breath actually. John never really understood the concept of privacy. If he was interested in something, he figured he was entitled to know all about it, regardless of whether or not it was any of his business. And he would probably have talked about it to other people if he thought they might be interested." She shook her head. "John was kind of a friend of mine, but he was a very difficult friend, if you know what I mean."

I certainly did. We all sipped our drinks.

"Are you coming to the screening tomorrow?"

"*At the Mountains of Madness*?" I exchanged looks with Dusty. "I don't think so. The tickets are pretty steep."

"I think it's already sold out. Daryl is trying to arrange another screening on Sunday. There's a lot of interest in it. I know Daryl has been fielding some offers to distribute it commercially."

"Seems a shame that the original cast and crew won't see any of that money," said Dusty.

"They're all dead by now." Jo finished her drink and looked around for a waitress. "It's in the public domain anyway."

I had a thought. "Is it though? If they never copyrighted it, then the copyright wouldn't expire?" But I immediately realized the flaw. If they hadn't copyrighted it, then it was fair game.

"I don't know about that, but Daryl talked to a lawyer and he thinks he can do whatever he wants with it."

"Daryl pretty much does what he wants anyway." Dusty, in case you didn't notice, was not a fan of Daryl Plimpton.

"He says that if you want to get something done, you should just do it, and worry about the legalities later."

"That sounds like something Daryl would say." I'm not much of a fan of Daryl Plimpton either.

"Daryl can get very caught up in being Daryl sometimes." She sounded pensive and I remembered that she had lived with him for a few months. But I was quite sure Daryl was in no way responsible for John's death. He would not have considered him worth that much effort. I don't know of anyone he would consider being worth that much effort.

"Was anyone offering a lot of money for distribution rights?"

Jo sighed. "Big in terms of Donald Trump? No. Big for Daryl Plimpton? Not so much really even there. I mean, he sure wouldn't turn down the money but he makes a good living doing these festivals. I don't begrudge him that because there's an awful lot of work involved and he does the lion's share of it himself, even when someone offers to help. He likes to keep everything under his personal control."

"The festivals seem to be getting bigger every year." I nodded my head back in the general direction of the Biltmore. "He's going to have to let some of the responsibility go or he's going to crash and burn."

"I told him that two years ago. He doesn't listen."

We had a second round of drinks. It was a little early in the day for Dusty and I but Jo seemed perfectly at ease and I felt a little bit guilty. Like everyone else, I had a tendency to take her for granted. She did a lot more work than she got credit for, and she was one of your basically nice people who get taken advantage of all their lives and never get credit for their accomplishments. I made a resolution to be more appreciative in the future.

But I didn't have time to be the big brother today. As soon as we finished our drinks, we left.

I was intending that we go to the dealers' room because I knew George Shackleton would be there. George specialized in old film magazines, movie stills, and autographs and he was almost a permanent fixture at film festivals. He always complained that business was bad, even when the money was coming in hand over fist, and I happened to know that his "cabin" in Vermont was twice the size of my house and sat in the middle of several acres of pine trees. There was one other commodity that George dealt in for which he wasn't paid, at least not in money. George was a compulsive gossip and he knew everybody in the business.

But my talk with George had to be postponed because a uniformed officer who looked vaguely familiar to me approached us as soon as we passed the reception desk. "Mr. Birch? Detective Bullard would like to speak to you."

He made it sound like a court summons, which wasn't all that far from the truth. "Do you need me?" asked Dusty. The uniform didn't seem to have an opinion on that matter so I said that I could manage on my own and that I'd meet her in the dealer room as soon as I was done. The uniform escorted me back to the private office where Bullard was working. I think he was afraid that I would make a break for it if he allowed me to go by myself.

Bullard was looking more harried than ever, but the hotel had provided a coffee urn so her day had to have improved a little bit. She was on the telephone when I entered and she nodded without interrupting the flow of words. I got myself a cup of coffee and dropped into one of the chairs. Her side of the conversation was not very informative, consisting mostly of single words like "yes," "no," and "really?" Eventually she closed the phone and gave me a weary look.

"Your friends aren't making this at all easy for me."

"Most of them aren't my friends, and if it was easy, they wouldn't be paying you the big bucks to take care of it."

Her snort of derision was no surprise.

"The only people on your list who have alibis for the time of your friend's death are Mallett, who didn't come, Hastings, and Plimpton. That's really a shame. I wouldn't have minded at all if it had been Plimpton."

"Sorry, but he's not the type anyway. He wouldn't have been willing to give up so much of his prescious time for John. He might have shot him but he would have forgotten the whole thing a minute later. He's too self absorbed."

"I eliminated you and Miss Rhodes as well."

"Decent of you, since we were home, together, without a motive."

"Yeah, but you did find the body. It could have been a conspiracy and you're smart enough to have arranged things so that you were first on the scene. That would explain any stray fingerprints."

"I'd have worn gloves."

"Or DNA."

"I would have arranged to visit John before I killed him, so that there was a legitimate reason for any stray hairs or follicles."

She nodded. "We've probably swept up enough in that room to identify twenty or thirty people – guests, hotel staff, people visiting guests in their rooms, pizza delivery guys, and everyone else. Some of them might even be from our murderer. We might even be able to match them to something in the databases, but maybe not. And we'd have to sample everyone in those categories to eliminate the innocent ones. And do you know how much one DNA analysis costs, let alone dozens?"

I admitted that I didn't.

"Well, neither do I. But it's a lot."

"How can I help? Do you need more names?"

"God no." She looked disgusted. "But I need a fresh set of eyes and you're it…them…whatever."

I stirred uneasily. "I try to leave police business to the police, regardless of what you might have heard. My expertise is in detecting fraud, not solving murders."

"But you've managed to catch a couple of bad guys despite that."

Three actually, but that would be bragging. "It was mostly luck, and I almost got killed myself a couple of times." Three actually, but that would be whining.

Bullard sighed. "Humor me. I'm not asking you to put your ass on the line. You know these people and I don't and I have to solve this within the next couple of days or my suspects are going to be scattered all over the country."

"Two countries, actually. No, three. Jo Parkin is from Canada and Nelson Whately is British."

"Whately's flight from London was just landing when the murder took place."

"Back to two."

Bullard picked up a sheet of paper. "This is our reconstruction of the sequence of events leading up to and directly following the murder. We're pretty sure of the facts here and the time of death agrees with what the coroner is telling me."

I settled back. I admit that I was curious. "All right. I'm listening."

"John Boncoddo checked in at precisely three o'clock, the earliest the hotel allows."

"That sounds right. John was always early."

"The bellhop, Martin, took Boncoddo up to his room, collected an inadequate tip, and left. That took about ten minutes. The victim then began to unpack his suitcase – his shirts were hanging in the closet and there were socks in one of the drawers. The hotel at that time was almost deserted. No one else checked in until after 4:30 and only three parties checked out. It was so quiet that the staff took turns going across the street to eat an early supper. There is no restaurant in the Driscoll. At 4:30 someone sent you a message using the victim's cell phone. We assume he was already dead by then and the coroner confirms."

I leaned forward. "The people checking out would have had luggage."

Bullard nodded. "Which might have been used to bring the weapons out after the murder. We're looking at them but I don't have anything but their names and addresses at this point."

"John definitely drowned?"

"Yes. But he was almost certainly unconscious at the time. The blow to the head wasn't immediately fatal but it would have been if left untreated. It's highly unlikely that he regained consciousness. We're pretty sure that the poison was injected next. The gunshot and the knife wound were so close together that it probably doesn't matter."

"Did you find the cell phone yet?"

"No. That appears to be the only thing taken from the victim, although we can't be sure. We haven't found the firearm yet either. It was a .38. We'll do a ballistic check but I'm not expecting anything there."

"How long do you think it would have taken to shoot, stab, poison, and hang the body after drowning him in the bathtub?

Bullard shrugged. "Less than half an hour if our killer worked steadily and to a plan."

I hesitated. "You know, you really shouldn't eliminate Dusty and I as suspects. We could be in cahoots. It would be even easier with two people."

Bullard met my eyes. "We've had a look at the security tapes. We were able to follow you around the Biltmore and the Driscoll's lobby. They don't have any coverage upstairs. Unless you have a third conspirator, you didn't do it."

"Good to know. I assume you checked on our friends the same way. Were you able to clear anyone else?"

"Plimpton didn't do it. Neither did Bates, in all probability, but there's a chance she could have managed it during one forty minute period when we couldn't find her. I think the chances are pretty slim. Bolduc and Strossi didn't arrive until later, and we didn't spot them anywhere, but they could have shown up earlier, left afterward, and then returned officially. Bolduc would be hard to miss and impossible to disguise and I'm inclined to say he couldn't have done it. Unfortunately, the Driscoll only has cameras in the lobby and the loading dock and there are two entrances that aren't covered at all, opening directly into the stairwells. Someone could have come in through one of those and walked up to the second floor before taking the elevator, and, they could use the elevator without being recorded. Or they could simply have walked all the way up and down."

"How about Jo Parkin? She was working for the festival and should have been in full view."

"She left the Biltmore at three and didn't come back until after five. She said she went shopping but didn't buy anything." Bullard went through all the other names we'd provided. Nobody else had even the ghost of an alibi.

Her cell buzzed and she answered. Her eyebrows went up and she nodded to herself. "Okay, I'll be right there." She put it away. "They just found your friend's cell phone. Want to come along?"

"Sure. Where was it?" I stood up.

"You'll be surprised."

I called Dusty while we walked back to the Driscoll and told her what I was doing. She was having a drink with Tanya Gregory, which surprised me, but Dusty in detective mode was a very different animal than I was accustomed to. She kind of scared me, actually, because she seemed to lack any sense of personal danger.

A uniformed officer was waiting at the front entrance and led the way to the basement. I assumed that the phone had turned up in one of the trashcans, but we turned toward the executive offices and entered the one marked: Michael Palotto, Chief of Security. Mickey was inside, sitting beside rather than behind his desk, with another officer and a technician. "I'm almost never in my office," he was saying loudly as we entered.

Everyone turned to look at us.

"Where was it?" asked Bullard.

The technician pointed to a filing cabinet. One of the drawers had been pulled fully open. "Way in the back. Turned off but the battery was still in it."

Bullard walked over and looked into the drawer. I retreated to a corner and watched Palotto, who was looking thoroughly miserable.

"I told this officer already, detective. Someone planted it there. I'm almost never in the office. I stay on the floor most of the time, or in the camera room."

Bullard's face was expressionless. "Do you keep this room locked?"

Palotto nodded vigorously. "All the time. I can't ask my people to be security conscious if I'm sloppy myself." But I could tell by the way his eyes moved away from us that he was lying.

"Who else would have a key?"

He hunched his shoulders as he thought about. "My two shift supervisors. The head of maintenance has a master. So does Mrs. Drake, the manager. That's all that I know of."

Bullard crossed and examined the door briefly. "Good lock. Hard to pick this unless you knew what you were doing."

"These offices were all brand new when they hired me. All redone. They should have spent the money on more cameras." That last sounded like a longstanding complaint.

"Can we take this now, Detective?"

Bullard waved her assent and the technician used a set of tongs to lift the cell phone out of its resting place. There weren't going to be any fingerprints, of course, but they had to act as though there might be.

"Just for the record, where were you between three o'clock and six yesterday?"

Palotto looked more frustrated than ever, but after a few seconds he spurted out an answer. "I was in a meeting with Mrs. Drake until just about four. I went down to the camera room and spent maybe twenty minutes there, then I had something to eat across the street." His eyes brightened. "I used a credit card. There'll be a record."

"We'll check it. Did you know Mr. Boncoddo at all?"

"I never heard of him until you had us come up to the room. I wish I still hadn't heard of him. There's nothing I could have done about it, of course, but it happened on my watch and the owners will hold it against me." Mickey was definitely lying now. My last fight with him in school had been because he was tormenting John, but I kept my mouth shut.

"Life isn't fair," said Bullard with absolutely no sympathy at all.

I confess to deriving a certain amount of pleasure from Palotto's discomfort. While still working at another agency, I had been assigned to help clear the name of a store clerk who'd been accused of taking merchandise home with her. It turned out her father was loaded and that she'd only been working because he wanted her to learn the value of a job. Ready2Go was a small chain of convenience stores whose margins were falling, in part because they were easy targets for shoplifters. So their management decided to shake down all of the clerks, accusing them of theft, claiming to have proof, and demanding restitution of amounts they apparently chose arbitrarily. The man responsible for this program was Michael Palotto, my high school nemesis, and I knew for a fact that he had reduced a number of those accused to tears. What goes around doesn't always come around, but when it does, it's one of the true pleasures of life. Mickey was two years older than me, but it could have been ten times that. He had gained weight and his face was heavily lined. He'd been married, had a kid, and been divorced all in one eighteen month period and he was still a bully, but now a bitter one.

Bullard and I left the office. "Why do you suppose it was left here?" asked the uniform standing at the door.

"Messing with us," said Bullard. "Not a smart thing, messing with us."

CHAPTER SIX

The three sets of guests who had departed the Driscoll were all strangers to me and none of them sounded like viable prospects, although naturally it would have to be checked. The first was a young couple name Yorke who were traveling with a toddler and an infant and whose home address was in Lawton, Oklahoma. They had been visiting relatives. The second was a Dr. Ngambo and he had only been in town to present a lecture at Brown University before returning to Botswana. The third was Mark Riley from Deming, New Mexico. He was in town for a job interview at Eblis Manufacturing up north of the city. Bullard would do a little digging, but not much. There was not even a tenuous connection to John or the festival.

Bullard delivered the information in a monotone. "I'm holding onto Room 415 for another day or two but I told the hotel they could have the others back."

It was too early for DNA results, and I didn't expect they would be helpful either. We were standing in the lobby, both of us trying to decide whether our conversation was over, when the bellhop who'd helped out the night before came by. He sketched a wave and that must have triggered something in Bullard's mind because she gestured for him to join us.

"Is there something I can help you with?"

"When you brought the dead guy up to his room yesterday, what did he have with him for luggage?"

I struggled to remember his name and then it came to me. Martin. Martin frowned in thought. "Just the one suitcase. He must have traveled a lot because it was pretty battered. The handle was loose."

"Was he carrying anything himself?"

"No. I remember because he put up both hands to keep the elevator door from closing. He was a little slow getting aboard. But now that you mention it, he had a shoulderbag of some kind."

"You mean a purse?"

"No, not a purse. It was black with a wide strap. I think it might have been a laptop computer."

Bullard looked at me. "Did your friend use a laptop?"

I had no idea. "He might have. He was into technology."

"We found a PDA in his room but no laptop."

"Maybe it'll turn up in the hotel laundry. Another ploy in the game."

Martin shook his head. "We don't have a laundry. We send everything out."

Bullard looked back at him with her irritated face. "Is there anything else you forgot to tell us?"

He looked taken aback and in fact retreated a half step. "I carry lots of bags for lots of people. I can't remember most of them by the time I'm back downstairs. And no one asked me what he was carrying until just now."

Bullard looked disgusted but she didn't press. "What can you tell me about the security office?"

"There are two of them. One is for Mr. Palotto, but he doesn't use it very often. That part of the hotel was refurbished three years ago. The other is where the guards hang out when they're changing shifts, and the monitors for the cameras are there."

"Does Palotto keep his office locked when he isn't there?"

Martin looked uncomfortable. "Most of the time." He was probably exaggerating.

"Who has keys?"

"The guard room is never locked. There's supposed to be somebody there at all times. Mr. Palotto has a key to his office, of course, and Mrs. Drake has keys to everything. I don't know about anyone else. Someone in maintenance, probably, because the cleaning crew goes in once a week."

The desk clerk rang his bell and Martin looked back and forth. "Is that all? They want me over there."

"That's all for now." Martin scurried off and Bullard looked at me. "I don't suppose you have any suggestions?"

"My crystal ball is cloudy today."

Dusty called as I was walking back to the Biltmore and asked where I was. "On my way back. Where are you?"

"Come up to room 612."

612 was the room shared by Muriel and Angela Bates, as I discovered when I arrived. The sisters were sitting on one of the

beds, Dusty was in one chair, and Bob Strossi was in the other. There was an open bottle of wine on the dresser, surrounded by plastic cups. I eased down onto the other bed.

"We're having an informal wake for John," Dusty explained. Strossi looked uncomfortable but didn't object. Muriel was looking solemn. Angela was keeping her eye ont Strossi and trying not to be obvious about it. It was obvious that their relationship wasn't as casual as she had tried to pretend, at least not on her side. And Strossi was here rather than watching Humphrey Bogart in *Angels with Dirty Faces* or Buster Keaton in *The General*, so maybe he wasn't completely disinterested either.

"The local news said it was murder." Muriel shifted her legs nervously. "I still can't believe it. Who would kill John?"

Strossi opened his mouth as though to provide an answer, but thought better of it and remained silent.

"He seemed kind of strange to me," said Angela in a small voice. "But I only met him twice."

"John never quite fit in," I explained. "He had no interest in the kinds of things boys usually like when he was in school, and he couldn't understand why the rest of us weren't fascinated by the things he was into. He was fascinated by old movies even in junior high. I didn't catch the bug until I was in my twenties."

"But I don't think he actually enjoyed them," said Muriel thoughtfully. "I think he enjoyed knowing all about them. He could talk about the technical side for hours but there were times when he didn't even seem to understand a plot. And he'd get annoyed if you told him you weren't interested in whatever it was that he wanted to talk about."

"He could really be insensitive sometimes," admitted Dusty.

"But once in a while he could be almost human." Muriel leaned back against the headboard. "One time up in Michigan we talked about our families and he was like a different person for a while."

"Was that while you were working out there?" I asked.

She nodded. "I worked mostly in the Lansing area but I made a few trips to check things out, once to a little town called Frampton in the Upper Peninsula. I convinced my boss to hire John as a consultant for a couple of days and he came out."

"You never mentioned what you were doing in Michigan." I had noticed her reticence on the subject in the past.

The wine seemed to have loosened her tongue. "Searching for old, non-commercial film footage, particularly about the early days of auto making. There was a lot around, but most of it was thrown out or badly stored. The Ford Company was financing the project. It was heartbreaking to find film so damaged that it couldn't be restored, but we did manage to recover enough to satisfy them. The documentary still hasn't been released though, and technically I've already said too much." She looked belatedly guilty.

"Did John do any of the restoration?"

She shook her head. "No. I think everything was done at Berkeley's film school. John was just there to look at some stuff and decide whether or not it was worth buying." But she looked away, out the window, and I had the distinct feeling that she was lying.

We took our leave after another few minutes and made our way downstairs. Strossi had made noises suggesting that he was restless, but he remained behind with the sisters. Dusty wanted to hunt down Tanya Gregory for some reason she wouldn't explain, but I wanted to go back to the Driscoll for a while, so we decided to split up again.

I don't read detective stories as a rule, but every once in a while Dusty would get enthused about one and I'd read it just so I could follow what she was talking about. I understood the formula pretty well. Once the murder was accomplished, the detective would discover that everyone in sight had good and sufficient reason to want the victim dead, but everyone would have an alibi or there would be some other combination of circumstances that meant none of them could have committed the crime. The problem here was just the opposite. Almost everyone could have managed to enter the Driscoll, get invited into John's room, and hit him over the head, all without being picked up on a security camera or spotted by any unwelcome witnesses. But no one at all seemed to have a good enough reason to have done so. John was annoying, even infuriating, but if he had provoked violence, it would have been a spur of the moment thing, an outburst of sudden rage. John's murder had been planned well in advance, completed with calm professionalism, and the note to the police and the games with the half dozen weapons and the cell phone suggested an ongoing game plan.

I was beginning to think that Bullard was going to have to face her nightmare scenario after all. This seemed almost certain to be a random killing, someone who wanted to taunt the police and prove that he or she could get away with murder. Which meant that all of the interviews and background checks were simply a waste of time. The killer might be one of the attendees, but it might just as easily be someone else entirely.

Bullard's best chance was that the killer might strike again, and this time make some mistake. That's a sad truth but inescapable.

The lobby of the Driscoll was crowded even though no one was lined up at the desk either arriving or departing. Martin and a young man, both in bellhop uniforms, were sitting at their station trying not to look bored. I walked over toward them and Martin stood up.

"Hello again, Mr. Burke. Is your wife with you today?"

"It's Birch and Dusty's not my wife." I thought I sounded a bit stiff and tried to lighten up a little. I wanted the man to cooperate with me with as much enthusiasm as possible. "Are you married, Martin?"

His face fell. "I used to be. My wife left me and took our daughter with her."

"I'm sorry to hear that."

Martin shrugged. "It's been thirty years, so I should be over it, right? What can I do for you, Mr. Birch?"

"I was wondering who I should talk to if I wanted to find out something about the way you assign rooms to your guests."

He frowned slightly. "I could introduce you to Malcolm or Denise and explain that you're with the police. Was there something specific you wanted to know? I fill in for them sometimes and I know the system pretty well."

"Maybe. When is a particular room assigned to a guest? When they make the reservation or when they check in?"

"It could be either. If the guest specifies something – some people want to be as near the ground floor as possible or want a non-smoking room, the room gets tagged as soon as the reservation is completed. Otherwise there is just a pool of guests and a list of available rooms and they get assigned when they check in."

John didn't smoke and always specified a non-smoking room, so it was possible to determine which room he'd be in even before he arrived.

"How hard would it be to find out? For someone not on the staff, I mean."

"Well, you couldn't just walk in and ask. But it wouldn't be a big secret either. There's a weekly staff meeting and they print out the next week's listing so they can review it for problems and staffing levels."

"What happens to the printout when they're done?"

"It gets tossed. I've seen them in the dumpster out back. There's no credit card or personal information."

"How about hackers? Could someone access your system from outside?"

Martin shook his head. "I wouldn't know. I can barely operate my DVD player. But I know our network is old because they keep talking about replacing it."

So someone might have chosen John in advance and it wouldn't be impossible for them to have found out what room he was going to be using.

"Do you have any new hires working here?"

"How new?"

"Oh, six months or less."

Martin shook his head. "Not a chance. One of the maids has only been with us for a year or so. Everyone else has been here longer." He beamed. "But no one as long as me. Thirty-nine years."

"I'll bet you've seen a lot of changes."

"I have indeed. About eight years ago they had to replace all the electrical work and they refurbished all the guest rooms at the same time. We were shut down for six months."

"That must have been tough on the employees."

He shrugged. "They gave us half pay while we were out, and most of us found temp jobs. I worked at the Biltmore for a while and considered staying with them, but I'd have been the least senior bellhop and you know what that means when business is off." He made a throat cutting gesture.

"I don't suppose there's anything particular about room 415?"

"I don't know what you mean, sir."

"I don't think I do either. Ghosts, famous visitors, suicides, anything like that?"

He smiled. "Any hotel this old has seen a few deaths, but I don't remember anything in particular involving room 415."

"Okay. Thanks." I turned away, still not quite sure what had led me back to the Driscoll. I walked over to the elevator, had to wait for the second car because there were so many people clustered around, and then rode up to the fourth floor. It was pointless. The door was locked. There wasn't even a crime scene tape. I opened the nearby door to the stairwell and walked down to the ground level, where a glass door opened to the lobby on one side and a solid one with a crash bar to the street on the other. The solid door was locked after eleven in the evening, but that didn't matter in this instance.

The stairwell went down further so I followed it. Another solid door said NO ADMITTANCE but it wasn't locked and I pushed it open. It appeared to be a large storage area cluttered with boxes. No one was around. I walked back up a level and exited onto the street. To my left was the loading dock. The overhead door had been pulled down and there was no one in sight here either. A small dumpster was just past the end of the dock. An alley led out to Weybosset Street. I could see people in the distance but I doubt that anyone noticed me. Someone could have entered and exited through this door carrying a bazooka and they probably wouldn't have been observed, particularly if they had a car nearby. There were no cameras here or in the stairwell.

I went back inside and made my way back to the lobby, where the crowd had thinned out somewhat. Johnny Weissmuller was swinging through the trees on a vine in one of the darkened rooms I passed and Jimmy Cagney was shooting at someone in another. A familiar face was standing at the desk and I veered toward her.

Margaret Drake was hard to read. She should have been either pleased with the crowd or unhappy about the murder, but she simply seemed to be detached. She blinked when I wove into view and there was a flicker of recognition in her eyes.

"It looks like a lively crowd, Mrs. Drake," I ventured.

There was an almost imperceptible nod. "You're with the police, aren't you, Mr...?"

"Birch. Paul Birch. I'm not officially with them, no, but Detective Bullard has asked me to help." I'd had a thought and I figured Drake was the most likely person to be able to scratch this particular itch without too much paperwork.

"The owners weren't happy about the publicity." It was pretty much a non-sequitur, but I understood what her concerns were. "Even if we are sold out."

"If you have a minute, I just had one question for you."

She hadn't really been looking at me but now she brought me into focus. "What do you want to know?"

"Could you tell me when the victim was assigned to room 415?"

"He registered less than an hour before the incident."

"I know that, but when did he reserve the room?"

She blinked and turned to the woman at the desk, repeating my question and providing John's name. The desk clerk pressed keys and looked at the computer screen. "Mr. Boncoddo made his reservations on the fourth of June and room 407 was assigned to him the following day."

I had just wanted to know how far back the killer could have known which room was John's, but now I felt a flicker of deeper interest. "He was in 415, not 407," I said.

The clerk frowned and punched some more keys. "That's correct, sir. He was reassigned to 415 just a week ago."

"Why would that have happened?"

"Sometimes a guest prefers to be near the elevators or the stairwell," Drake explained.

"Did he request the change?"

The clerk was still pressing keys. "There's no notation of it here. He swapped rooms with Edward Mrozek. I'm checking now to see if he put in a request." There was a brief pause. "No, there's nothing here either. But whoever made the change might have forgotten to fill in the reason. Sometimes we get rushed."

I thought about it. "Could someone have called in, pretended to be one or the other, and have requested the change?"

Drake and the clerk both nodded. "Unless there are conflicting requests, the guest would never even know what happened. Most people don't care particularly where their room is located, other than smoking and non-smoking. It's not as if we had a scenic view." Drake sketched a smile. "It's not something we make a point of documenting. Is it important?"

"I don't know." But it did raise an interesting question. If the killer had a specific target in mind and had looked up the reservation ahead of time but not within the past week, then the wrong person might have died. Maybe Edward Mrozek was the real target and John had just been in the wrong place at the wrong time. "Thank you for your help."

I stepped outside to find a quiet spot and called Bullard, explained what I had just found out.

"The killer might just have picked your friend out of the crowd and followed him up to the room. This might be a dead end." Bullard always played devil's advocate with theories that weren't her own.

"Maybe, but if they'd been followed, wouldn't the bellhop have noticed? He seems to be on top of things."

"Is this Mrozek person still checked in?"

I hadn't thought to ask and I said so.

"I'll do a quick background check and I'll send someone to talk to him. If we can find him. Is he one of your film freaks?"

"I didn't recognize the name, but there are about two thousand people here that I've never met."

"All right. I'll get back to you."

I called Dusty and she told me to meet her at the entrance to the dealers' room in fifteen minutes. I stopped and bought a cold drink from a sidewalk vendor and tried to figure out how I would have planned John's murder, first from the point of view of someone who knew him and then from the perspective of a stranger who selected him out of a crowd. The stranger scenario could not be dismissed, of course, but it didn't make sense to me.

I suppose someone could have been hanging around the desk when John checked in. They could have heard the clerk mention the room number, waited until the bellhop was gone, then knocked on the door. If it had been me, I would have had my various tools in a tool chest of some sort, and I would have told John that I was there to tighten a valve because the previous guest had complained of a leak. That would have gotten me inside. But a tool chest would have attracted attention in the lobby and there wasn't time to retrieve it from, say, a car parked nearby, then enter through the rear stairwell, climb upstairs, and knock. It was physically possible, of course, but it involved too many unpredictable elements. Anyone who had planned the elaborate death scene in room 415 would not have taken so many chances of being seen.

Most of the same objections applied if the killer was someone John knew. Instead of a tool kit, however, the murderer could have bundled everything into an ordinary suitcase, which would not have aroused any curiosity from potential witnesses and would seem perfectly natural to John. If I'd been planning a murder – and I wouldn't know the first thing about hacking into the hotel's registration system – I would have waited in the lobby until I saw John arrive. Once I was confident he was in his room – say by noting the bellhop's return to the lobby – I would have called John, told him I had something spectacular to show him, then asked what room he was in. Once the dirty deed was done, I could either leave through the rear exit unobserved or even just return to the lobby and walk away. I'd be carrying some sort of bag to the first choice was the better one. I would then have waited an hour or so before returning to register, or in some other fashion indicate my arrival, so that it would appear I hadn't been to the hotel earlier. There was always the chance that someone might have recognized me on my first visit, though, so I don't think I'd make a big deal about it, and maybe I'd have employed some simple disguise. An alibi that appears too good to be true often is, in real life as well as in detective stories.

If it was a stranger, I could not think of a promising line of inquiry, and I doubted that the police would be any better off unless Bullard knew something she hadn't told me. If it was someone from the film festival, then I was already doing everything I could think of. Something might come up in a conversation that helped, but I didn't think our villain was about to reveal himself by a slip of the tongue.

So I tried another approach. Who among our acquaintances did I think was mentally capable of devising and carrying off such an elaborate plan? Daryl Plimpton's name popped up immediately, followed by Bob Strossi. Both of them were organized and assertive. I drew a mental line under their names and added those who were certainly smart enough – Terry Wareham, Jimmy Gonsalves, Ray Riccello, Romeo Bolduc, and Helen Viele. The rest – Muriel Bates, Jo Parkin, and Tanya Gregory - seemed to me less likely, but that was probably my gender bias speaking. I decided to ask Dusty to rank them similarly so that we could compare impressions.

That reminded me that I was supposed to be meeting her and a quick glance at my watch sent me quickly on my way.

Dusty was leaning against the wall when I arrived and she wasn't alone. Tanya Gregory was with her. They both turned as I broke out of the press and Dusty gave me a bright smile. Tanya seemed subdued. "Is this the first time I was on time and you were late?"

"I got caught up in something. Don't gloat. Hello again, Tanya."

"Tanya has something to tell you." Dusty glanced around. "But we need to find someplace a little more private."

"Okay," I said. "But before I do, have either of you ever heard of someone named Edward Mrozek?"

Dusty looked blank but Tanya surprised me by nodding. "I know him. He's a friend of Ray's. They're working on some kind of project together."

"What kind of project?" I asked, trying not to sound pushy.

"I don't know exactly. They don't talk about it much around me. Ray came out and stayed with us a few days last winter and they talk on the phone a lot."

"Is he an actor or a writer?" Ray was always going on about doing another movie, but as far as I knew, talking was as far as he ever got.

"I think he's an accountant, but I really don't know." Her eyebrows rose. "If he's here I wonder if that's why Ray wanted to go off on his own this afternoon. I'll bet they're meeting someplace."

"The police are going to want to talk to him."

She looked puzzled. "Why? I don't think he even knew John."

I decided not to be too forthcoming. Bullard would slap my wrists if she thought I was compromising her position. "Just routine. He was staying a couple of rooms away and he might have heard something. Let's see if we can find a place to sit."

That wasn't as easy as it sounded. Two of the films had recently ended and people were milling around, waiting to use the restroom, clustered together in small groups, sometimes sitting on the floor. We headed toward the business offices and found a little waiting area with some couches and no warm bodies.

"Tanya was over at the Driscoll yesterday afternoon," explained Dusty. "And she may have seen something."

"It was probably nothing at all, but it did seem a little odd."

"When was this?" I asked.

"About three o'clock. Ray wanted to watch *Plan Nine from Outer Space* and I've already seen it too many times. I told him I'd meet him afterward and went to see *Arsenic and Old Lace*, but there was something wrong with the film and they substituted a Dagwood movie and like, blech! So I was hanging around the lobby, reading a magazine when I saw them come in together." She paused for dramatic effect. "It was Daryl and Terry."

"They were a couple once," I observed.

"Yeah, but she hates his guts now. That's why I was so surprised. There was almost no one around and I was sort of hidden behind one of those giant fake plants they have in the lobby, so they sat down right near me without knowing I was there."

"Maybe they were trying to patch things up."

Tanya ignored me. "You could tell neither of them wanted to be there. They sat kind of stiff, you know, and their voices were tense."

"Could you hear what they were saying?"

"Oh yes. Every word." She hesitated. "I really don't like to gossip and I wasn't going to tell anybody, but what with John and all, and Dusty was telling me how sometimes things that seem completely unrelated can be the key to solving a mystery, I wouldn't want to keep something secret that might be important."

"If it isn't relevant, we won't repeat what you tell us," I reassured her.

"You know Terry's been going through a bad spell."

I nodded. "I know. She's had bad luck with jobs. But this new one sounds promising."

"She had to sell her house last year, and whatever she got for it was pretty much eaten up by credit cards. She's only here this year because Jimmy Gonsalves is paying her way."

That I didn't know. Jimmy had always been something of an enigma to me. He was around a lot but he tended to blend into the scenery because he so rarely spoke. I knew nothing about his private life except that he did some programming and I wasn't even sure whether he was self employed or worked for Microsoft or something like that.

"Are they a couple?" I asked. It seemed unlikely, but I'd been surprised more than once in the past.

Tanya shook her head. "At least not romantically. I think Jimmy might be gay. Helen Viele came on to him at a party a couple of years ago and he didn't react at all."

"Then what is their relationship?"

"I think they're just friends. They both seem very lonely and they live in the same city now."

"Albany," said Dusty.

"Anyway, she was telling Daryl that Muriel had told her that Daryl might have stolen the copy of *At the Mountains of Madness* that he's so proud of. And Daryl told her that Muriel talked too much and had too much imagination. He said she had never met a melodrama she didn't like."

Daryl wasn't as imperceptive as I'd thought. I liked Muriel but she did tend to exaggerate minor setbacks into apocalyptic catastrophes.

"Terry said that he might be right but that there were questions he would have to answer and that she'd be asking a lot of them herself. Daryl got pretty mad then and asked her what she wanted. She told him that she wanted money."

I blinked. "Are you saying she tried to blackmail Daryl?"

Tanya shook her head, but her eyes were troubled. "I never heard her actually threaten him and she said he owed it to her for the work she had done for him when they were a couple. Daryl was real quiet for a while and then he told her that he would have to think about it and that he wasn't going to do anything until after the festival. Terry said that she could wait that long but that she had problems too. She gave him something but I couldn't see what it was, probably her address and phone number. Terry got up and went away, but Daryl stayed there by himself for a few minutes, then made a call on his cell. I couldn't hear any of that goes he got up and walked over to the front doors and left."

I confess that it was an interesting piece of gossip, but I couldn't see any way that it could be connected to John's murder. But then Tanya started talking again.

"Ray and I got back together after his movie and we came back to the Biltmore. We were looking at the program, when Tanya came over and asked if we had seen John Boncoddo. Of course we hadn't and we told her so, but she looked really upset and said something about needing to see him pretty badly. The hotel had told her that no one by that name had a reservation, so she was going to try the Marriott and the Driscoll."

I waited for more, but Tanya was apparently done. "Have you talked to her since then?"

Tanya shook her head. Her teased hair bounced. "Not a word. I saw Daryl later but I didn't speak to him. He seemed perfectly normal."

I wondered if Tanya had a thing for the melodramatic as well. Could she have misconstrued what she heard? She had never been a particularly good actress, though I thought she was probably smarter than she let on. It hadn't escaped my attention that she was more competent, assertive, and frankly more interesting company when she was away from Ray than when she was with him. Maybe that's how she kept their relationship stable. Maybe she wasn't such a bad actress after all.

"Thanks for telling us, Tanya."

"You won't let on to anybody that I said anything, will you?"

"Not unless we have to." Truthfully, I didn't see any way this could be connected to John's death. It turned out that it was, but my instincts are notoriously unreliable.

Tanya went off to find Ray and Dusty asked me what I thought. "Not much. I feel like I've picked up a few random pieces of a jigsaw puzzle, but I'm not even sure if they're part of the puzzle we're actually trying to solve."

"John did know a lot of people."

"Apparently he knew one too many."

CHAPTER EIGHT

The afternoon was better than half gone. We spent an hour wandering around, spotting people we knew more or less well and talking to most of them, but without learning anything. They all knew John, by name at least, but very little more. A few were sad, a few uninterested, and a few ghoulishly hungry for details about his death. We left them sadder, still uninterested, and unsatisfied.

Bullard called Dusty's cell and told me I could pick up my own if I stopped by the interview room, so we walked down that way. A uniformed officer whom I knew had seen me talking to Bullard earlier insisted upon seeing some picture ID before he'd give me my property. He probably didn't know where Bullard was at the moment, but she was "pursuing some leads," whatever that meant.

We were dithering about what to do next when Romeo Bolduc found us standing on the mezzanine. He appeared to be in a good mood but I noticed that he was breathing heavily and that his knees seemed the slightest bit shaky. Romeo always said that diabetes would kill him in the end, but if it had been a horse race, I'd have put my money on a stroke.

"What have the two of you been up to?"

I didn't want to say that we were investigating John's murder because technically we weren't supposed to be doing that, even if Bullard was looking the other way while nudging us in that direction, an interesting visual contortion. "Just getting caught up with people."

"Have you heard any more about John?"

"Only what's been on the news." Technically this wasn't a lie, since I wasn't sure that anything we had learned had any relevance at all. In fact, I was starting to lean toward random victim chosen by chance.

"Did you hear about the fight?"

Dusty and I exchanged looks. "What fight?"

Romeo was obviously pleased that he knew something we didn't. He had always been a compulsive gossip. "Helen Viele and Muriel got into it hot and heavy a couple of hours ago."

96

"I thought they hardly knew each other," said Dusty. "I wouldn't have said they had anything to fight about. Their interests don't overlap very much. And sometimes I think Helen only comes to find new guys to sleep with."

"Not just guys," said Romeo.

We knew that. Dusty had gently but firmly discouraged her during the Hartford festival. I had made a stupid remark to her about a threesome at the time and we slept in separate beds for a week before she accepted my apology.

"So what was it about?" I asked.

"It was about ten minutes long." Romeo grinned. "And very loud. They'd gone down one of the back corridors, I guess for some privacy, but they didn't realize it curved around and they were standing behind the back wall of the dealers' room."

"I didn't hear the first part," he admitted. "But Helen was swearing a blue streak and I've never heard Muriel talk that loud before. It was a while before I recognized her voice. Muriel kept shouting that Helen had promised not to talk about something, and Helen called Muriel stupid and petty and said she was making a big deal over nothing."

"Did either of them mention what the nothing was?"

"Not really. It had something to do with a bunch of money Muriel was expecting. Helen said she thought Muriel was getting hysterical over nothing. Muriel said something about Helen breaking her word. After that it was mostly name calling and someone got slapped."

I had started to notice a pattern. John and Muriel were both expecting to receive some unstated but apparently substantial amount of money in the near future. Ray Riccello appeared to be talking about doing a new movie, which meant he had found financing somehow. Jimmy Gonsalves had enough money to buy a broken down theater and refurbish it. Terry Wareham was trying to tap Daryl in return for keeping her mouth shut, subject unknown. Daryl was chronically short of cash despite his take from the festivals, so this was stranger than it might seem. Were these isolated bits of information related somehow, and was John's death connected?

"When did you say this happened?"

"About two hours ago. Someone banged on the wall and they went quiet real fast."

I was trying to decide whether or not anything I had learned recently was worth repeating to Bullard and decided that it wasn't unless something else turned up that tied things together when Romeo asked if we'd seen Daryl recently.

"Not since yesterday," I said after thinking about it for a second or two.

"He was looking for you a little while ago."

"Did he say why?"

"No, but he was asking people to keep an eye out."

So Dusty and I wandered back to the operations room. The faces had changed but otherwise it looked the same as during our first visit. A young man I didn't know asked if he could help and I told him we'd heard that Daryl wanted to see us.

"Mr. Plimpton isn't here right now."

"Do you know where he might be?" I was kind of hoping he'd say no, because I really wasn't in a mood to deal with Daryl's arrogant personal style just at the moment, but unfortunately I was to be disappointed.

"He said he'd be up in the hospitality suite."

"And where's that?"

It was, it turned out, not far from the main ballroom at the top of the hotel. There was a line at the elevators and this time it took two cycles before we were able to get aboard. Conversation was impossible since we were pressed tightly together – only one person got off on the entire trip and two more people got on in his place. Dusty spotted the sign for the hospitality suite – which was completely mobbed by people we didn't know who'd been drawn by the promise of free food and drink, although it was mostly chips and soda. I didn't see Daryl at first because he was around the corner near the bathroom talking to two people whom I knew by sight but not by name. He spotted us and cut his conversation short, moving in our direction.

"We can't talk here. Come down to my room."

He moved away without waiting to see if we were following him, which was also typical Daryl. Under ordinary circumstances, I think we'd have let him go just to see how far he'd get before he realized he was alone, but this situation was exceptional.

Daryl stalked to the far end of the corridor and opened the door to the stairway. He did at least have the grace to wait there until we caught up. "I'm only one floor down and the elevator is impossible."

I nodded agreement and down we went, Daryl leading. Two minutes later we were all standing in his guest room. The desk was covered with piles of paper and so was one of the two beds. Daryl dropped into one of the chairs and looked tired. I felt a twinge of sympathy before I realized that this was Daryl and most of his trouble was self inflicted because he always tried to stay in control of every little detail. He didn't invite us to sit but Dusty took the other chair and I was left with the uncluttered bed.

"Have you found out anything?"

His tone irritated me. "If we have, we would have notified the police. It's up to them how much they make public."

"I thought we had an arrangement."

"No, we didn't. I seem to recall your saying something about not being able to afford my rates. And even if you were willing to hire me officially, I would still be obligated to tell the police if anything relevant turned up. This is a murder, you know. And it's real life, not a movie."

"This is not the kind of publicity we need."

I had watched the morning news. "They hardly even mentioned the festival this morning, and not even by name. I don't think you're getting any publicity at all, good or bad."

"It certainly hasn't hurt your attendance," added Dusty. "The hotel is mobbed."

"I want to show you something." Daryl slipped a briefcase out from behind the desk and opened it. A moment later he handed me a single sheet of white paper. The individual letters taped to the paper had been cut from a variety of sources but the message was clear.

THIS YEAR'S FESTIVAL WILL BE YOUR LAST.

I handed it back. "When and how did you get this?"

"Six months ago, in the mail at my home."

"Did you keep the envelope?"

He fished around in the briefcase and retrieved a creased legal size envelope. There was no return address, obviously, but the postmark was Albany, New York. Which is where Terry and Jimmy were currently living.

"Did you show this to the police?"

"Not yet."

I sighed. "You obviously took it seriously or you wouldn't have brought it here with you." I was about to blurt out something about the note the police had received, but remembered at the last second that they hadn't made that public. "And when John was killed, alarm bells should have been sounding in your head."

"There's no reason to think they're connected."

"And there's no reason to think they're not." I didn't really think the note would help much, but it really irritated me that Daryl had kept this to himself. It wouldn't have made any difference to John, of course. That made me wonder if he had received a similar note.

"Have you and John been involved in any projects together?"

Daryl's eyes were immediately wary. "We've done some business outside the festivals. Nothing significant. Mostly I referred people to him. I've used him as a consultant on a couple of things. But we haven't even talked since last year's festival."

I tried a wild shot. "Have you been considering investing in his company?"

Daryl looked surprised, and then as amused as he ever allowed himself to be. "If I had a large chunk of money to invest, I'd find something better to invest in. I've been looking at a few businesses, but..." He let the sentence trail off. "You've known John longer than I have. Was there something in his past that could have led to this?"

I noted but did not pursue Daryl's suggestion that he had money to invest and answered his question. "I would have said no, and there's still a chance he was chosen randomly. But this note of yours makes that seem less likely." I pulled out one of my business cards and wrote Bullard's cell number on the back, then handed it to Daryl. "That's Detective Bullard's number. I strongly suggest you call her and tell her about the note."

Daryl's expression was briefly defiant – he didn't like to be pushed – but switched to resigned after a few seconds. There was something else there too, something I had never seen in his eyes before. Daryl was afraid. I would have been too.

He was still sitting there, note in hand, when we left.

"Now what?" asked Dusty.

"Now we go find someplace quiet so that I can get my thoughts organized."

"I know just the place."

She led me to the elevator and after a lengthy wait we rode down to the fifth floor. I asked where we were going but Dusty just smiled and kept walking. I followed her to room 550, where she took a room key out of her pocket and opened the door.

"Whose room is this and how did you get their key?"

Dusty gave me an impish smile. She was enjoying this and was going to prolong it for as long as possible. "It's our room. Mine actually. I found out they had a cancellation and snatched it up. I figured since we were going to be here really late tonight, it would be easier than driving home."

I started to object but she steamrollered over me. "I bought a travel pack with a portable razor and stuff while you were wandering around on your own this morning. There's also a shirt and a pair of socks. You'll have to make do for underwear. And I found this really gorgeous blouse." She opened the closet door to display her finds. "And a few other things. I really need to spend a day shopping."

I searched around inside my mind for more counterarguments, but gave it up as a lost cause. The deed was done, and it would be considerably more convenient, and I could manage for one night. "Darla is going to be mad at us. And hungry."

"Mad maybe, but not hungry. I loaded up her dish this morning, just in case. And I laid in some supplies." She gestured toward the desk, where I saw a package of lined pads and a box of felt tip pens.

My handwriting is better than Dusty's. Hers is, in fact, so illegible she struggles to read her own notes. She told me that she learned to type in fifth grade because her teachers couldn't read her deathless prose.

I made up a page for each of the people we had talked to. Normally I would have made two sub-entries, one for opportunity, one for motive, but since none of them really had an alibi except Daryl, I didn't bother.

"So, let's start with Terry Wareham. What motive could she possibly have?"

"If she really was trying to blackmail Daryl, then maybe this was part of a scheme of intimidation."

I thought about it. "Doesn't make sense to me. Daryl and John weren't close, and despite Daryl's complaints, the murder isn't having much of an effect on the festival. On the other hand, if she's capable of blackmail, she might be capable of worse. But I don't think Daryl has enough money to justify this kind of operation."

We couldn't think of anything else so we went on to the next – Muriel Bates.

"Muriel had a fight with Helen Viele," said Dusty. "That seems out of character. She's always been very quiet. And she knew John better than most of the others."

"But they were friends, and I don't think Helen had much to do with John. He wasn't her type. If Helen had been killed, then John might possibly be a suspect because he'd been rejected, but it doesn't work in the other direction."

"Both of them had affairs with Daryl at some point," I said. "But neither of them was involved with John."

"I can't see Muriel killing anyone. And if she did, she'd do it in a moment of anger, not methodically and dispassionately."

"Muriel also hinted that she's coming into some money."

"Maybe she made a loan to John and he reneged on repaying it."

That was pretty thin, and we'd still have to figure out where the money had come from in the first place, but I made a note.

We moved on to Jimmy Gonsalves. I spoke up first. "The only thing mysterious about Jimmy is that he suddenly has lots of money. He knew John pretty well, but not outside of festivals and conventions."

"We don't know that the money was sudden. I don't know about you but I've never heard Jimmy talk about himself. I know he does something in computers. Maybe he's assistant to Bill Gates or something."

"He seems tight with Terry. And he mentioned getting some kind of windfall."

Dusty shook her head. "I don't think there's anything romantic there. The body language didn't suggest any kind of intimacy."

"And it still wouldn't suggest a motive for killing John. Let's try the next."

Romeo Bolduc and John had quarreled, more than once, and quite loudly at times. His weight limited his mobility but it was just possible that he could have pulled it off. "But I can't see him actually being physically violent," Dusty objected. "He's like a big teddy bear."

"Actually, I think he could." Romeo and I had spent an evening in a bar once and he'd told me about his past. He'd been a marine in Viet Nam and a nightclub bouncer for a couple of years after that. He had killed at least three people in the war, and nearly killed a patron once afterwards, which is why he stopped working that particular job.

"The arguments were all petty, though. And he's pretty memorable. It would have been a big risk."

I had to agree with her about that.

Jo Parkin was another of Daryl's discarded girlfriends, but neither of us thought she knew John very well. We ended up leaving her page blank.

Ray Riccello was another one who seemed to have enjoyed a financial renaissance recently. I knew that John had disliked Ray, considered him a phony – with some justification, but even if Ray had been aware of John's opinion, it wasn't an uncommon one. Ray was hard to read, but I thought there was a bit of an edge there and I could see him killing someone if the motive was strong enough. I added a sheet for Edward Mrozek, Ray's new friend, but since neither of us knew a thing about him, it was otherwise blank.

Tanya George struck us both as the person temperamentally best suited to be a killer. I would never have realized that if we hadn't been in our present situation, but there was a kind of ruthless momentum in her life. Her goals might be relatively benign – she didn't seem to miss the world of acting – but she clung to them tenaciously. If Helen Viele made a play for Ray, it would not surprise me if her body turned up in a dumpster the next morning,.

Helen herself initially seemed to me the least likely of our potential suspects. I knew she was a good deal smarter than her air-head performance would suggest, but I think her casual attitude toward the world was genuine. She didn't really care about anything, certainly not so powerfully that she would kill to attain or protect it. On the other hand, there was a core of iron there. She didn't care about other people's opinions particularly, and she didn't like being interfered with.

Bob Strossi had an obvious motive. Despite his claim that he didn't bear a grudge about his brief stint working for John, I had noticed tension in his voice when he talked about it. He had a notoriously short temper, although I had never heard that he'd been physical except the one story he had told us himself about pushing John. He also had a methodical mind and was certainly capable of planning the complex murder scene in room 415. I didn't really believe that he had killed John, but Dusty and I agreed that he was the most viable name on our list.

"Is that all?" Dusty asked. "It feels like there should be more."

"'Just one. Daryl."

"But he's the one person we know could not have been in John's room. He has a solid alibi."

"I agree that he couldn't have done it personally, but he could have arranged to have it done."

"But why would he sabotage the festival?"

"He didn't. We just finished telling him that there's been no real effect."

"Do you really think that Daryl could have hired someone to kill John?"

I didn't hesitate. "I don't think it would bother him in the slightest. If John stood between Daryl and something that Daryl wanted, he'd have been eliminated one way or another. Maybe Daryl tried to buy something from him – his silence maybe – and that's why John was expecting to clear up his business debts."

"Do you think John was the kind to extort money?"

"I wouldn't have thought so, but then again, I wouldn't have thought it of Terry either, and she apparently is doing exactly that."

"Do you think it could be the same thing?" Dusty suddenly looked alarmed.

"I don't know, but I think we should drop a hint to Terry to be very careful this weekend."

CHAPTER NINE

We went through the list a second time, but were unable to add anything. Dusty was clearly discouraged. "We aren't getting anywhere."

"Which is why murder investigations are best left to the police." Although as far as I could see, Bullard was no closer to the solution than we were. Of course, she could have made progress which she hadn't mentioned. This wasn't a partnership, after all.

We wandered for a bit after that, mostly in the dealers' room, and I even picked up a couple of DVDs. Dusty found a book about silent films and started talking about a new novel set during the 1940s, a murder mystery. I wasn't really in the mood for another murder mystery just then so I changed the subject.

Somewhere along the way we ran into some old friends and before I realized what was happening, we'd been recruited into a party of eight for dinner. Muriel and her sister and Bob Strossi were the instigators – mostly Muriel – and Jo Parkin had already been invited. The last two were people I hardly knew – Lynda Harris and James Nicholson. Dusty knew Lynda from before she'd met me and had introduced us once, but she only came to East Coast festivals and not always then. She was tiny and the oversized glasses she wore made her look like a cartoon character. Nicholson I'd encountered once or twice before. He was a very charming person but I had never liked him. His insincerity seemed obvious to me and I knew he made some of the women uneasy, although I'd never heard that he misbehaved in any way.

Strossi had a rental car so we split into two groups of four. All of the restaurants within walking distance would be filled with festival people. Dusty recommended the Grist Mill, which was just over the line in Massachusetts, so I called to make sure they could take a large party and off we went. Harris and Nicholson rode with us, but there wasn't much conversation along the way. Neither of them were on our list of suspects. Neither of them knew John, although Nicholson knew who he was.

The Grist Mill was full but not crowded, and we waited less than three minutes before they were seating us. Angela had a mild case of the giggles for some reason and Strossi looked both uncomfortable and pleased at the same time. Muriel seemed preoccupied and didn't even seem to notice when the waitress handed her a menu. Nicholson had contrived to sit next to Dusty, who had never met him before, and I was curious to see what she would make of him. Jo Parkin was unusually talkative.

"We broke our old attendance record at eleven this morning and we're still getting a trickle of latecomers. Daryl was almost in a good mood when I gave him the numbers."

"How could you tell with Daryl? Did he smile while he was growling?" Strossi's sarcasm elicited more giggling from Angela.

"Daryl's not as bad as people say." Jo was almost pouting. "He takes a lot on his shoulders and no one really appreciates how much work he does."

"I'm sure you do, Jo." Muriel had shaken off whatever was bothering her. "You've been with him a long time." Muriel had been a co-founder, so she'd been there as long as anyone.

"This is my thirteenth year working at the festival, and I attended twice before that, including the very first."

"So what does everyone think about the murder? The cops are all over the place." Nicholson's choice of a ploy to change the subject was unfortunate, perhaps deliberately so. I could tell by his eyes that it wasn't a casual remark.

"Some of us were friends of John's," said Muriel angrily.

"Sorry. I wasn't trying to make light of it. I only knew him by name. Did he have a lot of enemies?"

"John was a bit of a goof," said Jo. "But he wasn't a bad guy."

"I'm on the same floor," said Lynda in a voice not much more than a whisper. "But the other wing. I wanted to change my room but the hotel is full."

"I don't think you have anything to worry about," said Dusty. "Just keep the chain on your door whenever you're in your room."

"Oh, I always do. And I put a chair under the doorknob too." That said, she subsided quickly, burying her face in the menu. The waitress returned and took our drink order.

We ordered and the talk turned to general subjects, mostly film related, and whatever his personality might have been, Nicholson's knowledge of noir films was extensive. Unexpectedly it was Lynda who dropped the bombshell. The conversation had drifted into one of those momentary lulls when no one had anything to say. Lynda had barely spoken since we'd arrived, but suddenly her head came up. "I think I might have seen him. The man who killed John, I mean."

Now I didn't know Lynda well – none of us did – but I remembered thinking once before that she had an overactive imagination. So I was skeptical right from the outset.

"Where was this?" I asked, keeping my voice as casual as possible.

"In the hotel. I think I came up in the elevator with him."

"What time would this have been?"

She pressed her lips together and I knew she recognized that I wasn't taking her entirely seriously. "A little before four o'clock yesterday."

The time was about right and I felt the faintest quickening of my pulse. "What makes you think he was the killer?"

She hunched her shoulders slightly as though expecting an attack. "He acted very strangely. I just managed to catch the elevator before the doors closed and he gave me a dirty look, then turned away so that I couldn't see his face any more. When we reached the fourth floor, he started for the door without waiting to see if I was getting out too, which he should have known since I hadn't punched any of the other buttons."

This was by far the longest speech I'd ever heard from Lynda. The words came out as though they'd been immersed in soda water which was then rapidly shaken under pressure.

"He stood in the elevator lobby when we got out and didn't go off in either direction. I was all the way down to the door of my room and he still hadn't moved. I know because I was afraid he might follow me and force his way into my room."

"Did you see where he finally went?" asked Angela.

Lynda shook her head. "No, I was afraid to open my door. I stayed there until suppertime."

"What did he look like?" I asked.

"Oh, like a guy. Thirtyish, I guess. Dark hair with a little bit of gray. About your height and a little heavier."

"How was he dressed?"

"Just normally. I don't really notice clothes. I think they were dark."

My next question was the important one. "Was he carrying anything?"

"Yes he was. He had a canvas dufflebag over his shoulder, and he had a brief case too."

Was it possible that she had actually seen John's killer? "Have you told the police about this?"

Lynda looked suddenly alarmed. "No, of course not. I'd be afraid the killer would find out and come after me."

I'll spare you the next ten minutes during which Muriel, Dusty, and I managed to convince her that she'd be safer if she talked than if she kept it secret. I'm afraid I was a bit unkind. I kept reminding her that the man she had seen had seen her as well, and that if he was concerned that she could identify him, he'd come after her whether or not she talked to Bullard. She was teary eyed by the time we were done but she had agreed to repeat her story to the police. "But after we eat, please. I'm really hungry."

So we ate.

I didn't trust Lynda to follow through without strong encouragement, so when we got back to the city and had the car safely parked, I called Bullard immediately. She didn't sound as though she was in a good mood, and her mouth was full. I explained that we'd found someone who might have seen a suspicious looking character on the fourth floor of the Driscoll at the right time.

"Have you now? And who is this person and where would I find them?"

"Her name is Lynda Harris and I'm with her now. Where should we meet you?"

There was a brief hesitation. "The interview room at the Biltmore. If I'm not there when you arrive, wait for me."

She wasn't there when we arrived. Either she had farther to go or more likely she was going to finish whatever she was eating first. A bored looking policewoman was sitting inside reading a magazine and once I'd told her we were meeting Bullard, she ignored us completely. About ten minutes later, Bullard showed up.

"So what have we got?"

I introduced Lynda, who was tongue tied at first, but finally managed to get the whole story out. Bullard plied her with a few questions, none of which she could answer, and asked her if she'd be willing to work with a police artist. Lynda seemed to have gained some self confidence from being the center of attention and agreed readily. Bullard took out her cell, called someone, and it was obvious from her half of the conversation that she was meeting some resistance, but eventually she told us that someone would be over in half an hour. "Jackass thinks his job is nine to five," she told me in an aside.

There was no real reason for Dusty and I to remain there and I grew increasingly restless. Dusty read my mood and offered to stay with Lynda. "There's no reason why you should stick around." Bullard had no objection so I left.

Now that I was free to go where I wanted, I couldn't think of any place I wanted to be. To be truthful, the events of the last twenty-four hours had started to catch up to me. I felt emotionally drained and physically tired. It would not be true to say that I no longer cared about what had happened to John, but the sense of immediacy, the urge to do something about it, had somehow evaporated when I wasn't looking. I wanted to go home and watch something mindless on television, or better yet, one of the two movies I was stowed away in the glove compartment of my car. But I couldn't very well do that since we had a room for the night,

So I went up to the room and lay down on the bed for a while, trying not to think, maybe take a nap. But that didn't work either. I was restless and I had that annoying feeling that I was forgetting something or overlooking something obvious. I looked through our notes again, but my mind refused to work. I was stuck in neutral.

So finally I went down to the bar. I wasn't in the mood for company, but unfortunately company was in the mood for me, in the form of Helen Viele.

Helen and I had some history together. It was brief and I didn't regret it and it was the year before I met Dusty. I actually think it was John who introduced us in Memphis. I hadn't been involved with anyone since Audrey and I had split up almost a year earlier. The agency was only two years old and I was really struggling to make ends meet. Twelve hour days and six day weeks are not conducive to an enduring romantic relationship.

We were at a room party at the time and after a while I got tired of breathing second hand smoke. As I started to leave, Helen caught me by the arm. We had exchanged perhaps a few dozen words by then and hadn't unearthed any interests that we shared. I had duly noted that she was an attractive woman, but she wasn't extraordinarily attractive.

"You look like you could use a drink and I know I could" It wasn't the slickest line I'd ever heard, but the logical response was to take her to the hotel bar and in due course up to my room where we spent the rest of the evening and about half of the following morning. Like I said, I don't regret it at all. There was obviously no long term commitment, no deep emotional attachment, or any complicating side issues. If I hadn't met Dusty the following year, it's entirely possible that the night would have been repeated with the same lack of consequences. And yes, Dusty knows all about my past entanglements. She and Audrey even go out for a drink together occasionally and I often wonder if they are comparing notes.

Almost the only time I'd ever seen Helen without a male companion in tow was when she had a female one instead. So it was a bit of a surprise to see her sitting at the bar by herself, idly playing with her drink. I debated pretending that I hadn't seen her, but that seemed churlish so I sat down on the next stool.

She glanced in my direction and nodded. "Where's your better half?"

"Busy. I'm waiting for her to finish." I didn't want Helen to get the wrong idea. Her own apparent inability to forge a lasting relationship had apparently convinced her that everyone else felt the same way.

She glanced away. "Do you ever worry about getting old, Birch?"

I shrugged even though she wasn't looking my way. "I try not to worry about the things that I can't change."

"Very logical. How old do you think I am?"

I had the sudden feeling that I was standing in the middle of a minefield. Truthfully, I would have guessed thirty-five, but I decided to be tactful. "Early thirties."

That brought an unpleasant laugh. "I just turned forty."

"You don't look it." I could say that confidently because it was true.

"I feel it though. It's a little harder to get out of bed in the morning, it takes a little longer to get the face looking right, and I have to pay more attention to what I eat."

"We all have to deal with that sort of thing." I was a bit uneasy because I didn't want to hurt her feelings and she wasn't being her normal, predictable self.

"It's different for a guy. It's not fair." I couldn't argue with either of those two statements so I said nothing. "A worm like Daryl doesn't even have to work at it."

Now frankly I had never thought of Daryl as being good looking, but when I considered the matter now, I realized that he probably was, after a fashion. He wasn't athletic but he was trim, the short beard that would have made me look silly was distinguished on his strong chin. He had piercing eyes, a sharply defined nose, and still had his own hair, although I suspected that he colored it. Helen had lived with him for a couple of months, which was probably her personal record by quite a bit. I remembered that she had money, enough that she didn't have to work and could travel around the country to attend not only this festival but other industry related gatherings as well. I had the impression that she traveled a lot and when I thought about it I realized I had no idea where she called home, if there was any place that she called home.

"I know he doesn't have the greatest personality, and you're probably wondering why I stayed with him so long."

To be truthful, it had never occurred to me to wonder, but I nodded as though I had, and now that she brought it up, it did seem a bit mysterious.

"I made the mistake of falling for him. Oh, not all the way. It wasn't the one true love of my life or anything like that. I think he just happened to be there at the right moment. But for the first time I decided that I wanted something to last a little longer than one night or at best a long weekend. Maybe I got jealous of people like you and Dusty or Ray and Tanya. Maybe I just figured I was missing out on something and wanted to find out what it was like to be in a stable relationship." She chuckled and took a drink. "I suppose I could have found someone a little more stable than Daryl Plimpton to experiment with, but he was available and apparently willing and things just kind of fell together."

This had all taken place about eighteen months back, I remembered. I wondered why it had resurfaced now. "Daryl can be a bit trying," I said quietly. "But he's an oddball. I wouldn't spend much time blaming myself if a relationship with him didn't work out."

"Yeah, I know." She had finished her drink and waved her glass at the bartender. "You don't have to listen to me feeling sorry for myself."

"I hate to see you looking so glum. If you want to talk about it, I'll listen. If you don't, I can go away."

"No, stay." The bartender appeared with a replacement for her empty glass and she nodded toward me. "Give him another of whatever he's having and put it on my tab."

I automatically started to protest, then cut myself short. If Helen wanted to buy me a drink, then she wanted me to stay and, presumably, to listen.

"Daryl has a nice place out in California, you know. Big house, lots of land, way out in the country."

"I'm surprised he can afford it."

"He can't really. He inherited it. Most of the land is rented out to a local farmer and about half the house is closed up. A Mexican woman keeps it reasonably clean. She's probably illegal. I know he pays her in cash. The taxes aren't bad that far out but the upkeep must be daunting."

"How long were you together?"

"Three months and one week."

"What finally made you leave?"

"He threw me out, actually. Told me that he'd decided he didn't like having someone living there with him and that I'd have to go." She drank a little and I finished my first just as the second arrived. "It was real sudden. No warning at all. And I was kind of surprised because I was helping out with the finances a little here and there and I knew he needed the extra cash."

"Maybe you scared him. He's lived alone for so long that he might have felt as though he was losing control." I hesitated and decided to plunge onward. "Do you still have feelings for him?"

Helen shook her head. "I don't think I ever really did. I think I was attracted by the idea of being in love with someone and was trying it on for size. To be honest, I don't really care for his personality. No, I don't miss him at all. He can be charming but he's all caught up in himself, and toward the end he was being so secretive that it was like a caricature of someone with a secret."

"Secretive about what?"

"I don't really know. I didn't care particularly and I never tried to find out. But he went away for a week and when he came back, he wouldn't talk about the trip and he was different in bed. Preoccupied. Maybe even a little bit worried. He told me I'd have to leave about a week after that and I went."

"Sounds like it was more about him than it was about you."

Helen nodded, took a sip, and looked directly at me. "You and I would never have made a good couple."

"Probably not."

"And it wouldn't have been your fault."

"It wouldn't have been anyone's fault. We're all pieces of a jigsaw puzzle. Sometimes we fit together, sometimes we don't."

"Sometimes I think I'm in the wrong puzzle box."

"Maybe you're just a corner piece. You don't have as many connections, but when you do find one, it's going to be important to the puzzle as a whole."

"We're straining the metaphor a bit, aren't we?" She laughed then, and so did I. "That feels better," she admitted. She finished her drink. "I'd better get going. If I don't connect with someone soon, I'm going to end up sleeping alone tonight. Now that would be depressing." She stood up and put some money on the bar. "Thanks for listening."

"Easy job. Just sit and look attentive."

"No. Actually listening is hard work, and you're one of the few people I know who's good at it." And then she was walking away.

I had just finished my drink when my cell buzzed. It was Dusty. "Where are you?"

"Hotel bar."

"Can you come back here? Something interesting has happened."

So I went back to the interview room. There was a new uniform standing – or actually slouching – outside the door and he didn't challenge me when I passed. Apparently I was expected.

Dusty, Bullard, and Lynda Harris were still there, along with a youngish man with a skinny moustache whom I didn't know. He was the only one standing and was clearly preparing to leave. I assumed, correctly, that he was the police artist. Lynda looked mildly bewildered, Dusty had a cheery smile on her face, and Bullard looked grumpy and thoughtful, which wasn't remarkable since that's how she always looked.

Dusty beckoned me over. I could see two or three charcoal sketches on the table, all vaguely similar, but none of them looked even remotely familiar to me. I assumed this was the person Lynda had seen carrying the canvas duffle bag and Dusty quickly confirmed my opinion. The guy with the moustache never acknowledged me as he walked past and out the door.

"He doesn't look particularly memorable," I said.

"Ah, but he does," said Bullard. "I talked to this man just about two hours ago."

"Who is he?"

Bullard picked up one of the sketches. "This, my friends, is Mr. Edward Mrozek, a guest in this hotel."

"And a friend of Ray Riccello," I added.

"Who has recently hinted about a new movie project, which requires capital," said Dusty.

Bullard stood up. "I think I need to ask Mr. Mrozek a few more questions. I would like Miss Harris to identify him in person and since the two of you were so helpful, I have no objection if you come along." She gave me a look. "So long as you remain silent observers."

"Our lips are sealed," I promised.

Lynda looked terrified. "I really didn't see him all that well." Her voice trembled.

Bullard managed not to look disgusted but I could read it in her body. "No one is going to leave you alone with him, Miss Harris. You'll be perfectly safe."

Actually, no one was ever perfectly safe, but I wasn't going to say that out loud.

The four of us stepped outside into darkness. In the distance we could see dancing lights and hear the strains of music being played along the banks of the Providence River, which snaked through the city. There was a Waterfire tonight, which pulled thousands of people into the city and had drawn off some of the festival goers as well. Large iron cradles had been installed at intervals throughout this part of the river and a few times each year they were loaded with firewood and set ablaze while sidewalk vendors working out of tents provided cold drinks and food to the crowds. Dusty and I had been several times in the past, but it was still special in its way.

It was a short walk to the Driscoll and no one said much of anything. Lynda looked as though she was being marched to her execution and Dusty took her arm reassuringly. A uniform was waiting for us in the lobby and we all rode up together in the elevator to the fourth floor. The crowd waiting to use it made some caustic comments when he cut the line but Bullard flashed her badge almost automatically and they subsided.

Mickey Palotto was waiting for us when we got off, along with two more uniforms. Mickey was looking almost as uncomfortable as Lynda, but then again, that was his normal expression. There were nods and Bullard told us to wait there with Lynda while they checked out the room.

Mickey's master key proved unnecessary because when they knocked, someone called out from inside and unlocked the door, keeping the chain engaged. Bullard showed her badge and the chain came off. From where we stood, I could only see Mrozek's profile, but it looked a good deal like the sketch. Bullard and the others went inside and there was some muffled talking. After a couple of minutes, one of the uniforms beckoned for us to join them.

It looked like any other hotel room. Mrozek was a bit fuller in the face than Lynda had remembered and his hair was longer, but otherwise she'd done a pretty good job. He was standing in one corner of the room, looking alternately nervous and angry. There was a canvas duffle bag on the bed, smaller than I'd expected, not much more than an overnight bag. It was empty now, or nearly so.

Bullard glanced at Lynda. "For the record, is this the man you saw in the elevator yesterday?"

Lynda had to try twice and her voice was fainter than ever but she confirmed that it was.

"What's this all about?" asked Mrozek, somewhat testily.

"Are you aware that a man was killed on this floor last night?"

"Of course I am. I could hardly miss it with all the comings and goings last night. What has that to do with me?"

"We're just checking the movements of anyone who was seen on this floor at the time the death occurred. You could be a potential witness."

"I didn't see anything." Anger was triumphing over nervousness.

"Did you see Miss Harris here?"

Mrozek looked at her and she shrank back. "Possibly. There was a young woman in the elevator with me when I arrived but I didn't pay any attention."

"May I ask why you're visiting Providence? I notice that you aren't listed as attending the film festival."

"Actually, I am." He reached over to the desk and picked up one of the festival's badges. He handed it to Bullard.

"Strange Developments? Is that a company name?"

"Yes it is. We invest in indie film projects that appeal to our founder, Daniel Ruderman. I'm here to talk to some people whose proposals seem promising."

Bullard glanced at the duffle bag. "You travel light."

"Yes, I do. I don't like checking bags. There's too much chance of them getting lost or delayed."

I could tell by her body language that Bullard was losing interest. "Did you know John Boncoddo, the deceased?"

"No I did not. I understand that he worked with vintage films. They don't fall within our purview. We're only interested in new work."

Bullard glanced at me, inviting me to ask a question. So I did. "Is Ray Riccello one of the people you're meeting?"

Mrozek nodded. "Yes, in fact, he is. His proposal is actually the most interesting one we're currently considering." His tone warmed a bit. "Vampires vs the zombie apocalypse. I know it sounds odd, but he submitted a fascinating précis." Mrozek looked as though he was about to launch into a summary but Bullard cut him off.

"Do you own a firearm, Mr. Mrozek?"

"No. I've never had a reason to want one."

"How did you arrive in Providence? Train? Bus? Automobile?"

"We're based in San Diego, detective. I flew, of course." And he certainly couldn't have brought a weapon in his carryon bag.

"Did you see or hear anything unusual in the area after you reached your room yesterday?"

"Not that I recall. I took a shower as soon as I arrived, and unpacked of course. Watched the news. I didn't leave the room until about five when I decided to find someplace to eat. There was a bellhop in the elevator and I asked him what he recommended and he suggested a very nice Chinese place. When I came back an hour or so later, there were policemen everywhere."

Bullard handed him a card. "If anything should occur to you that you don't remember at the moment, please give me a call at that number. We're sorry to have disturbed you but you understand that for the safety of everyone in the hotel we have to check every possibility."

Mrozek seemed mollified. "Of course I understand. I wish you the best of luck."

We all stood outside the door of 407. Bullard glanced at Lynda. "I think that's all we need from you, Miss Harris. Thank you for your cooperation." Lynda glanced around, as though unsure that she actually had permission to leave, and then she walked briskly off in the direction of her own room. I was pretty sure she was going to cry.

"Sorry about that," I said, although I really wasn't.

Bullard just shook her head. "Don't be sorry. It was a possibility and had to be checked out. I'd have been pissed if you hadn't brought her to me. And we'll check this guy out." Her mouth tightened. "But it would be nice to get something tangible to wrestle with. My suspects are all going to be leaving the city tomorrow."

"Actually," said Dusty, "that's not entirely true. The festival goes through Monday night because of the holiday. Some people will leave, of course, but the names we gave you are all hard core fans. They'll probably all be here until late Monday or even early Tuesday. I know Daryl and Jo Parkin and Muriel Bates will all be dealing with things right until the end. Probably Terry Wareham too."

"And if the killer's isn't on your list?"

She shrugged. "Can't have everything your way. Would you want things to be easy?"

Bullard never hesitated. "Yes, all the time."

CHAPTER TEN

We all rode down in the elevator together in utter silence. When we reached the lobby, Bullard told the uniforms they could go home. "That's where I'm headed." She nodded in our general direction and walked away.

"So where to?"

I glanced at my watch. "I think we just missed Daryl's big announcement."

"Color me disappointed."

"How about we go up to our room and rest our feet?"

"Sounds like a plan."

The crowds around the river were thinning rapidly as the last of the fires died down. I could smell burnt wood as a faint breeze tickled the night air. The Biltmore lobby was a lot less crowded. The announcement had been made in the ballroom far above us and the elevators were just starting to bring people down.

When the next load emerged, Jo Parkin was among the crowd emerging and she grabbed Dusty's arm before we could move past. "Did you guys miss the big announcement?"

"I guess we did," I admitted. "Is Daryl running for the Republican Presidential nomination like everyone else?"

"Very funny. No, he's signed a deal for the DVD release of *At the Mountains of Madness*."

"Is that all?" Dusty shook her head. "We've been expecting that for over a year."

"Well, almost all. It's going to be released in a colorized version as well as the original black and white."

Now this might not seem like a big deal, and on the cosmic scale of things it really isn't. But there are some purists – with whom I confess I sympathize – who believe that it is wrong if not actively immoral to tinker with an original creation. Cleaning up noise in the picture or soundtrack or sharpening images is okay, because those are things that the people involved in the original production would have done, but adding color, re-editing or adding scenes, even changing the aspect ratio could get you roundly cursed.

"That must have gone over well," I said.

Jo blinked at me. "Well, mostly. There were a few people who weren't happy about it, but they'll come around when they see the end product."

"Have you seen it?"

"No, of course not. The work hasn't been done yet. Daryl just signed the deal a couple of weeks ago. As soon as the distributor pays the advance, he's going to take the original print to a studio that specializes in colorization. They expect it to be on sale in time for Christmas."

So Daryl was indeed coming into some money. Could Terry have learned about this in advance? Was that why she had approached him? It also occurred to me that John would have been furious. John had been a purist and colorization was right at the top of the list of things he wouldn't tolerate.

The other elevator arrived and disgorged more people. I told Jo we'd catch up to her later and followed Dusty into the car. We were the only people going up. "What do you think of that?" asked Dusty.

"I think Daryl just made a lot of people happy, and another lot of people very unhappy."

When we reached our room, I realized that I was exhausted and my feet really did hurt. I'd spent a big chunk of the day standing or walking, and I'm usually desk bound most of the time I'm not in bed. It was getting toward ten o'clock, my normal bedtime, and I was developing a headache. I took off my shoes the moment the door latched behind us, and Dusty disappeared into the bathroom.

Dusty's shopping trip hadn't included sleepwear, so I turned down the air conditioning and started to undress. I had my shirt off when I noticed that the little red light on the telephone that indicated we had a message waiting was blinking impatiently. I had a strong impulse to leave it until morning, but even if Dusty didn't see it – and I know she would be able to resist the urge to find out what it meant – it would blink persistently in the dark and keep me awake even if I put a pillow over my head.

So I sighed, took a deep breath, and picked up the receiver. The desk clerk told me that Romeo Bolduc requested that I call his room. She provided the room number. I thanked her and broke the connection. Dusty had just come out of the bathroom wearing just her underwear and I was seriously considering letting Romeo wait until morning, but I knew it would bother me so I dialed his number.

He picked up right away.

"Romeo, this is Paul. What's up?"

"Hey, man. Look, I've been thinking a lot about what happened to John. And I remembered something peculiar from a while back. I don't know if it's worth telling the police, but you know about that sort of thing so I wanted to run it by you."

"I'm not a policeman, Romeo."

"I know that, but just give it a listen. This was about a year ago – just before we had that big argument - so it probably doesn't have anything to do with anything, but you never know, do you?"

I admitted that we were all troubled by universal, unending ignorance.

"John and I were both at the Seattle festival and we ended up sitting together through a set of old detective movies – *The Old Dark House,* the first Bulldog Drummon, and something else I don't remember. Afterwards we went to lunch together, just the two of us because not a lot of the regular crowd were attending that year. Anyway, we were talking about how as lot of the old mystery movies only worked because some of the characters withheld information that would have cleared things up earlier, and a lot of the time they really didn't have a reason to do that except to help the plot along."

I stirred impatiently but I knew from experience it would be counterproductive to try to get Romeo to speed things up.

"We'd had a couple of drinks with lunch and you know John doesn't usually indulge and gets kind of silly when he does."

I nodded, realized Romeo couldn't see me, and confirmed that I knew what he meant.

"So then he tells me he wants to ask a hypothetical question. What do I think is the right thing to do when someone suspects that maybe a crime has been committed, but isn't really sure. So I tell him that I'd go to the police and let them figure out if it was worth looking into. But, he asks, what if that person has personally benefitted – completely innocently – from the crime and might lose that benefit if it turned out that his suspicion was correct. Well, naturally I told him that didn't make any difference and he started adding other little bits, like the possible adverse effects on a perfectly innocent third party, and stuff like that. Anyway, to make a long story short, he hung so many bells and whistles on the story that I finally agreed that there were instances when it would be better to remain silent, particularly if the crime involved was something minor, like petty theft. And I thought that satisfied him, except he got real quiet for a while and then he thanked me but that he still wasn't sure what the right answer was."

"That all sounds pretty vague." Dusty was no longer wearing anything at all and I really wanted to cut the conversation short.

"Well, I'm no dummy and I had figured out by then that this theoretical question of his was real. I thought it had something to do with his company, like maybe one of his clients was involved with something shady like manipulating the books or something. So I said if it was something like ripping off the government in tax returns, I didn't think he was obligated to say anything. At least not morally."

Romeo was a libertarian, sort of. He hated taxes, distrusted the government, but wasn't comfortable with his conservative friends because he advocated gun control, gay marriage, and legalized pot. To be honest, I don't think Romeo ever really grew up, and I don't think he'd thought about the issues enough to have an integrated, functional political stance, but that's a whole other story.

"That sounds right to me." Dusty was posing and right then I wouldn't have cared if John had told Romeo he knew about a plan to assassinate the President.

"So he thought about that for a while and then he gave this big sigh and said something about how it was too late anyway, that the damage was done, and that he really didn't know for certain that anything illegal had happened. By then he wasn't even pretending that it was hypothetical anymore."

"That's an interesting story, Romeo, but there's no way to prove there is a connection to what happened to him, if there is one."

"No, I guess not. But Paul, John was really upset right at the end. I could see it in his eyes, and his hands were shaking."

I thanked him, hung up the phone, and what I did next is none of your business.

There are people I know who claim to be psychic in some fashion or another. They insist that they can sense when it's going to be a bad day, or that they can evaluate a person's character based on intuition alone, or in some other fashion reach an accurate conclusion even in the absence of evidence. I've read detective novels where the private eye or police investigator has a kind of instinct and knows when a crime has been committed despite appearances to the contrary. I've always thought this was a load of nonsense. Sure, there are instances when there are subliminal cues that suggest a conclusion we can't necessarily reach by a logical examination of the facts, but at least there is a chain of cause and effect there.

So when I dropped off to sleep about an hour later, I had no presentiment of doom or danger, no uneasiness, no reason to believe that John's murder was not an isolated event. To be completely honest, I had been drifting away from my earlier feeling that the culprit was someone within our group and toward the possibility that John had just been chosen by chance. It was still a tragedy, of course, just as it would have been if he'd died of cancer or been killed in an automobile accident. But it would have been a discrete event, over and done with, not likely to have any lingering impact.

That misconception would not survive the night.

I awoke complete disoriented. The room was dark and Dusty hadn't stirred. She could sleep through a category nine earthquake. It took a few seconds to recognize that the buzzing sound was the telephone and a couple more to remember that I was in a hotel room. I caught one foot in the dangling sheet as I got out of bed and nearly fell onto the armchair beside the bed. Then I reached the desk, stubbing my toe along the way, and lifted the receiver.

"Yes? What is it?" I glanced over at the clock. It was just after three.

"Is this Paul Birch?" It was a gruff male voice that I didn't recognize.

"Yes, that's me? What do you want?" I am rarely in a good mood when roused directly from deep sleep.

"Detective Bullard would like you to come up to room 612 right away."

"What's this about?" A little bell went off in my head. I knew who was in room 612.

"I couldn't tell you that, sir. I just know that Detective Bullard told me to call and have you come as soon as possible."

I almost asked another question but stopped myself. Even if the officer – and I was quite certain I was talking to a policeman – knew the answer to my question, I very much doubted that he would answer. "I'll be right there."

Dusty woke up while I was pulling on my pants. "Whassup?"

"Bullard just called. I have to go up to 612."

Dusty sat up and shook her head. "That's Muriel's room."

"I know."

She swung her legs over the side of the bed and stood up. "I'm coming too."

I knew better than to argue with her.

We went up in the elevator together. Neither of us said anything. Both of us dreaded what we expected to find. It would have taken something dramatic to get Bullard back to the Biltmore after going home for the day. Something like another murder or two. Angela and Muriel were sharing that room.

When we got out of the elevator, the corridor was crowded – mostly with uniformed policemen. I counted at least eight. One of them was directing traffic and I identified myself. "Bullard wants to see us." I didn't waste my breath asking what had happened.

We weren't allowed inside 612, but through the open door we could see Angela sitting on the end of one of the beds. She was crying and there was a medic standing over her. We identified ourselves again to the guard at the door, who passed the message along, but it was another ten minutes before Bullard came out to see us.

"What's happened?" I asked.

"We have another victim. She was on your list. Muriel Bates. Shot once in the head just above the ear. Died instantly."

"How's her sister?" asked Dusty.

"Shaken but not physically harmed. She was unconscious when we arrived, drugged. Both of them were probably drugged. There was an empty bottle of champagne and a fruit basket. My money's on the champagne."

"No enhancements this time?"

Bullard shook her head, then hesitated. "Actually there are, but in a different way." She turned to Dusty. "Do you think you could help us with the sister? The EMT doesn't want to give her anything to calm her down because we don't know what drug was administered."

"Of course. Can I go in?"

Bullard bit her lip. "We'll bring her out. The technicians are still going over things. The night manager has opened up a room one floor up. If you could take her there, one of the officers will escort you."

Angela came out with the EMT and a policewoman a few seconds later. She was shaking violently and her face was streaked with tear lines. She looked much smaller than I remembered. Dusty put an arm around her and they all walked off toward the elevator.

"So why am I here?" I wondered aloud.

Bullard looked at me as though I had asked a very dumb question, which was perhaps the case. It was obvious now that the death of John Boncoddo had not been random, that someone was targeting festival attendees, and almost certainly members of our particular circle of friends. Daryl was not going to be happy when he found out.

"We have some more peculiarities here. I was kind of hoping that one or more of them might strike a chord with you. Something that might point toward an actual person instead of a large mob."

"What kind of peculiarities?"

She beckoned to a technician. "Give this gentleman a pair of gloves."

The technician, a rather attractive redhead, looked as though Bullard had committed blasphemy in the Vatican, but she took out a pair of plastic gloves and passed them over. "Don't touch anything," she cautioned me. "Move around as little as possible. Don't interfere with anyone."

I followed Bullard into the room. Muriel was lying on the bed farthest from the door, on her back, looking almost peaceful. There was a dark stain under her head but not as big as I would have expected. "Probably the same weapon that didn't kill Boncoddo," said Bullard.

A metal cart had been pushed up against one wall. There was a fruit basket on it, but I couldn't tell if anything had been taken. Beside it was a bottle of champagne, half empty, and three glasses – hotel issue water glasses. There was also an ashtray with a cigarette butt. "Muriel didn't smoke," I said. "I don't know about Angela. We just met her yesterday."

"We checked with room service. The fruit basket was sent as a gift by an unknown party. They don't know anything about the champagne."

I thought about it for a second. "Someone sent the fruit basket, then followed it to find out what room they were in. Showed up later with the champagne and drugged them." But all three glasses were empty. How had the killer managed not to succumb himself, or herself? And if that was the case, Angela would be able to tell us who was responsible. "That doesn't work, does it?"

"It's close," Bullard admitted. "Room service delivered the fruit with a note that read 'From an Admirer.' It was addressed to the sister, who says she thought it was from someone named Bob."

"That would be Bob Strossi. They've been dating, sort of."

"A couple of minutes later there's a knock on the door. The older sister answers it and someone delivers the champagne. The sister didn't see anyone because she was in the bathroom doing her hair. The unknown party must have opened it because it's not likely they could put poison in a champagne bottle without popping the cork."

"There's a third glass."

"And two more in the bathroom, still wrapped in paper."

I thought about it. Hotel rooms usually provided two or four glasses, never five. "It's not from this room," I said.

"Bingo. But it is from the Biltmore. Has the logo on the side. But it's a slightly different shape. This came from the bar."

"So the third party drank some of the champagne. That doesn't make any sense."

"That's what I would have guessed, and the sister says they never had any company. Whoever brought it was gone by the time she came out of the bathroom and the bottle was open. She says they drank a glass and were watching television when she started to get sleepy. The killer must have come back after they'd both passed out."

"But how would anyone get into the room?"

"There's a master key missing from housekeeping. We checked that right away. Their security here is pretty good so someone knew what they were doing."

"Why leave the glass though?" I wondered.

"I think it's part of the game. I wouldn't be surprised if there are finger prints on it, but they won't belong to the killer." She gestured toward the cigarette in the ashtray. "And I'll bet there's DNA on that, but likewise it will point to some perfectly innocent person. So will the other clues."

"Other clues?"

Bullard managed to look annoyed and amused simultaneously. "We found a business card under the bed. It belongs to a Mr. George Flint, who lives in Florida. He stayed at the Biltmore about two weeks ago but hasn't left Tampa since then. I talked to him on the telephone a few minutes ago. I assume he's not part of the vintage film community."

"Not to my knowledge."

"Then there's the button. I can't show it to you because the techies have already taken it away, but you can take my word for it that it matches those found on the uniforms of the housing staff, bellhops, and desk clerks here at the Biltmore. The logo is unmistakable."

"That might be coincidental."

"It was sitting on the counter beside the bathroom sink, in plain sight."

"Not a coincidence then."

"And then there's the cell phone. The victim's cell was on when we arrived. A number had been entered but hadn't been called. It was to a small film related company in California."

"John's company." I thought about it. There might be a good reason why Muriel would have wanted to talk to some of John's friends. But she would hardly have done so in the middle of the night. "Do we know when it happened?"

"The fruit basket was delivered at eleven, almost exactly. The young lady who brought it up noticed nothing unusual. The sisters were surprised and one of them said it must be from this Bob guy. I guess he's the boyfriend."

"Strossi," I said. "I don't think it had progressed to boyfriend and girlfriend yet. When did she die?"

"Preliminary time of death is anywhere from eleven to one."

"I assume Angela recovered and raised the alarm."

Bullard shook her head. "No, in fact she was still unconscious when we arrived."

"Then how did you know?"

"The killer sent us another message. The email arrived just before midnight, followed by a phone call a few minutes later. We actually did trace the call. It came from the lobby downstairs. We're still talking to people but no one seems to have noticed anything."

"What did the caller say?"

"There's a dead body in room 612 of the Biltmore."

"Nothing else?"

Bullard shook her head. "The email came through one of those anonymous sites so we don't expect to have any luck there either."

"Why would the killer bother? Angela would have recovered at some point and would have raised the alarm."

"I couldn't tell you. My guess is that our friend is playing a game of sorts, trying to get us spread out over so many lines of inquiry that we can't focus on one that might be critical. There are so many clues this time that if he inadvertently left a genuine one, it would be nicely camouflaged. Come over here."

She led me over to the small table that stood between the two beds. "Right there was a long red hair, presumably human, but we won't know for a while yet."

"Muriel and Angela are brunettes."

"We also found a matchbook cover from the Hot Club."

I frowned. "I thought they closed down."

"They did, quite a few years ago. And someone knocked a bottle of talcum powder off the sink. It was scattered all over the floor when we arrived, and there was a footprint in it. "A sneaker, fairly small, probably worn by a woman."

"Obviously faked."

"Obviously. There was no sign of a struggle. The two women simply passed out. The killer came in and shot the older one once in the head, sprinkled the clues around, and left."

"Had to have been planned well in advance."

"I don't think there's any doubt that the two murders are connected."

"Which means it also has some kind of connection to the festival community." That was good news in a way for Bullard, because it meant that we weren't dealing with a random psycho. The bad news was that pretty much all of the likely suspects would be leaving town over the course of the next two days.

"Was there anything else?"

"There was a pen that came from a car rental agency in Michigan."

"Muriel was out there on some kind of a job for a while a couple of years back. That might actually have belonged to her."

"It was stuck into an orange from the fruit basket."

I didn't know what to make of that. "Anything else?"

"One more thing. We found a cell phone case." She paused for dramatic effect. Obviously there had to be more. "It was personalized with the owner's initials. JB."

"It was John's." I didn't have to see it to know. It was a perfect fit.

"It appears so."

"Okay, why am I here?"

"You're my native guide, or resident expert if you prefer. I don't know these people and I don't have enough time to do as thorough a background as I'd like. I'm hoping you can cut a few corners. We're on the clock here. Not to mention that there's nothing suggesting that our friend has finished his killing spree yet."

I felt a sudden thrill of fear, for Dusty as much as myself. We were both part of this particular social circle so we were potential targets as well. Bullard must have seen the revelation in my face because she nodded. "And yes, you'll both be safer if you're working with us."

"That might just be more of a challenge."

Bullard had no response to that. "Can you think of anything specific that might tie these two together? Some connection other than the obvious one?"

I shook my head. "They were never a couple. They lived a thousand miles apart. As far as I know they never saw each other except at festivals like this." I thought about that for a second. "Wait a minute. John visited her once when she was working in Michigan, but I don't have any idea why."

"You said she was working out there. What was she doing?"

I shook my head. "Searching for lost footage for a documentary. She said something about a confidentiality agreement. I was never interested enough to ask the details. Her sister might know more about it."

"Whereabouts in Michigan?"

"I don't know that either. If she ever mentioned it, I've forgotten. I got the impression it was out in the sticks somewhere. Not Detroit. Angela would know."

"Then let's go talk to Angela. I'm hoping she'll be a little more coherent now, particularly with some familiar faces around."

CHAPTER ELEVEN

We took the stairs up to the seventh floor and Bullard led the way to 726. The door was cracked open and there was one of the ubiquitous uniformed officers standing outside. Bullard pushed past and I followed. Angela was on the bed, but sitting up. Dusty was sitting in an armchair beside the bed and a female officer was seated in the opposite corner.

"How is she?" Bullard directed the question at Dusty but Angela answered herself.

"I'm feeling better." Her voice was steady but she looked pretty rocky.

"Do you think you could tell us what happened again? You were a little out of it the first time through."

She nodded. "I'll do anything I can to help."

"What time did you and your sister get back to your room?"

"About half past ten. We stopped and had a nightcap in the hotel bar with a friend."

"Who would that be?" asked Bullard.

"Bob, Bob Strossi. He wasn't feeling too well and went back to his room so Muriel and I decided to call it a night."

"Did you notice anyone following you?"

"No. There were some people in the elevator with us but they all got off before we did. And there was no one in the corridor when we reached our floor."

"Did you or your sister receive or make any phone calls?"

"No. Muriel was pretty tired and I don't really know many people here. We came in and Muriel turned on the television to catch the news."

I glanced a question at Bullard. "It was still on when we arrived."

Muriel ignored us. "We talked a little bit, unwinding, and took off our shoes. I was just about to take a shower when someone knocked on the door. It was room service with a fruit basket. I thought it was from Bob but his name wasn't on the card. I only had a glimpse of the woman who delivered it."

"Was there anything unusual about the person who brought the basket?"

"Not really. She was kind of pretty but you could tell her smile was part of the costume, if you know what I mean. Muriel gave her a tip and she left."

Bullard glanced at me. "Her name is Madeleine Kelly and she's worked her for three years." She turned back to Angela. "The champagne came later?"

"Yes, about ten minutes."

"Did you happen to notice what time it was?"

"A little after eleven. I was in the shower by then." She shifted slightly on the bed. "I didn't look at the clock until I came out and it was twenty past."

"Do you know who delivered the champagne?"

"Muriel didn't say anything and I was in the shower. She told me that the champagne was supposed to come with the fruit basket and someone had made a mistake and sent it up separately."

"Did she say anything at all about the person who delivered it?"

"No. It didn't seem important."

"Okay, when did you open the champagne?"

"It was already open when I came out of the bathroom. Muriel was pouring herself a glass and she asked if I wanted one and actually I was in the mood for a drink so I said yes, that we couldn't let it go to waste now that it was open."

"Was the champagne on a separate cart?"

"Yes, just like the first one. It was in a bucket with ice."

Bullard glanced at me again. "We only found one of them in their room. We're trying to run down the second but there's not much chance of it. It wouldn't be hard to borrow one. My guess is that the dope went into the bottle when it was opened."

Angela picked up her story. "We went back and sat down on the bed and drank champagne while we watched the news. I remember getting sleepy and setting my glass down after a while, and then the next thing I knew was when you people were waking me up and asking me questions and Muriel was dead." Her voice broke a little but she visibly took control of herself. "Why would someone want to kill Muriel? She never hurt anyone in her life."

Angela started to cry then and Dusty put an arm around her shoulders. Bullard glanced at me. "I think we're done here for the moment."

Dusty looked up. "I'll stay with her."

We stepped outside the room. "You didn't ask her about Michigan," I pointed out.

"It can wait." Bullard didn't often show her human side. "What time did things close down tonight? The movies, I mean."

"The dealers all close up shop at nine. The panels run until eleven. Most of the movie tracks end then too, but there was one scheduled to show horror movies until dawn."

"So people would have been up and about."

"A few of them. We tend to be an older crowd, and most of us are in bed by eleven."

She sighed. "So almost anyone we talk to is going to have an unconfirmed but perfectly natural alibi. I notice no one on your list was married."

"Now that you mention it, no, none of them are. But some of them may be sharing rooms." I thought about Helen. It was unlikely she was spending the night alone.

Bullard took out her notebook. "Everyone you named is staying in the Biltmore except Riccello and Gregory, who are sharing a room at the Driscoll. Gonsalves and Wareham are at the Marriott."

"Are you going to roust them all out at this hour?"

She shook her head. "What's the point? They can wait until morning. I don't suppose you'll be going back to bed."

"Hardly."

"Show me where they're still watching movies."

We rode the elevator down to level two. One of the function rooms was dark but a flickering light betrayed activity. The two of us slipped in through the door and let it close behind us while our eyes adjusted. On the screen at the head of the room, Elsa Lanchester was incoherently refusing to be the mate of Frankenstein's monster. There were about a dozen people in the audience, at least two of whom were clearly asleep.

"Recognize anyone?" asked Bullard.

I shook my head and walked down one side of the room, scanning the profiles. As far as I could tell, there was no one here that I knew. I went back to where Bullard was standing. "No luck." We left the room.

"I didn't really expect anything but it was worth a look." She yawned and covered it hastily. "I might as well go home and sleep while the lab people do their thing."

"But you won't."

"No. No, I won't. Do you know what really pisses me off?"

The question was supposed to be rhetorical, but I answered it anyway. "The killer is playing a game with you. Too many weapons. Too many clues."

She nodded. "There's an inconsistency there." I didn't understand what she meant and said nothing. "If it was just a game, then the choice of victims wouldn't be significant. Anyone would do. But our two victims knew each other and they were in different hotels. The odds against their being chosen at random is pretty high. That means there must be an actual motive, but if there is a motive, why the subterfuge?"

"You said earlier you thought the killer was trying to overload the investigation, provide too many paths to follow simultaneously, possible cover up if a real clue was inadvertently left behind."

"I know, but now that we know there's a link, we have a genuine line of inquiry to pursue. The little trimmings aren't going to divert us from that. Not much anyway."

I had a wild thought that I couldn't support logically. "Maybe whoever it is wants you to find out the truth, just not too soon."

Bullard looked interested. "What makes you think that?"

"Well, assume scenario one, that our murderer had a genuine motive to kill both John and Muriel. Why do it here? Why not murder John out in California and Muriel back in Chicago? The chances of the two cases ever being connected would be vanishingly small."

"It might be a matter of convenience. Less traveling around."

"A small price to pay to elude the law. Instead our attention is drawn to the connections between the two victims. The bizarre circumstances surrounding the two murders accomplish the same thing. I can't imagine how but in some way John and Muriel managed to offend someone to the point where murder seemed justified. I think that we're meant to find out the truth. Whoever is responsible for this has some kind of endgame in mind. I think you're meant to solve the case, but not right away."

"We're a long way from that point, unless someone turns up and confesses."

"That's what bothers me. We don't even know how many links there are in the chain."

Hubbard frowned. "You don't think this is over with. You think someone else is going to be killed if we don't figure it out."

"Yes I do. And quickly. You said that your suspects are going to be running off in every direction pretty soon, but that holds true for the potential victims as well."

Bullard nodded. "I get your point."

Bullard went back to police headquarters, hoping to nudge the technicians into working faster, so I went back to our room and napped a little in a chair. I woke when Dusty came in, looking a bit haggard. "She's asleep. I'm taking a shower."

I was too awake now to doze so I took out our notes and went through them again. The only line of inquiry I could see at this point was the visit by John to Muriel while she was working in Michigan. It wasn't much to go on and was probably completely innocuous, but there was nothing else to do.

Dusty emerged from the bathroom, toweling her hair. "There's a police woman staying with Angela for the time being."

"I doubt she needs protecting," I said. "If she was on the killer's list, she'd have died last night."

I had a quick shower myself while Dusty dressed and then the two of us went downstairs and walked over to a donut shop for coffee and bagels. The morning paper was out but there was no mention of Muriel's death and no one in the coffee shop seemed to be aware of it. That wouldn't last much longer.

When we got back to the hotel, there were only a few people in the lobby, and about half of them were journalists. "I guess the news is out." I glanced around. "Let's see if Bullard is back."

She was in the same conference room as before and she looked exhausted. The uniform at the door didn't question our presence this time, although he was holding reporters at bay, and

Bullard glanced up to acknowledge our presence before returning to a conversation on her cell.

When she was done, she sketched a smile. "I was kind of hoping you two would show up. I'm going up to talk to Miss Bates again. So far the press hasn't figured out where she is but someone tipped them off that there was a survivor this time, so they're panting and straining at their leashes."

"There are a bunch of them staking out the elevators and watching the stairwells," I told her.

"Which is why we're taking the service elevator." She stood up. "Let's get this over with."

Bullard had secured her own key so we rode up alone and without being observed. There was no one in sight on the seventh floor. Bullard knocked and the door was opened cautiously by the policewoman.

Angela was still awake. The hotel had provided coffee and the fixings and she was sitting in a chair with a cup in one hand.

Dusty fussed over her a bit, but Angela was definitely in a different mood than she had been the last time we'd seen her. She was sad, of course, but angry as well. She acknowledged our concern and turned to Bullard. "Have you found out who killed my sister?"

"We're working on it. We could use your help."

"Whatever you want."

Dusty and I sat down on a bed. Bullard remained standing. "I understand your sister lived in Michigan for a while."

"She was there for about eight weeks. That was about a year ago, no, closer to two years now."

"And whereabouts in Michigan was that?"

"She had rented a room just outside Lansing. I don't remember the address but I could get it for you."

"What was she doing there?"

Angela took a deep breath. "She was looking for footage connected to the early days of the automobile industry. It was some kind of joint project between one of the big car companies and Michigan State University. She wasn't supposed to talk about it because they figured if people knew who was interested, they'd ask more for any footage they might have."

DEATH IN BLACK AND WHITE

"Is that why she signed a confidentiality agreement? Why would it matter now if the project is done with?"

Angela looked puzzled. "I never heard anything about that. She was always pretty open about what she was doing, at least in general terms. She liked the work, she found some things that no one knew existed any more, and she told me that everyone was very pleased with her. She talked about it a lot after she got back. Sometimes I got tired of hearing about it, in fact."

"There was never any hint of tension? No problems?"

"None that I know of. They stipend she had was for twelve weeks and she finished up a month early. As far as I know, everyone was happy with her work."

"Did you know that John Boncoddo visited her during this period?"

Angela nodded. "Right at the end. She was tying up loose ends by then and was taking a week off. John slept on her couch that first night and they went off together the next morning. I thought they were getting to be more than friends but she told me later that it was nothing like that. She just wanted his opinion about some film she was trying to buy."

"Had she ever done anything like that before? I mean, any kind of relationship with a man, or woman for that matter, that was out of character for her?"

Angela hesitated. "She went and stayed with Daryl Plimpton for a while, but that didn't work out. I never thought it would. I hadn't met him at the time but her description was pretty grim. I never understood why she did it."

"Do you know where they went? John and your sister, I mean."

"Yes. They went to a little town called Frampton in the Upper Peninsula. But they had to stay in another town – Foster City, I think it was – because there were no motels in Frampton."

"What was the attraction? It sounds like the middle of nowhere."

"She never said exactly. Told me they were going up to talk see someone who had a collection of old films."

"And how long were they there?"

"I don't remember. Just a few days, no more than a week."

"Did she ever say anything about the trip after she got back?"

Angela hesitated, clearly searching her memory. "Nothing in particular. She said it was pretty up there and that they'd had a nice visit and that she was thinking about going back some time. I think there was still some kind of negotiations going on."

"Do you know who they were visiting?"

She shook her head. "I don't think she ever mentioned a name. Does this have anything to do with…with what happened?"

"I don't know yet. That's what I'm trying to find out. Did she and John ever get together again?"

"Not that I know of, except they probably ran into each other at festivals. And she might have talked to him on the phone, I suppose. I was living with her by then and since she got a full time job as soon as she got back from Michigan, she didn't travel again until the next festival."

Bullard seemed to have run out of questions, but then one more occurred to her. "Do you know the exact dates of the trip to Frampton?"

"No, not off hand. But I could find out if I had my laptop." She stood up. "Can we go back downstairs yet?"

Bullard hesitated. "You're better off here. The press might find out which room you were in. I'm going to have the hotel move your things here, but right now Officer Krane is going to go retrieve your laptop for us."

Krane, the policewoman, gave a little jump at the sound of her name, then nodded and disappeared.

Bullard reassured Angela that her sister had never regained consciousness and hadn't felt any pain. She promised that the killer would be caught, which was at least partly wishful thinking, but Angela seemed to accept it. Then Krane was back with the laptop, two of them in fact. "I didn't know which was yours."

Angela took one of them and began booting it up. The rest of us waited while she brought up her online diary and searched for the right entry. "She went to Michigan on September 5. That was Lansing." She searched some more. "It was October 23 when she went up to Frampton with John. I think they left on the 30th and John flew home. Muriel finished up in Lansing and drove back a couple of days after that."

"Did she ever say anything else about trip to Frampton?"

Angela closed the laptop. "Not really. She just said John had come up to help her evaluate some footage and that they were going to do some sightseeing while he was there. She seemed to think it was a big deal at first, but she was pretty discouraged when she came back."

"John wasn't the touristy type," I said. "He wasn't into scenery or woodsy things. I can't imagine him spending a week away from a city without a good reason."

"Was there anything between the two of them?" asked Bullard.

"You mean were they sleeping together?" Angela looked at her as though she'd grown a second head. "Obviously you never met John. Muriel said he was asexual. They were just friends."

Bullard was groping for something to work with. "Did your sister ever refer to the trip again?"

Angela gave it some thought. "She talked about Lansing some times, but I don't think she ever mentioned her trip with John except to say that he was pretty boring after a while and that she might go back some time."

"Did she act any differently when she got back? Depressed? Excited? Secretive?"

"Not that I noticed. But I was working long hours then and we didn't see a lot of each other. And we'd been living a thousand miles apart for five or six years by then. People change."

Bullard was silent so I spoke up. "Your sister implied to some people that she was expecting to come into some money soon."

Angela nodded. "She told me she was expecting a commission for some work she'd done a while back."

"Did she say what it was?"

"No, but I never asked. She did lots of small assignments like that. Muriel worked with the film department at the University of Chicago off and on, and a couple of other places. Sometimes she would have to wait months to be paid."

We all ran out of questions about then. Dusty asked how she was feeling and Angela said she was all right. She had decided to remain in the room for the morning to avoid the reporters, who would hopefully pick up a different scent by lunchtime.. "I called Bob's room and he's going to come by later on." Bullard was mildly dubious but she sent the policewoman home and we left. Dusty came with us this time.

"I don't suppose she said anything earlier that might help," Bullard said quietly as we walked to the elevator.

"Only that Muriel had spent a half hour with Daryl late yesterday. She told Angela they had to talk about some project they were both working on."

"I think it's time we talked to Mr. Plimpton."

But we had to put that plan on hold because Daryl wasn't in his hotel room or in his makeshift office. "He went to breakfast with some people," said a bored looking young woman who barely looked up from her computer screen. "I didn't catch their names."

Bullard had a list of room numbers. She called the Marriot and spoke to Ray and Tanya, who had ordered breakfast from room service and hadn't heard the news. Then she tried the rooms in the Driscoll and Biltmore with zero success, Everyone else seemed to have gone out for breakfast, so that's what we did.

CHAPTER TWELVE

We didn't stay with Bullard when we returned to the hotel. She was going set up shop in the conference room again and begin tracking down the people whose named we had provided. Dusty and I went up to our room, went through our notes again with a mutual lack of enthusiasm. I noticed in the program schedule that Romeo was leading a panel discussion at the Driscoll which would be winding up in half an hour and suggested that we try to catch him when it ended. I recalled that he knew Bob Strossi better than most of us, and I was mildly suspicious of the latter's sudden interest in Angela Bates, for no particular reason except that he was the only person who seemed to be acting out of character.

We were sitting on a low sofa with a good view of the door that led to the panel when Ray and Tanya appeared. They came over and sat down facing us. "What's going on, guys? The police practically woke us up this morning to ask us where we'd been all night."

There had been no official announcement, but rumors were clearly spreading through the festival. I was hesitant to reveal anything without permission but Dusty made that moot. "Muriel Bates was murdered last night."

They both looked shocked but neither of them had been very close to Muriel. "What happened?" asked Tanya.

"The police aren't saying much yet," I answered quickly in case Dusty intended to reveal more.

"Poor Muriel," said Tanya quietly. "We were never really close but one time she and my cousin Wendy and I all went out drinking together and she could be really fun when she loosened up."

"Well, we were in bed early and we never left the room," said Ray.

Tanya squirmed a little. "That's not exactly true," she said quietly. "I couldn't sleep so I went for a walk."

Ray looked irritated. "I thought we weren't going to tell anyone about that."

Tanya didn't look at him. "Ray didn't know I was gone because he was sound asleep, so he didn't really lie to the police when they called. I didn't realize until just now what it was all about. I mean, we knew something was up, obviously, which is why we haven't said anything about it."

"What time did you go out?" I asked.

"I don't know exactly. Maybe around eleven? I think I was gone for about an hour but I didn't look at the clock when I came back."

"Where did you go?"

"I just came downstairs and went out front. It was a nice night. I wandered a little but not far because I don't know the city very well. Then I went upstairs."

"Did anyone see you?"

"There were a few people around, but no one that I know."

I didn't think that someone could leave the Driscoll, walk to the Biltmore, order from room service, deliver the champagne, steal a room key, and murder Muriel, then return all within an hour, but then again, we only had Tanya's word for how long she was gone.

"You need to tell Detective Bullard about this. I don't think it will matter in the long run but if someone mentions seeing you and you're caught in a lie, even unintentionally, it won't look good."

Ray seemed reluctant, but finally agreed that it was the best thing to do. They left us and, I hoped, went straight over to the Biltmore to amend Ray's earlier account.

The panel broke up a few minutes later and we waited until Romeo emerged. He was wearing a Humphrey Bogart tee shirt this morning. Dusty waved to attract his attention and he came over and dropped wearily onto the sofa Ray and Tanya had just vacated. "I hate these early morning panels," he complained. "My brain needs a while to wake up and the audiences are always thin and half asleep."

"I'm sure it went fine," I said. "I assume you know that there's been another incident."

His face twisted. "Not another like John?"

"Not quite, but Muriel Bates is dead."

He aged a decade before our eyes. "Shit! Not Muriel. She was such a sweet kid."

"We're trying to figure out if there was some connection between her and John that we didn't know about."

Romeo just stared for a few seconds, then visibly shook himself back to the present. "No, not that I ever heard of. They knew each other, of course, but there was nothing unusual about it. John was never really interested in dating. You know that. And I don't think Muriel ever really got over her brief fling with Daryl."

I let a couple of heartbeats pass silently. "How well do you know Bob Strossi?"

"I've talked to him a few times. He doesn't have a lot of self confidence so he tends to bluster. People think he's standoffishness but it's really not. Once he relaxes, he can be good company."

"Did you know he was seeing Muriel's sister?" asked Dusty.

"Angela? No, I didn't. She's even quieter than her sister." He blinked. "Is she all right? I know she came this year because I saw her yesterday."

"She's shaken, but I think she'll be okay." I switched the topic back to Strossi. "You know Bob used to work for John."

"Yeah, for about a year I think. There was some kind of big blow up and either he walked out or got fired."

"A little of both apparently. Do you know what he was doing exactly?"

"He's not a technician, so he wouldn't have been involved with actually restoring prints, which was John's main line of business. But John filled in with other things. He designed the packaging for some of the smaller DVD distributors, wrote copy, provided stills. At one point he was talking about reviving his own imprint and that was around the time Bob was hired. Bob has worked in distribution before, so that might have been the connection. I told him it was a bad idea. The big distributors have the market tied up and they're not much interested in oldies but goodies."

"Did John ever replace Bob after he left?"

"I have no idea, but I'm pretty sure John had dropped the project, or at least put it on the back burner. He was running short of cash, laid off a couple of people, and was looking around for work. There was nothing he could use to expand."

"The police are going to want to know where you were last night," I said.

"What time?"

"Eleven to one."

Romeo snorted. "In bed, of course, and alone, of course. At my age, ten o'clock bedtimes come back into style." He hesitated. "Did she suffer, do you know? I always liked Muriel."

I shouldn't have said anything without Bullard's approval, but what the hell. "She never felt a thing."

"Well, there's that at least."

Martin, the bellhop, was on duty when we went downstairs, but there didn't seem to be much activity. Dusty had gone to the little gift shop to see if she could pick up some aspirin so I was reading the newspaper headlines through the glass window on the pay box when he spotted me. I really didn't want to talk to him but it would have been rude to walk away.

"Good morning, Mr. Birch. I didn't expect to see you again. There's still one policeman here but I haven't seen the detective since yesterday morning." He glanced around. "Is your young lady with you today?"

"Gift shop."

"Ah. That was my wife's weakness as well. Never met a gift or antique shop she didn't like. She was a movie fan too. Mary would have loved to be here this weekend. My mother-in-law was in the business for a while but never made a success of it. Unfortunately I never cared for movies. I don't even own a television. Just another thing we didn't have in common."

"Are you still in touch?" I asked without interest.

"No. Mary died a while back. And then my daughter followed not long afterward. I suppose I always thought somewhere in the back of my mind that we'd all get together again at some point, and now that will never happen. Take my advice, Mr. Birch, and never put off anything that really matters to you."

I had a thought. "Didn't you say that you worked for the Biltmore once?"

He nodded. "For about six months."

"How hard would it be to steal one of those room service carts?"

He frowned. "Well, it's been a while and they might have changed things, but the hardest part would be getting it out of the hotel."

I shook my head. "What if I just wanted to pose as room service?"

"Oh, that would be ridiculously easy. A lot of guests push them outside the door when they're done with them and they sit there until morning. But the hotel staff all wear uniforms. If someone saw you pushing one in street clothes, they might ask questions."

"Okay. Thanks."

Then Dusty appeared and we almost made our escape.

Mrs. Drake caught us before we could leave. She was standing near the check-in counter and she recognized me and beckoned us over. "Detective Bullard has released Mr. Boncoddo's room and his luggage, but she hasn't yet provided us with the name of the next of kin. I understand that you were friends with the...gentleman."

"Casual friends," I admitted. "As far as I know, he had no living relatives. I can give you his home address in California, but he lived alone. He had his own business. Someone there might be able to help you." I gave her the name of John's company, which Bullard had ascertained, and the business phone number in my cell phone. "I doubt anyone will be there today, as it's Sunday."

"There is also the matter of the telegram."

Dusty and I exchanged looks. "What telegram?" I asked.

Drake spoke to the desk clerk who retrieved a small envelope from somewhere out of sight. "It arrived first thing this morning."

It was sealed, naturally. "I don't know if it's important, but you should turn that over to Detective Bullard."

Drake looked at the envelope distastefully. "I suppose you're right, but I had rather hoped that our involvement in the matter was over with."

It was not, and not by a long shot.

Drake called Bullard from the desk and told her about the telegram. I imagine Bullard was saying she would send someone right over but Drake mentioned that we were with her and the next thing we knew we were enlisted as messengers. There was no point in worrying about fingerprints since it had been delivered by a uniformed messenger who was known to the clerk who was on duty at the time.

Bullard was alone except for a sleepy looking uniform who sat in one corner of the conference room trying to look alert. She accepted the telegram without comment and carefully opened it.

It was from someone named Roland Staines and it announced his resignation effective immediately from his position as general manager of Revivify, Inc – John's company - for "reasons well known to you."

"That's John's company," I said unnecessarily. "I don't think anyone there will have heard that John is dead."

"Do you know this Staines character?" asked Bullard.

"I don't know anyone who worked for John, except Bob Strossi, of course."

Dusty spoke up. "Jo Parkin worked in the office there for awhile, but it was only over a summer. She didn't like California and moved back east."

Bullard dropped the telegram onto the desk. "I don't see how this can be connected but I suppose we'll have to check it out."

That's when Daryl Plimpton showed up, escorted by another officer. He didn't look happy.

"What do you want now, detective? In case you haven't noticed, I have a festival to run here. I don't have time to waste." Daryl glanced at Dusty and I disdainfully.

Bullard didn't look impressed. "Are you aware that there has been a second murder, Mr. Plimpton?"

"Yes, I heard something about it when I came back from breakfast. But I'm sure it doesn't have anything to do with the festival. This is a good sized city. I'm sure you have murders here all the time."

"Not as many as you might think. Are you aware of the identity of the second victim?"

For the first time Daryl looked a bit uncertain. "No. Should I be?"

"Her name was Muriel Bates."

Daryl was obviously staggered by the revelation. He went pale and his hands clenched, then quickly relaxed. "I know Miss Bates, of course."

"In fact you were at one time cohabiting with her, were you not?"

Daryl glanced at us with open dislike. "That was a long time ago and it was never serious."

"Could you tell us where you were last night from, say, ten o'clock on?"

Visibly taking control of himself, Daryl nodded. "I was working in our operations room until shortly after nine. I was the last to leave so I locked up myself. I had an appointment to meet with some people in the hotel bar at half past nine."

"Could you give me their names?"

"Arthur Baldwin, Candace Wells, and Vernon Foulkes. They all work for a film distribution company."

"How long were you in the bar?"

"About an hour. Vernon went up to his room early but the other two were still with me. We talked for another few minutes in the lobby, and then I also went to my room. They were going to go outside for a smoke first."

"Did you leave your room again that evening?"

"No. I read my email and did a little work on my laptop, then went to bed. I didn't check the time but it was before midnight."

"Did you make any telephone calls or have any visitors?"

"No. After eleven there were only a couple of movie programs going on. Unless there had been some kind of emergency, no one would have had any reason to disturb me."

Bullard made a show of going through her notebook. "Do you know anyone named Russell Staines?"

"Never heard of him."

"How about Edward Mrozek?"

"No."

"Had you spoken to Miss Bates at any point this weekend?"

Daryl was quiet for a few seconds. "I said hello to her on Friday morning. She introduced me to her sister, but I don't remember her name. I've seen her in the corridors once or twice since then but I can't tell you where or when. We remained on amicable terms but we were not particularly close."

"Are you aware of anything unusual that may have involved Miss Bates recently?"

Daryl's eyes moved away and I didn't need a lie detector to know he was about to tell an untruth. I doubt that Bullard missed picking up on it. "We've hardly talked in the past year. Muriel wasn't entirely happy that our relationship had ended and I tried to avoid her. Emotional scenes are very distracting."

"So if we check your telephone records, we won't find any calls between the two of you during the past six months."

"I didn't say that. I talked to her a couple of times about the festivals. She often volunteered to help and she was very reliable. That's how we originally met. And she called me a few times socially, probably to see if there was any chance of our getting back together. I didn't encourage her, but she was persistent." I was skeptical of Daryl's explanation. Even if Muriel had still entertained feelings for him, and I doubt it, she would never have had the temerity to make advances on her own.

Bullard stared at him quietly for almost half a minute. "How long do you plan to stay in Providence, Mr. Plimpton?"

"The festival ends Monday afternoon. Tomorrow. There will be some administrative things to take care of after that, so I'll be here Tuesday morning. I plan to drive back either that afternoon, or if things take longer than I expect, to stay over another night and go back on Wednesday."

"I would appreciate it if you gave me a call when you decide to leave. You have my number?"

"Does this mean that I'm a suspect?" He was clearly indignant.

"Everyone is a suspect, Mr. Plimpton. Until I say otherwise."

Daryl was the last person on our list of names to provide information about their whereabouts when Muriel was killed. When Bullard summarized what she'd learned from the others, I remarked that the only person with an alibi was Angela.

"I'm far from ruling her out," contradicted Bullard. "We only have her word for the sequence of events. She could have ordered room service herself, drugged her sister, murdered her, hidden the weapon outside the room, then taken more of the drug herself."

"She doesn't have much of a motive."

"No one appears to, but somebody did or she wouldn't be dead."

We promised once again to check in if we discovered anything interesting, but I think both Dusty and I were pretty discouraged by this point. There were obvious connections between John and Muriel, but those within the festival community offered no motive and those without were largely unknowable to us. The chances of their being random victims was vanishingly small, so some connection must exist somewhere, but we weren't likely to find it. Hopefully Bullard's greater resources would turn something up.

There were more people up and about since the program was now fully underway. The dealers' room was particularly packed as people realized that they were getting near the end of the festival and that all those purchases they had earlier deferred needed to be addressed soon. We wandered a bit and Dusty paid entirely too much for a reprint of a lobby poster for *The Third Man*, but I found it hard to concentrate. There was a ghost of a common thread that bothered me. John and Muriel had gone to the Upper Peninsula of Michigan two years ago on a project that even Muriel's sister did not know much about. They were both expecting to come into an unspecified amount of money in the near future. They had both been murdered, almost certainly by the same person. Bob Strossi had left Revivify at about the same time as the Michigan trip, give or take a couple of months. Russell Staines had just resigned as well. Strossi had been making advances toward Angela Bates even though I had never known him to show any interest in female companionship at previous festivals. Ray Riccello was also apparently about to receive funding for a new indie film and Jimmy Gonsalves had come up with enough money to buy an old theater. Terry Wareham had approached Daryl for money, and Daryl always lived on the financial brink, so why would she have thought he had available cash now? Or had she known in advance that Daryl was planning to sell the rights to *At the Mountains of Madness* to a distributor?

Dusty tapped my shoulder. "Earth to Paul. You're blocking traffic."

I was indeed, having come to a stop in the middle of a narrow aisle. I apologized vaguely to people trying to edge past me and allowed myself to be led toward the exit. We had just reached it when someone called our names.

It was Helen Viele.

She already knew that Muriel had been the second victim so it obviously wasn't a secret any longer. As far as I knew they had never been more than casual acquaintances but she seemed genuinely sad as well as shocked. "Who do you think will be next?"

So this is where I confess that I was very slow on the uptake. I was certain now that the murders were related, but for some reason I was reluctant to speculate that there might be more links in the chain. If the Michigan trip was the key, then the only two people connected to it were already dead. Bullard was ahead of me on this because she had already arranged for a visible police presdence at both hotels for the next twenty-four hours, but particularly in the evenings. She also wanted the hotels to advise all guests to keep their doors chained and not allow anyone inside whom they didn't recognize. Of course, if the killer was one of us as I suspected, this warning wouldn't do much good.

This would all prove to be ineffective, but at least Bullard had made an effort to avert a further tragedy.

Helen had missed breakfast and wanted us all to go over to a nearby donut shop for crullers and coffee. My inclination was to decline, but Helen actually looked a bit forlorn and lonely and in any case Dusty agreed before I could say anything.

"I went back to my room first thing this morning and there was a policeman waiting for me. A detective. He wanted to know where I'd been all night, so obviously I knew something was up, but I didn't really want to tell him without checking first."

"With the guy whose room you were in?" Dusty beat me to the punch.

"Yeah. He wasn't really here for the festival, just on business. And he's married."

"Well, he won't be ecstatic when the police call him to check on your alibi," I said.

"Well, the thing of it is that I wasn't really there all night. I mean, we hooked up after midnight in the bar, just before it closed."

"Hunting outside your usual territory, aren't you?" asked Dusty. Dusty knew about Helen and I and it was before we'd met, but I still sometimes saw a hint of cattiness.

"You go where the game is. Anyway, Edward and I hit it off right away and he told me he and his wife had an understanding which is, I know, one of the oldest lines in the book, but I really didn't care if he didn't, so we went up to his room and it was fun but it didn't mean anything. I got up early and went for a walk but nothing was open yet so I decided to go back to my room to shower and change and there he was waiting for me. The detective I mean."

I had one of those moments of intuition that are supposedly reserved for women. "His last name wasn't Mrozek, was it?"

"Yeah, I think it was. Do you know him?"

"Sort of." Wheels were turning inside my head. "Who made the first approach in the bar? You or him?"

Helen frowned and then we were at the donut shop so she didn't answer until we had our orders and were huddled at a tiny table that rocked somewhat ominously in one corner. I asked her again.

"I guess it was a little of both." She looked puzzled. "Why do you ask?"

I decided to make light of it. "Sorry, but everything looks suspicious to me this morning."

"I get that. But Ed is all right. He was just looking for company for the night."

"Did he mention what kind of business he was involved in?"

"He says he spends all of his time moving money around. I think he's some kind of investment counselor, but I really didn't ask and he didn't volunteer. And there wasn't a lot of talking going on anyway." She gave me an arch look that Dusty didn't see, or at least pretended not to see.

For someone who had managed to keep herself slender and healthy looking, Helen could pack away the food. She had four

152

crullers and two cups of coffee before she pronounced herself fit to deal with the rest of the morning. We started back to the Biltmore and the conversation turned to reminiscences about Muriel. "Did you know that Muriel and I were a couple once?"

Dusty stumbled and I stopped dead in my tracks. "A couple how?" I asked.

A shadow of a smile came and went on Helen's face. "Shocked you, didn't I? It wasn't much of a success but she invited me to stay at her place while I was on my way back home a couple of years ago. No, three years it must have been. It was just before she went to live with Daryl. I could have told her that would never work."

Helen was going too fast for me. "Go back a bit," said Dusty.

"Her sister was going to be out of town for two weeks and she invited me to stay as long as I wanted and I'd never really seen Chicago before except to pass through the airport. My cousin Wendy was going to be there for a couple of days and I hadn't seen her since we were little kids, so the three of us went out to dinner. And the night that Wendy went back home Muriel and I split a bottle of brandy and then we were in bed together. It wasn't a big deal, or maybe it was for Muriel. I stayed a week and we shared the same bed, but I could tell that Muriel was uncomfortable and I finally got her to talk about it. I think it was a little too sudden and clashed too much with how she was brought up. We didn't fight or anything, but the next day I left. She was a little bit uncomfortable with me after that but I don't think anyone noticed."

"Muriel never seemed the daring type to me," I admitted.

"She was deeper than you think." Helen started to walk again so we hastily followed. Just before we reached the Biltmore's main entrance, she stopped and turned around. "I think that might be why she moved in with Daryl a few months later. I think she was trying to prove something to herself, or maybe just figure out how she really felt about sex. Daryl was hardly the best test case."

"No," I observed. "But they did stay together for a few months."

"I barely made it through one night with him. He's too self absorbed to be fun."

"Muriel had more secrets than I would have guessed," said Dusty.

"She kept to herself," said Helen. "She never mentioned that week again so I kept it under my hat. I was kind of sorry it put some distance between us afterwards."

"When exactly was this?" I asked.

"Right after the Hartford festival, so that would have been 2012."

That would have been almost a year before Muriel went to Michigan. The affair with Daryl had taken place late in 2013. "I don't suppose she talked about a job she was going to take in Michigan, tracing old documentary footage."

"No, not that I remember. She did say she was working with one of the big universities, but I don't remember which one or what it was about. Why? Is it important?"

"I don't know what's important and what isn't at this point. But while she was living in Lansing, she made a side trip to the Upper Peninsula for a week with John Boncoddo, some little town named Frampton. And John and Muriel are both dead and no one seems to know why they went there."

"Oh, I can tell you that!" Helen looked pleased with herself. I felt my pulse quicken.

"You know about Frampton?"

"Well, sort of. I've never been there, but I know whereabouts it is and I think I know why Muriel went there. I have no idea why John would have gone along. They weren't a couple, were they?"

"Definitely not." Although in fairness, I wasn't even sure of that.

"Well, I told you that my cousin Wendy was with us in Chicago for a while, didn't I?"

Dusty and I both nodded. "Muriel and Wendy really hit it off. Wendy had recently become deeply interested in old movies, which I hadn't known, but it was so recent that she didn't know much about organizations or festivals or anything like that. She didn't have a lot of money and probably couldn't have attended anyway. She and her mother lived in the grandmother's house in Frampton because there was no mortgage and the cost of living was low out there. Her mother and grandmother had both died earlier that year in a car crash and the insurance was enough that she treated herself to the Chicago trip, but that was the first time I'd seen her in like fifteen years and the last time too."

"What was her last name?"

"Taft. She and her mother changed their names back after the divorce. Does any of this matter?"

"I don't know if it does or not. Do you have a telephone number for your cousin?"

Helen's mouth twitched. "Not any more. She died about a year later."

"How did she die?" I had a powerful feeling that I knew what the answer was going to be, but I was wrong.

"It was another accident. That side of the family was cursed, I swear. She fell down the cellar steps and cracked her head. It was a couple of weeks before they found her and the rats had been at her." Helen shivered a bit. "I only found out about it because I wrote her a letter and it came back marked deceased. I had to call the state police to find out the details. They sent me a copy of the newspaper clipping."

"Do you still have it?"

"Probably not. We weren't close, obviously, but she seemed nice. It was a real shame."

CHAPTER THIRTEEN

I didn't know if Frampton had anything to do with the murders, but the fact that John had accompanied Muriel there was intriguing. Helen was going off to watch a Hopalong Cassidy double feature so we found ourselves alone in the lobby. I took out my cell and called Bullard.

"Yes?"

"I might have something for you. Didn't you say you were going to check out Frampton, Michigan?"

"Probably. But there's not much to go on and they don't have a local police force so I'll have to work through the state police. And I don't have much to give them, just a date, a couple of names, and no local connections."

"I have a connection." I summarized what Helen had just told us. "Wendy Taft died a few months later," I concluded. "She supposedly fell down a staircase."

"Are you suggesting that your two friends murdered her?"

"No, of course not. There's nothing to suggest they ever went back to Frampton and the death might well have been an accident. But at least it gives us a point of reference."

Bullard let me hang for a few seconds. "All right, I'll make the call. It's not as if I'm backed up with promising leads."

"Anything turn up yet?"

"Sure. Everyone was in bed so no one really has an alibi. No one can figure out how the key was stolen from housekeeping unless it was an inside job. No one saw anything suspicious. The fruit basket was charged to Celia Winslow in room 212, who never heard of Muriel and who is visiting her son's family and doesn't like being questioned by the police. The call was made from her room twenty minutes before it was delivered but she was eating at Hemenways at the time and has witnesses. None of the local liquor shops sold a bottle of that particular champagne during the last two days, but it's fairly popular. There are no fingerprints in the Bates' room that shouldn't be there. The case is almost solving itself."

"Someone planned this out pretty thoroughly."

"You're telling me? I gotta go. If I hear anything I'll be in touch."

Although Frampton could be a wild goose chase, it felt right to me. Neither Dusty nor I had brought a laptop with us, so we went to the dealers' room and found Bud Collins, who had sold me most of the vintage posters in my office and who knew me by sight. The hotel had free Wi-Fi and he had a laptop. Dusty and I squeezed around behind the table and did a quick search.

The aerial view of Frampton looked like a patch of wilderness with an occasional swatch of roof visible if you looked closely. There was one through road and a handful of subordinate ones, many of which looked to be unpaved. The business district was about a block long and there was no street view so we couldn't tell what was there except for the gas station at the corner.

Frampton had no newspaper. There was a weekly for the surrounding area, but it had ceased publication in 2013. The population was just under three thousand. They sent their kids to a regional school and the fire department was all volunteer. A small plane had crashed there in 2010, killing the pilot, who was alone, but it was attributed to an unfortunate encounter with a flock of Canadian geese. Google couldn't identify any restaurants, tourist attractions, hospitals, or much of anything else within the town limits. A search on the name Wendy Taft didn't even turn up her obituary, but she was mentioned as the only surviving relative of Adele and Mary Taft, mother and daughter, who were both killed instantly when they were struck a glancing blow by a tractor trailer just outside Crystal City, Michigan.

I thanked Bud for the loan and Dusty bought a set of postcards featuring movie stills.

We spotted Jimmy Gonsalves and Terry Wareham looking through a table of assorted memorabilia. I was still curious about the source of Jimmy's apparent windfall, although it no longer seemed as promising as it had when I'd jotted down a note about it in our room. Dusty and I joined them, exchanged muted reactions to news of Muriel's death, and then stood about somewhat awkwardly. Jimmy had never been much of a talker and Terry was clearly much subdued by recent events.

"We're thinking about leaving early," she confessed. "The police are warning everyone about strangers and even people we know. It's pretty scary."

"They think it might have had something to do with a business deal John and Muriel were involved in." It wasn't technically a lie. "I don't suppose either of them came to one of you about investing."

Terry's laugh was uncomfortable. "I can barely pay the rent, let alone invest in something."

"How about you, Jimmy?" I tried to make the question sound casual.

"I haven't really talked to John for a couple of years. Muriel never said anything about it. I would have turned them down anyway. My new theater is going to use up all my free money for a while."

I asked a few questions about the project, trying to elicit something about the source of his funding, but without success. I couldn't tell if he was deliberately avoiding the subject because he always answered in very short, direct sentences, and my questions were necessarily indirect. I made a mental note to remind Bullard about Jimmy's sudden affluence but I felt a little bit guilty about it. The odds were long that Jimmy had nothing to do with any of this.

Dusty and I had an uneventful lunch in the hotel restaurant. We were by ourselves and didn't see anyone we knew more than very casually except that Ray Riccello and Tanya Gregory were leaving as we came in. They both looked preoccupied. I thought I heard Romeo Bolduc's booming voice in the corridor once but if so, he was bound elsewhere. We were waiting for the check when my cell rang. It was Bullard.

"Where are you?"

"Just finishing lunch. What's up?"

"My call to Michigan had some interesting results and since you came up with the lead, I thought you might want to be here when they call back."

I gave the waitress my credit card. "What kind of interesting results? Did Muriel and John do anything that would have made the police interested in them?"

"Nope. Not a thing. There's no record of their ever visiting the town, although the motel confirms that they did stay in Foster City on the dates in question. Separate rooms."

"So what's so interesting?"

"I'm expecting a call back at half past one. They had to track down the officer in charge of the investigation. It was his day off."

"What investigation?" Getting information from Bullard was like pulling teeth.

"Just come up to the conference room and you can listen to it yourself."

We only had fifteen minutes once the check was paid, so we went directly there. Bullard was talking to Jo Parkin, but she turned and left with a wan smile in passing as soon as we arrived. There were two uniformed officers present, one of whom was the woman who had stayed with Angela.

"Why so mysterious?" Dusty and I sat down without being invited.

"Because I don't know that much myself and misery loves company. Captain Winston of the Michigan State Police has only been in Frampton once but he remembered that there had been some controversy about a death there, ruled accidental."

"Wendy Taft."

Bullard nodded. "It seems that the investigating officer wasn't entirely satisfied that it was an accident, but he didn't have enough to make a case for a more thorough look. They're understaffed, of course, and there's the usual pressure to close out investigations unless there are compelling reasons not to. There was no family left to keep the pressure on so this one faded away really fast."

I realized then that I had been expecting something like this, and I was convinced now that the two deaths were linked to the Michigan trip. I also felt cautious optimism. It seemed likely that the killer had achieved his or her goals now and at least there probably wouldn't be any more deaths. But John and Muriel had been in Frampton several weeks before Wendy Taft died and there was nothing indicating that they had ever returned. Had something they had said or done preyed upon Taft's mind enough that she had committed suicide, which had then been misinterpreted as an accident? And did someone else know the truth?

Bullard's phone rang exactly on time. She put it on speaker and introduced us. "Mr. Birch and his...associate have been helping us with our inquiries."

Winston introduced his own companion, Detective Abe Larson. I guessed that Larson was quite young based on his voice and his obvious deference to Winston.

"I'm going to let Abe tell you the story his own way," said Winston. "The closest I ever got to the case was when you asked me to look up the paperwork."

Larson started by telling us what we already knew. Wendy Taft had been living with her mother and grandmother and had been ever since she was twelve years old in 1980. Most people assumed that Mary Taft was a widow like her mother, but she was actually divorced from her husband, whom no one local had ever met except, presumably, her mother and daughter. Adele and Mary Taft were both killed instantly in an accident near Crystal City in 2011. Wendy Taft was in her forties by then and she inherited both estates, which consisted of the house where she lived, two small bank accounts, and a pair of insurance policies that barely covered the funeral expenses. Mary Taft had recently retired from her job as teacher at the regional high school. They had no near neighbors, which was not unusual in Frampton, but people who knew them had nothing bad to say about them.

Wendy had worked several low paying jobs over the years, mostly in Foster City, as clerk in a convenience store, house maid at the same Motel where John and Muriel had stayed, although years earlier than their visit, and most recently as receptionist for a pediatrician. She was reportedly very good with children. Although she had dated occasionally when she was younger, there had never been a steady boyfriend and no one was aware of any sexual partners during the ten years preceding her death. She had been a friendly, outgoing person who had a lot of friends but none of them really close.

The pediatrician had relocated to Flint a few months after the car crash and Wendy had started collecting unemployment. She had been looking for a new job, but there weren't a lot of opportunities in the area at the best of times and these were hardly the best of times. All she'd been able to find were some short term assignments filling in at a local library, a brief stint as a waitress at a bar, and some odds and ends. She had mentioned to a few people that she was feeling very discouraged, but none of them recognized any signs of severe depression.

Wendy paid almost all of her bills electronically. Her mail, which was very light, was delivered through a slot in the door so no one noticed that it had started to accumulate. No one investigated until a thunderstorm brought down a power line and one of the service crew spotted a rat crawling through a broken window.

"She'd been dead at least two weeks by then. We found her at the foot of the basement stairs. The rats had been at her for so long that the bones were partially disarticulated. The medical examiner determined that the cause of death was a blow to the back of the head which could have happened if she fell backward off the steps and landed on the cement floor. There was a broken step about two thirds of the way up, a fresh break."

"But you didn't think it was an accident?" asked Bullard.

Larson hesitated. "I didn't think that it was clearly an accident. For one thing, the basement hadn't been in use for a long time. There was a thick layer of dust everywhere, except on the steps. It was almost as if they'd been swept clean."

"There must have been a furnace," I suggested.

"No, sir. It wasn't that big a house. There were two fireplaces and a cord and a half of firewood. The stove was electric and there were a couple of space heaters. She might have gone down to look for something, but if so, she didn't look far because there were no tracks in the dust. If she'd been carrying something down, we would have found it but there was nothing in the area except the body."

"Was there any sign of a break in?" asked Bullard.

"The back door was unlocked but the house was secure otherwise. The window was probably broken during the storm. But things were unsettled." He hesitated, then went on. "I couldn't tell you exactly why, but I'm pretty certain that the house had been searched recently. There wasn't a mess, but I believe someone had been looking for something. At the inquest, the suggestion was made that Miss Taft had been trying to find something she had mislaid, and finally started down to the basement. There were some old boxes of paperwork – bills and receipts and a big stack of National Geographics, but not much else. The step might have snapped under her weight and down she went."

"But the damage was to the back of her skull, you said." Bullard was frowning.

"She could have spun around trying to regain her balance. I didn't think that was likely given how narrow the stairs were, but I suppose it's possible. Anyway, I checked with the neighbors – none of whom lived within sight of the house – and a couple of them mentioned that there had been a second car in the driveway a couple of weeks earlier. The deceased owned a gray Volkswagen minivan. This was a passenger car. It was either blue or green or black and no one looked at the license plate."

"So she had company," said Bullard.

"Was the car there overnight?" I asked.

"I wasn't able to determine that. There was nothing substantial to justify pursuing the investigation any further, particularly with a verdict of death by misadventure."

"What happened to the property?" I really didn't want to fly out to Michigan, but it might be worth a look.

"Sold when the estate was settled. The new owners turned it into a real estate office."

So there was no need to go to Michigan. I felt both relieved and frustrated.

"Is there anything else you can tell us?" asked Bullard.

"No, not really. I just had the feeling that the scene had been staged, but there was no physical evidence, and I could have been wrong."

"Well, thanks for taking the time to fill us in."

"Do you mind if I ask why you're interested?"

Bullard nodded to herself. "There's a possible link to a couple of deaths we're looking into. Both victims were known to have visited Miss Taft."

"Could they have been driving the mystery car?"

"Not unless they came back, and there's no indication of that. They visited a couple of weeks earlier. It's possible that it was coincidental. One of our victims had met Miss Taft previously."

"If anything comes of it, I'd appreciate it if you'd let me know. I won't say that the Taft case gnaws at me or anything like that, but I'd like to know the truth."

Bullard took down Larson's cell number. "If anything comes up, I'll let you know."

It had been an interesting conversation, but when I thought about it afterward, it really didn't tell us much. It was remotely possible that some unknown party had decided that Wendy Taft had been murdered, but had the time frame wrong and had tracked down John and Muriel to exact revenge. But I didn't buy it. A day or two off, maybe, but two weeks had passed. No one who carried off two murders with such precision would have made such a simple mistake.

"There has to be a link there," I said aloud.

"Well if you can connect any of the dots, you let me know." Bullard was obviously disappointed. "Otherwise that was no help at all."

I didn't say anything to Bullard because I was still working it out in my mind, but I had put a few random pieces together and they seemed to fit. Five people at the festival were or had been expecting a financial windfall of some kind – John Boncoddo, Jimmy Gonsalves, Muriel Bates, Daryl Plimpton, and Ray Riccello. John and Muriel were linked to Wendy Taft, but that wasn't true of any of the others. Ray's funding was somehow connected to Edward Mrozek. Jimmy's was a complete mystery. If there was a common thread among all these people, I couldn't see it, but it was too much of a coincidence to believe that there was nothing there. Some of the links had to matter.

Almost by chance, the puzzle became somewhat simpler only a few minutes later. I spotted Terry Wareham talking to someone at the festival's help desk. "Got a minute?"

"Sure. Just a sec." She finished her business with the volunteer and the three of us found a corner that was the most private area in the lobby. "What's up?"

"How well do you know Jimmy Gonsalves?" I asked bluntly.

Her eyebrows rose but she answered. "Not very well until recently. My new job is just outside Albany, so we get together for dinner once in a while. We're not a couple or anything. At least not yet." Her eyes dared me to make a crack.

"Do you have any idea how much Jimmy paid for this theater project of his?"

"Not offhand. But he downplays it a lot. It's actually a very nice piece of property. I'd guess something like half a million, but some of that might have been borrowed."

It was still significantly more than I had expected. "I don't suppose you'd know where he got that kind of money?"

Terry was frowning now. "What is this all about?"

I would rather not have explained, but it was obvious that Terry was alarmed if not outright angry. "John and Muriel were both expecting to receive significant amounts of money. I was just trying to figure out if there was a common source."

Terry relaxed, but not all the way. "That much I can tell you. I don't know what they were involved in but Jimmy's money is his own. He designs and programs computer games under a pseudonym. You should see the house he lives in. It has more bedrooms than some motels."

I was rather startled to have stumbled into a dead end so quickly. "Did he ever mention having any kind of business relationship with John or Muriel?"

"No, and I doubt it. Jimmy always works alone. He subcontracts the work he doesn't want to do. And all he has talked about for the past year has been how he was going to buy this derelict theater and restore it."

I glanced at Dusty in case she'd thought of something that I hadn't, but she just shrugged as if to stay I'd stumbled into a sand trap on my own and it was my job to get out of it. "Okay. I figured there was nothing to it but I had to ask. Thanks, Terry."

She softened enough to smile as we were leaving, but her eyes were still hard I suddenly realized that Terry's interest in Jimmy was more than just friendship. I silently wished her luck.

"What are you thinking?" asked Dusty as we walked back into the lobby proper.

"I'm not sure, but there's money in this thing somewhere. I would sure like to know more about Edward Mrozek."

"Bullard said she was having his background checked."

And so it was that I called Bullard's cell once again.

"I hope this isn't another complicated lead that goes nowhere?" She was testy, and I really didn't blame her.

"I just wondered what you might have found out about Edward Mrozek."

"Why?"

"Because I'm running out of ideas and he's one of the question marks. He's talking about financing a movie for Ray Riccello and that's not cheap even in the days of direct to video and CGI."

"You might as well forget Mrozek. He's just a front man for a group of investors back in California. He' s never been in trouble with the police, not even a parking ticket. Unless he has a secret life that he keeps well hidden, he's exactly what he says he is."

"All right. Thanks." That left three people – John, Muriel, and Daryl – and two of them were dead. I turned to Dusty. "I think we should go talk to Daryl."

But that turned out to be more difficult than we expected. He was not in his temporary office, but he'd been in and out throughout the festival so that meant nothing. He wasn't in his hotel room either, or at least he wasn't answering his telephone. We took a quick walk through the festival areas without finding him, but activities were spread over five different floors in the Biltmore and three in the Driscoll. He could have been sitting in the dark in one of the movie rooms and would have been effectively invisible. We also asked people and a few had seen him during the course of the morning, but no one since shortly after noon. Jo Parkin said that he'd planned to go over to the Driscoll to deal with a dispute about the length of time for which one of the function rooms had been reserved.

"He said he'd take care of it, but I haven't heard from him since."

So we walked over to the Driscoll. Our old friend Martin was busy with an elderly couple's baggage but he nodded as we went by. The desk clerk didn't know anything about any disagreement but directed us to the woman who handled such matters. Her name was Patricia Burgess and she had a depressingly neat office and a professional but meaningless smile. She did indeed know about the problem with the Sturgeon room – the function rooms were all named after fish for some reason – and wanted to know if we represented the festival.

"No," I explained hastily. "The person you want is Daryl Plimpton. We were told that someone called from here and asked him to come over, and we're looking for him."

"There's nothing to discuss. The contract clearly states that the room be cleared an hour prior to the end of the contract to allow us to set up for the next function. I informed the individual running the camera and he said he'd take care of it. No one has been in contact with me since then so I assumed that the matter was settled."

So we went to the Sturgeon room and managed to cajole the young man working the projector out into the corridor. "What's up?"

I explained why we there and asked if he had seen Daryl. "No, man, not since yesterday. There's no problem though. I added up the running times and we'll be all done just about on schedule, so there's no problem after all."

"You didn't call Daryl and tell him to come over?"

"Never. Daryl and I don't communicate much."

"And you haven't seen him at all today?"

"Like I said, no, I have not."

Something else had been gnawing at me for a while without showing its face. I asked Dusty if she still had her program with her.

"Sure." She fished around in her shoulderbag and pulled it out. The movies were listed in the order they were being shown, with an index by title in the back, along with a separate list of panel discussions and other events. A black embroidered box drew special attention to the showing of *At the Mountains of Madness*, with a list of the cast and a squib about how it had been believed lost for several decades.

My thoughts jumped a little gap and landed on a major assumption, but the ground seemed firm. "I need to call Bullard." I pulled out my cell.

Dusty was very good at reading my moods. "What's wrong?"

"I think I know what the connection was between John and Muriel, and if I'm right there's going to be at least one more murder. And I think I know who it's going to be."

CHAPTER FOURTEEN

As it happened, Bullard was on her way over to the Driscoll, so I just told her that I thought I'd stumbled upon something significant. She agreed to meet us in the hotel lounge. A waitress came by to solicit drinks but I chased her away. "We're just meeting someone."

Bullard arrived a couple of minutes later, waved off the same waitress who was looking a bit miffed now, and joined us. "What have you got?"

I summarized the chain of reasoning, such as it was, that made me concentrate on the people who were expecting a financial windfall and why I had eliminated Jimmy and Ray.

"I've thought about the same thing and I could have told you about Gonsalves and Mrozek a while ago if you'd asked. Both of them were perfectly willing to talk about it when I asked."

"There's also Daryl Plimpton."

"Yes, but we know where his payoff is coming from. He sold the rights to that weird movie."

"How did he get the rights anyway?" asked Dusty, who was obviously only a step behind me.

"It was never copyrighted," I told her. "The people who were involved could probably mount a troublesome legal case, but none of them are alive anymore and the three men all died single and childless. There are probably some relatives somewhere, but it would probably take a lot of effort to track them down. I don't know where Wendy Taft comes into this, but I think either she was a descendant of one of them, or in some other way came into possession of a complete copy. Muriel met her, found out or at least suspected something, and asked John along when she went to visit so that he could tell her whether the film was in good enough shape to be useable. Daryl must have come into it later."

"So you think Daryl and our two victims were all involved in acquiring the film, and someone is killing them because they were left out of the deal?"

"Yes and no. I don't think money is actually the motive, although it might be. There's really not enough to matter. I know that John and Muriel were looking forward to their share, but ten grand would have been enough to excite either of them. I'd be surprised if Daryl got as much as a hundred grand total, but I suppose it might have been more. And it's not likely the split was equal. He'd find a way to get the lion's share."

"And Wendy Taft is dead and can't provide her side of the story." Bullard was starting to look interested. "I think we need to talk to Mr. Plimpton again."

"We tried to find him but he's not around," said Dusty.

Bullard used her cell to call and arrange for a quiet search of both hotels. "I asked them to have hotel security open his room, just in case you're right and we're already too late."

"I hope that's not the case. You might also have someone from the festival staff page him. They must have his cell number." Neither Dusty or I had ever had a good reason to call Daryl.

Bullard quickly gave instructions over her cell. "So if money wasn't the motive, what was?"

"Wendy Taft. I think someone believes that she was murdered and is looking for revenge."

"We'd have to trace how Taft got hold of the film."

"The only woman in the cast was Adele Leslie. Taft's grandmother – who would have been about the same age – was named Adele."

"That's pretty thin, but we can find out for sure."

"If I were you, I'd get hold of that motel in Foster City and find out if they had anyone named Plimpton staying there at about the time that Wendy Taft had her accident."

Bullard sighed, but she made another call, this time to Officer Larson of the Michigan State Police. She explained briefly what she was looking for, then ended the call. "He's in the area so he'll check right away and call me back."

"This might just be another wild goose chase," I cautioned, but my instinct said that I was close to the truth.

Bullard just grunted.

An hour later we were back in the conference room at the Biltmore. A reasonably thorough search had turned up no sign of Daryl Plimpton. He was not in his room, which showed no sign of a struggle. Calls to his cell went to voice mail because it had been turned off. He had missed his two o'clock appointment with the board of trustees who were to choose the following year's festival location – the board were figureheads who just rubber stamped whatever Daryl wanted. The people from the distribution company had checked out and left early that morning. Daryl had charged breakfast to his room but there had been no activity on his account since, although he could have eaten outside the hotel or paid cash or credit inside. No one could remember seeing him since noon or perhaps slightly afterward. Everyone who knew Daryl agreed that this was not typical of him. He was psychologically incapable of standing back and letting the festival run itself; he had to be seen as its driving force.

Abe Larson called back and confirmed what I had suspected. Daryl Plimpton had spent three nights in Foster City at the right time. I found it hard to believe that Daryl would actually have committed murder, even to acquire a copy of *At the Mountains of Madness*, but I no longer doubted that Wendy Taft had been the source. Bullard requested more background information on the family and the state police were trying to find someone who might be able to help.

At four o'clock, there was still no sign of Daryl and I had a growing conviction that the news would not be good when he finally turned up. Bullard had pizza delivered, much to the disgust of the hotel staff, but we did buy soft drinks in the lounge. The snubbed waitress had apparently gone off duty by then, replaced by two others in anticipation of the evening crowd.

Dusty went out for a while and returned to tell us that rumors were spreading about Daryl but that the tone was more curiosity than alarm. Daryl didn't exactly have a lot of friends, or any for that matter. But things were beginning to wind down now anyway. Although there was another day of movies and panels to come, it would be foreshortened and a lot of people attending would be leaving that evening or the following morning, depending on their travel arrangements.

Just before six, Abe Larson called again. He had managed to locate Reverend Winslow Holt, retired, who knew the two older women reasonably well, although Wendy had not been much of a churchgoer. Holt's deep, resonant voice was muted by the cell phone but not by much. "Adele was a fine old lady but not particularly outgoing. She used to volunteer for church work – bazaars and suchlike – while her husband was alive, but when Arthur passed away – it was lung cancer - she withdrew into herself. Her daughter, Mary, had moved away in 1964 or 1965, lived in Denver for a while, I believe, then went East somewhere and and got married. I never met the husband because the only time she came back to visit, she came with just the baby. That would be Wendy."

"What was Adele's maiden name?" I asked when he paused for breath.

"Leslie. Only child of Ted and Grace Leslie. Her husband was Arthur Taft."

"And what was Mary's married name?"

"I don't know offhand, but she changed it back after the divorce, when she and Wendy moved back here. Wendy would have been about eleven then."

"Did the father ever come to visit?"

"Not to my knowledge. Mary always said that it had been a clean break and there had never been any talk about visitation rights or anything like that. I always thought there was something funny about that but she wouldn't talk about it."

"Was anything ever mentioned about Adele's connection with the movie business?"

Reverend Holt sounded surprised and possibly mildly offended. "Never heard of such a thing. Adele was a proper lady and never worked a day in her life, just kept house for her husband and raised her daughter."

I saw Dusty's lips tighten at this cavalier dismissal of the work involved in keeping a house and raising a daughter, but she didn't say anything.

Bullard asked a few more questions. No, there had never been anything to suggest that there were any family secrets. "But most of us have them, don't we?" He didn't know much about Wendy, who was an irregular churchgoer and in any case he had been retired for five years now. "I don't believe the Lord ran out of work for me but the church elders thought otherwise." Bullard thanked him for his help and Larson spoke up before we could break the connection.

"When this Plimpton guy checked in, they took his license plate number. It was a rental car. Turned it in at Sawyer Airport. I didn't see any point in trying to find out what flight he took."

Bullard couldn't see a reason either. "Thanks for the prompt work. I hope this is going to help, but Mr. Plimpton has gone missing on us."

Larson whistled. "Sounds like you're having an interesting weekend."

By six o'clock, the Biltmore had emptied out considerably. Three of the five movie rooms had ended their programs and the ballroom was closed. About a third of the dealers had packed up and left, but the rest were waiting for the last minute sales on Monday. Bullard had ascertained the departure times of everyone remaining on our list. Jimmy and Terry were traveling together and were planning to leave at around noon. Ray and Tanya had moved to the Biltmore for their last night because they didn't like the Marriott. Helen Viele was staying until Tuesday morning, as was Romeo Bolduc, Jo Parkin, and Bob Strossi. Angela had planned to leave Sunday night but had extended her reservation for at least one more day. Edward Mrozek had already checked out and had taken the airport shuttle.

Someone had managed to track down Russell Staines in California. He was resigning in order to take a better paying job with Anchor Bay Studios and didn't know anything that seemed pertinent except that "John had this super secret job that he did mostly by himself about a year and a half ago, but he was always doing weird things like that."

Dusty suggested another scenario – that Daryl had killed both John and Muriel because they knew too much about how he had acquired the film, or to keep from giving them their share, or both. That presupposed that Daryl had murdered Wendy Taft and that somehow the other two had figured this out. It was a bit of a reach, but I had to admit that we couldn't rule it out. But if so, why had Daryl disappeared and drawn attention to himself?

"Has anyone mentioned the Frampton connection to Daryl?" She looked back and forth between Bullard and I. "If he didn't think we had any idea about Wendy Taft, he could assume that we had nothing to link him to the two murders. Maybe he's going to show up and claim he was abducted or something so we'd think he was another prospective victim and he escaped somehow."

That was a happier outcome than the one I was expecting, that Daryl was dead and it was just a matter of time before we found his body. And I didn't think Dusty really believe in her own theory.

In any case we didn't have much longer to wait.

It was about half an hour later when Bullard took another call. I could tell by the way her voice changed that it wasn't good news. I think Dusty sensed the same thing because she put a hand on my arm. The call only lasted a few seconds but that was long enough.

"They found Daryl, didn't they?" asked Dusty.

"Not exactly. They received another anonymous email though. I need to visit room 316. I can't let you into the room but I'd appreciate it if you kept yourselves available."

"Of course," we said in unison.

It was room 316, all right, but not in the Biltmore. That one turned out to be occupied by Camille Caldarone, who was attending her first festival and didn't know much of anyone. The three of us then walked briskly back to the Driscoll where Detective Doyle was checking out their room 316. It was obvious that something was up because there were already uniforms standing in clumps and our friend Mrs. Drake was looking fretful. Mickey Palotto stood beside her, clearly uncomfortable. The bellhop on duty was a burly young Hispanic. There was only a handful of guests in sight and some of them cast curious glances at the intrusion, but there was no sign of actual alarm.

We went up in the elevator with Drake and Palotto and left the rest waiting for the next car. It's good to be the chief detective, or close to her.

The door was closed when we arrived and Doyle was waiting for us with another uniform. "This room is supposed to be vacant," said Drake quietly. "The last guest checked out early this morning."

Palotto produced the pass key and opened the door, then stepped back. Bullard motioned for us to move out of the line of fire, then cautiously eased the door open. "This is the police. Identify yourself at once."

There was no answer, of course. Two of the uniforms had drawn their weapons and Bullard stepped back to let them clear the room, with Doyle close behind. They moved quickly, disappearing inside, and then we heard one of them shout an expletive. Obviously they had found something. A voice came from beyond the door. "We have a body, Detective, but there's no one else here."

Bullard went in, was there only a few seconds before all three of them came back out. The first of the technicians had arrived by now and she gestured for them to go inside. I didn't have to be a mindreader to anticipate what she was going to say when she came over to us. "It's Plimpton and he's dead. Very dead, in fact. I don't think you're going to want to see him."

"Was it like the others?" asked Dusty.

Bullard shook her head. "Not remotely. The first two were executions and it's likely neither of them knew what hit them. This was slow and painful. He was tied, gagged, and mutilated. I don't know what actually killed him but I'd guess blood loss. No sign of a bullet wound, but that will have to be determined."

I didn't ask how he'd been mutilated. I didn't want to know, and as it happens I never did hear the details. The cause of death turned out to be a bullet after all, but the coup de grace had followed a lot of pain and had probably been welcome when it finally came.

"The first two were simply jobs to be done. There was no real emotion involved. This time it was personal." I hadn't meant to speak out loud, but Bullard nodded.

"Looks that way."

Bullard offered to call us when they knew more, but we ended up sitting in the elevator lobby while the technicians and others went back and forth. Drake disappeared almost immediately and Palotto followed a short time afterwards. It was over an hour before we spoke to Bullard again.

"They'll be taking the body away shortly. He's been dead about four hours, maybe five, so that means no earlier than two o'clock. The housemaid says she had this side of the floor all made up before noon. All of the mutilations were inflicted while he was still alive, I'm sorry to say."

"Someone should have heard something," Dusty said.

"They might have, but he was gagged pretty well, and the killer probably turned on the television to mask the sound. There was no window dressing this time. No bogus clues, no extra weapons."

"I wonder what that means." I had a feeling that I knew, however. "What did the email say?"

"It suggested that we take a look at room 316 to avoid an innocent guest having an unpleasant surprise. It didn't mention which hotel."

"Considerate of our killer. Do you suppose omitting the hotel name was intentional?"

"Yeah, a real gentleman. Or lady. Who knows why he did what he did? Maybe it was another delaying tactic. Maybe he just forgot. We'll have to check everyone's alibi again, of course."

I was about to say that I thought that would be a waste of time since there was no discernible link between anyone else and Wendy Taft or Frampton, but then I realized that I was wrong. Wendy had been Helen's cousin. Helen cultivated an image of herself as a flighty libertine, but I knew that wasn't the whole story. She could be very intense if she wanted to. I tried to imagine Helen shooting two people in the head and found I could do so quite easily. There was a hard core in Helen; she led the kind of life she did because that's what she wanted. I wouldn't have cared to be an obstacle in her path. But while I could accept the possibility that she had killed John and Muriel and even Daryl, she would never have resorted to torture, not even in Daryl's case. Or at least so I thought. But I might have been underestimating her.

"I'd give priority to Helen Viele. Wendy Taft was her cousin." I felt like a traitor saying it, but there it was.

Bullard had a list of cell numbers and she called each of our remaining suspects, asking them to come over to the Driscoll. A new interview room had been established in 301. She was able to reach everyone except Helen. That call went to voicemail. Dusty and I sat in on the subsequent, very short interviews but we didn't ask any questions. There had been no official announcement but it was obvious that there had been another incident and by now pretty much everyone knew that Daryl had gone missing. No one met our eyes except Jo Parkin, who looked stunned. Terry Wareham was crying. Bob Strossi showed up with Angela Bates. They seemed the least affected but I didn't know if Angela had ever even met Daryl, and I knew for sure that Bob had never liked him and wouldn't be shedding any tears.

Unfortunately, no one had much of an alibi. The medical examiner estimated that all of Daryl's injuries could have been inflicted in less than thirty minutes, but it might have been an hour or even longer. He'd been dead since somewhere between two and three. Terry, Joe, and Romeo had all been wandering around on their own during the crucial period. Bob and Angela had had lunch together, but she'd gone back to her room right afterwards and Bob had walked down by the Providence River for about an hour.

No one had seen Helen Viele since early that morning. They were still looking for her when Bullard suddenly took out her cell and made a call to Michigan. "Yes, Detective Larson, I was wondering if you could do my one more favor. Could you find out who inherited the Taft property? And you might ask around to see if anyone has ever heard of Helen Viele. She was Taft's cousin. Thank you."

"She said she'd never been to Frampton and hadn't seen Wendy since they'd been kids," said Dusty.

"People say a lot of things. Doesn't mean any of it's true."

The technicians finished with the room about six o'clock but Bullard locked the door and posted a guard. "At least until we have lab results," she explained.

"The killer must have had a key," I pointed out, even though I was quite sure she'd already thought about that.

"This place isn't nearly as secure as the Biltmore. All of the housemaids have keys and no one checks to make sure they turn them in at night. Half a dozen of them have been misplaced over the last year or so. And you can make a key at the front desk in about ten seconds if you know how."

"Wouldn't it be obvious if someone came around behind the desk?"

"Not if they picked their moment. The desk clerks at night are on alone and they're supposed to do paperwork in the little office behind the desk when nothing is happening. There's no line of sight from there. And they have to answer the call of nature at some point. And for that matter, these are older model locks. There are electronic devices that can bypass them, like skeleton keys."

"How would they know the room was going to be empty?" asked Dusty.

"If it was me," said Bullard, "I'd wait around in the lobby until I heard someone checking out and mentioning the room number. Then I'd wait an hour and go up to the third floor. If the housemaid was on that floor, I'd make myself scarce. If not, I'd check the room to see if it had been made up. Then I'd lure my victim over with some kind of fake message. I'd use my gun to subdue him, force him to tie his ankles together, then lie on his back while I did his hands."

"He would have resisted," I pointed out. "He must have known by then that this was the same person who killed John and Muriel."

"Which is why I am inclined to think it was a man, someone strong enough to overpower him."

Helen was an athletic woman who was much stronger than she appeared, as I remembered from our one night together. Daryl was tall but he was soft and clumsy. There was no doubt in my mind that she could have handled him physically without much difficulty. In fact, Dusty could have done the same and she's considerably smaller than Helen.

The head technician had not been hopeful. "Lots of prints, hairs, and incidental traces but it's a goddamned hotel room. It would have been more surprising if it had been clean." The rope was ordinary clothesline. There was no sign of whatever had been used to inflict what were apparently gruesome wounds, "but there might be traces of metal that will show up at the autopsy." Even if there were, it would almost certainly be pointless to try to trace them. Contrary to various television detective shows, laboratories could not perform miracles of identification.

We all went downstairs to talk to Margaret Drake, who had retreated to her office in disarray. "The owners will be very unhappy," she told us the moment we joined her. "Nothing like this has ever happened here before." Actually, she was wrong. There had been a double murder in the Driscoll in the 1930s, but it had been the Grand Union Hotel at the time.

Bullard had been looking tired almost from the first moment we'd seen her, but then again, she almost always did. But now she was looking discouraged, and that was something I hadn't seen before. "I asked you to talk to all the housemaids to see if any of them had seen anything unusual in a guest room."

"Yes, and we did that, but other than a couple of movie props that I told you about already, no one noticed anything."

I glanced at Bullard because this was the first I'd heard of any suspicious movie props. "There was a fake cutlass and a toy guillotine," she explained off handedly. "Both of them were bought from the exhibitors in the Biltmore."

"We've had a lot of people standing around but that's not unusual in an event like this." Drake gestured broadly with her hands. "And they're almost always in groups. Your people have already asked if they heard anything this afternoon, but except for the housemaid, no one would have any reason to be on that floor during the early afternoon, and we know that she was done and had gone on to the next floor before the…incident. No one has checked in on that floor today and the departures were all well before noon."

"How about delivery people?" Bullard was grasping at straws now.

"They're supposed to check in at the desk, but they don't always bother. We had one delivery that we know about around that time, but it was flowers to some newlyweds on the sixth floor."

I was restless. This was routine and Bullard had to go through the motions, but Dusty and I didn't have to waste our time providing background. I stood up. "Dusty and I aren't doing any good here. We're going to walk around a little."

Dusty's face reflected her own relief at the prospect of leaving. Bullard just nodded without looking up.

"Where to, Sherlock?" Dusty asked.

"I want to sample the rumor mill. Some version of the truth will have escaped captivity by now."

So we trudged back to the Biltmore and made our way to the festival operations room. It looked quite different now. About half of the electronic equipment had already been removed and a lot of the printed material had been bundled up for removal or disposal. The young man at the first desk was a stranger, but Jo Parkin and Terry Wareham were huddled together in the far corner, so we joined them.

Jo looked a little weepy but Terry clearly wasn't in mourning. She might, however, have been just the faintest bit frightened. That was fair. I wasn't entirely easy myself. Three people in our circle had died violently in a very short period of time. Even though I was convinced that they were connected somehow, and that Dusty and I were not, I couldn't be sure until the motive was exposed. And even if we were not, the killer might think that we were.

"I can't believe this is happening," said Terry by way of greeting.

"Unfortunately, it is. I assume people are talking about it."

"A couple of people who were scheduled for panels this evening have already told us they're leaving early. It's difficult to talk coolly about the role of private detectives in noir films when you're in the middle of a real life serial killer story."

"At least most of the festival is over with," said Jo. "But I'm worried about next year."

"Do you think people will be worried that there will be more murders at the Salt Lake City festival?" asked Dusty.

"No, probably not. But we all know that Daryl was the glue that held this whole operation together. He was egocentric and rude and domineering and all that, but he never lost sight of the mission. He's the reason we've lasted so long."

I had to admit she had a point. "Isn't that why we have a board of directors?"

"Yes," said Terry. "And the two of us are it now that Daryl is gone. We need to find a new member who has a sense of organization." She gave me a meaningful look which I very carefully avoided acknowledging.

"You could hire an event manager," suggested Dusty.

"Do you know how much those people charge?" Jo looked as though she was talking about a criminal offense on a par with homicide.

"I wonder how this affects the deal to distribute *At the Mountains of Madness*?" I asked the question quite deliberately because I wanted to see their reaction.

Terry looked thoughtful, but Jo shook her head. "I don't think it will. He told me he signed the last of the paperwork this weekend. I'm not sure who will end up getting the money though. Daryl never mentioned any relatives and he was the kind of person who would be too convinced of his own immortality to have bothered with a will."

"Did you ever hear how he managed to find a copy?" If Terry had been trying to blackmail Daryl because she knew something about the film's provenance, she might be reluctant to let on, but now that Daryl was dead, I hoped that her reasons for keeping it a secret no longer applied. But to my surprise, it was Jo and not Terry who answered.

"He bought it from a member of the family of one of the actors. He told me that the family didn't want their names brought into it so a condition of the sale was that he couldn't reveal the source. I think it was some connection to Ernest Gilles because supposedly he had a couple of illegitimate children and one of them must have had a copy in a closet somewhere."

"What made you think that?"

"Daryl dropped a couple of hints."

Dusty glanced at the growing stack of cartons in one corner. "What's going to happen to all this stuff? Didn't Daryl usually store it at his house?" The boxes contained unused membership tags, ribbons, lanyards, attendance lists, undistributed flyers for the Salt Lake City festival, literature from New Orleans and St Louis, who were competing to be the next site in the rotation, and other material that could be reused.

"Romeo is going to take most of it in his van. He has a walk in attic where he can store everything, at least until we figure things out."

"Romeo might be a good replacement for Daryl," suggested Dusty.

Both women shook their heads. "We already asked. He said that he might have been willing when he was younger but he lacks the energy and mobility to run things now. He agreed to serve on the board if we can't find anyone else, but only if we get someone else to do the actual organizing."

I was feeling restless again. If either Jo or Terry knew something, they weren't going to talk about it in this setting. "Has anyone seen Ray and Tanya?"

Jo nodded. "They switched hotels and they're staying over until tomorrow afternoon. Tanya wants to hit the local mall again. Ray never liked Daryl so he was hardly heartbroken."

I took a step back. "Well, good luck to both of you and hopefully we'll see you again next year if not sooner."

Terry frowned. "Are you leaving already?"

"Not right away. We want to say goodbye to a few people first."

As soon as we were outside the room, Dusty tugged on my arm. "Why did you say we leaving? You had me extend our stay for tonight."

"We're not, but right now I don't think I want people to know what our plans are from minute to minute."

"Do you think there's going to be another murder?"

"I don't know. But I have the feeling this isn't over with yet."

"That sounds ominous."

"Let's go up to our room," I said. "I need some place where I can think about this."

CHAPTER FIFTEEN

Dusty picked up our notes when we arrived, but I waved them away. "The three elements we need to resolve our motive, method, and opportunity. I'm sure the motive is connected to Frampton, Wendy Taft, and *At the Mountains of Madness*. I'm sure now that she was the one who provided the surviving copy, that Muriel or John or both of them somehow found out about it and told Daryl, and Daryl eventually acquired it as about the time that Taft died."

"Do you think he killed her?"

"I don't know. It might have been coincidence, or an accident, or there might be another explanation that hasn't occurred to me. But even if Daryl had nothing to do with her death, it certainly looks as though he did, and whoever our murderer is might well have leaped to that conclusion. That's the obvious motive, but there might be others. There might be something about the movie itself that someone doesn't want revealed. If Daryl hadn't already signed the distribution deal, it could have been tied up indefinitely. I'm not sure what the legal situation is now."

"How could a seventy year old adaptation of an old horror story be so dangerous?"

"I don't know. I haven't even seen the movie and if I had, I might not have noticed anything. Daryl has shown it to half a dozen audiences already."

"Maybe one of those people saw whatever it is."

"Might be. But no one keeps records about who attends screenings at film festivals. No, I think we have to ignore motive for the time being. And it looks like everyone on our list of suspects probably had opportunity. I think we need to do a step by step reconstruction of the three murders." I didn't mention that the only person we knew of who had an actual connection to Wendy Taft was Helen Viele. Although I was emotionally convinced that she wasn't the person we were looking for, I had to admit to myself that she had a hard inner core and was one of the strongest people I knew mentally and emotionally. If she felt justified, she would be completely capable of killing someone.

Dusty picked up the hotel pen. "All right, I'll take notes. Legible ones. Where do we start?"

"The first question is how the killer – let's call him Mr. X – knew that John was staying at the Driscoll. The majority of the guests were registered at the Biltmore and the Marriott, so they would be more logical places to watch for him."

"I would have emailed John a while back and asked casually where he was staying."

I shook my head. "Emails are too permanent. You wouldn't want to leave a record."

"Telephone then. And if I was really paranoid, I'd use a disposable."

"This all assumes that Mr. X is someone that John knew personally. What if Mr. X is a stranger."

Dusty thought about it. "I'd call the hotels and ask if John Boncoddo had booked a room and what his arrival time was. They'd tell me that, wouldn't they?"

"Maybe. Probably. He could even pretend to be John and say he was just checking to see if his secretary had made the right reservation. So you know he's checking in on Friday at the Driscoll and you watch for him in the lobby. You're carrying a suitcase or something like that with all of your paraphernalia, but you don't want to hang around too long because someone might notice, even in a hotel. A bellhop might have offered to take his bag for him. He would have to have a good reason to keep it, and that would make him memorable. I don't think that's what happened."

"He might have checked it until he needed it," suggested Dusty "Or what about waiting in the little park across the street? It's not likely anyone would pay attention to someone sitting there pretending to be reading a book or something."

"Good point. It would make it harder to spot John when he arrived, but it could be managed. I don't like the checkroom idea as much because once again someone might have remembered him. But Mr. X has to take some risks after all. Now, how does he find out what room John is in? The hotel wouldn't give that information out."

"Not unless you bribed one of the desk clerks."

I thought about that for a few seconds, but dismissed it. "Too dangerous. The clerk might realize the significance after the murder and confess."

"Mr. X could have ridden up in the elevator with John." Dusty frowned. "No, that wouldn't work. If it was someone he knew, they would have talked. And didn't the bellhop say that they'd been alone all the way to the room?"

"Yes, he did. Even if it was a stranger, he would have been too conspicuous. The bellhop would have noticed him and there might have been someone in the corridor when they got out of the elevator. And where would Mr. X have concealed himself while Martin – the bellhop – was in the room with John? That just doesn't work."

Dusty frowned. "Okay, I've seen John arrive but I don't know what room number he's in. The desk won't tell me but they'll connect me by phone. So I call John and ask him his room number so that I can come up."

"Which probably but not necessarily means that John knew Mr. X." It was becoming more and more probable that the killer was someone we knew. That turned out to be true, of course, although it was a bit more complicated than I realized at the time. "Meanwhile, John has dismissed the bellhop and has started to unpack. Some of his clothes were already in the dresser, but he hadn't hung up his shirts yet."

Dusty picked up her narrative. "I carry my bag up to his room, knock, and he lets me in. I knock him unconscious, run the bath and add the salt, drown him, and then confuse the scene with other weapons for reasons unknown or maybe just to annoy the police. I find John's cell phone, pick your name out of the list, and send the message. I tape the note to the door and drop off the room key at the desk. Why did he choose you?"

"Probably because I'm local and would not be checked into the hotel. That increased the likelihood that I wouldn't show up prematurely and upset the scenario. When Mr X. left John's room, he took the cell phone with him and at some point planted it in Mickey Palotto's office, where the lock could be easily bypassed if it was even engaged." I remembered Palotto's uneasiness when asked about that.

"Why bother?"

"Just to add to the confusion I imagine. Remember, we still haven't found John's missing laptop. I suppose he could have had a digital copy of the movie, but I don't understand what difference that would make to the killer. And I don't see any way that Palotto could be connected to all of this." I was silent for a few seconds. "But note down his name and circle it. We never really asked him if he knew anyone from the festival."

"He knows you," she pointed out. "If he was the killer, that might explain why your name was chosen."

"Good point. Maybe we should talk to him some time soon. And we forgot about the threatening message Daryl received months ago."

"Do you think the killer sent it?"

"I don't know. It could be coincidence, or it might have been something he did impulsively, before he began working on a more elaborate plan."

Dusty scribbled a note. "So what next?"

"We don't have any idea what Mr. X did from that point until shortly before Muriel's death. Somehow he acquired a pass key for the Biltmore, but that might have happened earlier. Once again, he somehow learned that Muriel and Angela were in their room. That's less problematic because he could have heard them say something beforehand or he might have called their room. In any case, he arranged for the fruit basket and charged it to another room."

"How could he do that?"

"He already had a passkey, remember? All he had to do was wait until he knew a specific room was empty, slip inside, and use the phone to call room service. They would have had no reason to question him. Once he was certain that the cart had been delivered, he went up to their room with the bottle of champagne."

"How would he manage to get a hotel uniform?"

"We don't know that he had one. Angela never saw him, remember? In fact, she never heard the voice distinctly. It might even have been a woman who delivered the bottle. It was almost certainly Mr. X because he had to open the bottle in Muriel's presence in order to slip in whatever he used to knock them out, but he or she was gone by the time Angela came out of the bathroom. And that tells us something."

Dusty frowned, but figured it out almost immediately. "Muriel didn't know Mr. X. She would have said something if Romeo or Helen or Daryl or somebody showed up claiming to be from room service."

"Right. So either Mr. X is not part of our inner circle, or the situation is more complicated. There might be two different people involved, or one person who had some kind of disguise, although that would let out Romeo for certain. Let's call the second person Miss Y."

"That would certainly make things easier to manage. One of them could be someone we know and who could find out where their victims would be and when, and the other could do the actual murders while the first was providing himself, or herself, with an alibi."

"Right, except that none of the people on our list actually has an alibi for any of the murders. If there are two of them, why didn't they take advantage of that fact to establish one?"

"Because the people with the ironclad alibi are almost always the killer?"

I sighed. "You've been reading too much detective fiction. In real life, ironclad alibis almost always are in fact ironclad."

"They might have gotten their plans screwed up." Dusty pouted, but she already saw the flaw. Whoever was responsible was very organized. They might just possibly miscalculate the alibi in one case, but not three times in a row.

"Back to our narrative. Mr. X waits a while, then calls the room. No one answers, so it is safe to assume that the sisters are unconscious. He still has the passkey so he goes inside, probably knocked first just to be sure, then kills Muriel rather quickly, and leaves."

"But he sends a message to the police. He did the first time too and we forgot to note that." Dusty scribbled a bit to correct the omission. "Why bother?"

"I think it was a crude attempt to convince the police that this was the work of a serial killer and that the victims were being chosen at random. If we hadn't found out about the Frampton connection, we might still believe that was the case."

"Okay." Dusty drew a horizontal line under her last entry.
"So now another night passes. The next thing we know of is
when Daryl disappeared late this morning."

"I don't think this one was as well planned. I suspect that at
this point Mr. X was either improvising or changed his plans
when an opportunity presented itself. He was obviously keeping
track of Daryl's whereabouts. Up until the time that he went over
to the Driscoll, Daryl had never really been alone except in his
room at night. The fake room service ploy wouldn't work again
so he had to be convinced to go somewhere where he could be
subdued, in this case room 312 at the Driscoll."

"He was lured there by a bogus call about the room conflict."

"Which wasn't common knowledge, but wasn't a secret
either. There really was a disagreement about the room. It had
already been resolved by the time the call was made, but Daryl
would not have known that. I would have thought Daryl would
have been suspicious if he'd been directed to a guest room
though."

"So why did he go there?"

"My guess is that he was met when he arrived by Mr. X,
Miss Y, or an unwitting intermediary, and sent up to the room
where he died on some pretext. Mr. X was waiting for him, tied
him up, and beat him rather savagely. There was a lot more
emotion this time. John and Muriel were executed painlessly,
remember; Daryl's death was an act of rage."

"So Mr X had a passkey for the Driscoll also?"

I shook my head. "Not necessarily. Their security system is
so old you can circumvent it with an electronic master key. Or he
could have stolen one from one of the housemaids. They all have
access to extra copies so if one disappeared, it could be replaced
without anyone else knowing about it."

"But how would he know the room was empty?"

"He probably noticed that the chambermaid had finished with
that floor. It wouldn't have been too tricky to identify an empty
room – just knock on a door, open it if there was no answer, and
leave quickly if there were any personal possessions."

"And then another message to the police. Why?"

"Whim, maybe. I think Mr. X expects to be caught
eventually. Maybe even wants to be found out. He just wants to

finish the job first. If that's the case,. Daryl might not be the end of the chain."

"But who else could there be? Muriel could have found out about the movie's existence, and then she told John who evaluated its condition for her and probably did the restoration later on, and Daryl was almost certainly the one who actually bought or stole it and who may or may not have killed Wendy Taft in the process."

"There may have been other people involved," I said. "But unfortunately the three people who might have identified them are all dead."

We were both quiet for a while. Dusty finally spoke up. "We still don't know how Taft happened to have a copy, do we?"

"No, but I'm pretty sure her grandmother was the same Adele Leslie who appeared in the movie. For some reason, she must have kept a copy but never told anyone about it. We all know about the legendary *At the Mountain of Madness* but the general public does not. And I suspect that Adele became very religious at some point. Her pastor didn't seem to think much of the acting profession. There are a lot of reasons why she might have kept quiet about its existence, but I don't think it matters." It probably didn't, but that led me to my next thought. I called Bullard.

"I hope you have good news for me because the crime scene people are shaking their heads and muttering under their breath. Not a good sign."

"Not news, no, but a possible lead. Can you call our friend in Michigan again?"

"You're going to break my budget for long distance calls. What did you want to know?"

"I was curious about the terms of Wendy Taft's will."

"I can ask," she said. "But today's Sunday. Court buildings aren't going to be open until tomorrow. Make that Tuesday. Tomorrow is a holiday."

I'd forgotten that. There was nothing I could do about it and I had the feeling that if more drama was going to happen, it would be all over by then. "I don't have anything else to suggest."

"I'll ask Larson to look into it. We've talked to people here and no one saw or heard anything. I can't even find anyone who saw Plimpton arrive."

"Whoever lured him over didn't want to be seen with him. They would have whisked him away as quickly as possible."

"That's how I see it. I'll talk to Larson."

Dusty and I played with our outline for a while, trying to figure out if we could eliminate anyone from our list by positively locating them elsewhere, but we couldn't rule out anyone but each other, and that was assuming that Mr. X didn't have an accomplice. Despite what I had said earlier, I really didn't think that was the case. Well, let's be honest. I really hoped that wasn't the case because the delivery of the champagne bottle to Muriel pretty much eliminated everyone that actually knew her personally who was attending the festival. The only good news was that I was ready to eliminate Romeo as a suspect. He just could not physically have accomplished everything without having been seen by someone. Nor could I figure out any reason why he might be incensed by the recent history of *At the Mountains of Madness*.

Dusty wasn't happy that we hadn't figured everything out and began grasping at straws. "What if someone like Bob Strossi was Mr. X? He could have told Muriel that he ran into the person from room service and offered to bring up the champagne to save them time."

"I don't think they're supposed to do that."

"The Dorrance isn't exactly a top notch hotel. They're shorthanded and they don't pay well. If Mr. X handed them a tip, I'd be surprised if they didn't bend the rules a little. He'd have known their names and room number and would say that he was headed there already."

"Okay, except that we know that no one ordered it from room service, remember?" It would have relied too much on the idiosyncrasies of whoever was delivering it and I didn't believe that Mr. X would have resorted to anything that uncertain..

We sat in silence for a while before Dusty made me feel even more uneasy. "There is one person in the chain who is still alive."

I glanced up quickly. "Who is that?"

"Helen Viele. Didn't she introduce Muriel to Taft in the first place?"

I had completely forgotten that. No, that's not true. I remembered it but I just hadn't taken the mental step of connecting those particular dots. It might mean nothing, but it might mean that Helen was in line to be the next victim. Or, a little voice whispered, she might be the killer. What if she is the heir to the Taft estate and wants to reclaim the rights to *At the Mountains of Madness*? I took out my cell and called her.

It went to voice mail. Apparently she was still out of touch. I glanced at my watch. It was just after four. "Helen's not answering her phone."

"Try her room."

There was no answer there either. Now none of this would have been alarming under ordinary circumstances. Helen rarely spent time in her room at festivals – even at night let alone the middle of the day – and I happened to know that she didn't like cell phones and often kept hers turned off. Normally I wouldn't have given the situation another thought. But the present situation was not even remotely normal.

Bullard snapped at me when she answered this time. "What is it now?"

I ignored her tone and reminded her of Helen's connection to the Taft family. "I can't locate her and there's a chance she might be next on the list."

Still grumpy, Bullard admitted that I might be right. "We haven't been able to track her down or find anyone who has seen her recently. She hasn't checked out and her luggage is still in her room. We're working on it. I left a voicemail for Larson, by the way."

"Thanks. It might be another dead end."

"That's where I spend most of my life."

We bought sandwiches from a street vendor outside the hotel and spent the next hour wandering around the Biltmore looking for Helen Viele, asking a few people who knew her when they had last seen her. One of the dealers whom I knew slightly said she had come past his table at mid-morning with a heavy set man he didn't recognize. "He had a name tag but it was flipped around on the lanyard so that I couldn't see it."

Romeo was sitting on one of the couches on the mezzanine and he looked awful. His face was red and his hair was damp with sweat. "I'll be okay. I just overdid it a little. I guess I'm going to have to do something about this extra weight I've been carrying. It didn't bother me so much when I was younger, but now running up a staircase is like a marathon. I should know better."

He hadn't seen Helen at all that day, but when I expressed mild concern, he shrugged it off. "You know as well as I do that Helen doesn't come to these things for the movies. They're just the excuse. She comes to meet guys she never has to worry might call her back and get serious."

"Nothing wrong with that," said Dusty.

"Hell, no. I envy her. I was never that self confident, even when I was young enough that I might have found willing partners." He chuckled. "I was never Cary Grant, even when I was young and skinny, but I wasn't Arnold Stang either. I was even engaged once."

"What happened?" I asked.

"We both came to our senses."

My cell buzzed right about then and it was Bullard. "I talked to Larson and it turns out his cousin is a lawyer in Frampton, which is part of the reason he was so interested in the Taft case."

"Did his cousin handle the probate?"

"No, but he knew quite a bit about it. Wendy Taft died intestate so another lawyer named Woodruff was assigned to handle it by the court. They apparently tracked someone down who came out to Frampton and sold off the property. Neither Larson nor his cousin knows who it was and Woodruff is currently on a river cruise in Europe."

"Does he at least know whether it was a man or a woman?"

"Nope. He's going to ask around but I think we're out of luck until Woodruff gets back."

"Have you located Helen Viele yet?"

"Not yet, but there are a lot of places she could be and a lot of them are places we can't really look into, like hotel rooms. I gather Ms. Viele is, shall we say, sexually active."

"Enthusiastically so," I admitted.

"We've left messages in various places for her to get in touch with us. Her cell phone was sitting on the desk in her room, incidentally."

I sighed. "She didn't like them. Called them a necessary evil."

"Pretty much all evils are unnecessary, don't you think?"

Dusty and I walked over to the Driscoll, figuring we could be just as useless there as anywhere else. The crowd had grown even more anemic, but that wasn't unusual at this stage of a festival. Many of those attending had a long trip home and since Monday would not have any particularly attractive program items, there was no compelling reason for them to stay another night. More of the dealers would have packed their wares and decamped by now, although others would wait until the very end, determined to squeeze the last dollar out of the stragglers. And every item sold was that much less to be shipped or carried home.

The small information desk for the festival was still there. There were copies of the program but no one was manning the station to answer questions. We poked our heads into the film rooms and the one ongoing panel, but if Helen was in the audience at any of these, she was doing so in disguise. That wasn't as farfetched as it sounded. Although there had been no costume party this year, there had been at some of the previous ones. Helen had come as Barbarella for one and I hadn't recognized her. She had worked for a while for a special effects company in Hollywood and had picked up a few tricks.

I was suddenly and uncomfortably aware of the fact that this skill would have made it possible for her to remain in close proximity of the victims without being recognized. Although I felt guilty about suspecting her, I was also angry at myself for not having considered this possibility earlier. And Helen wasn't the only one who could easily have disguised herself. Ray Riccello was a director, Tanya a retired actress, and Terry Wareham had once worked in costuming for an independent studio that had managed to turn out only two very bad films before folding. Romeo probably had the necessary knowledge as well, but no one had enough to disguise his bulk.

"Where are you?" asked Dusty, and I realized I'd been standing silently for a while.

"Tracking down a train of thought." I explained what I had been thinking, but she looked doubtful.

"I don't see where that helps us. No one, stranger or otherwise, was seen near any of the murders. I suppose whoever delivered the champagne might have been disguised, but why bother? If it was someone Muriel knew, they could have invited themselves in to share the bottle, or made up some other story. Since Muriel wasn't going to be alive much longer, it didn't matter if she knew who was there."

"But Angela would have been. If whoever it was had stayed any longer, Angela would have been able to identify the killer, so it would have been necessary to kill her as well, and she doesn't seem to have any direct connection to Wendy Taft."

Dusty bit her lip. "Okay, I concede the point. It was only luck that Angela was in the bathroom and didn't see the delivery, so yes, it could have been someone they both knew but if so whoever it was probably wore a disguise."

We checked the lounge and the bar and were headed back toward the lobby when Bullard called back. "I heard from Larson again. This case must have really bugged him because he's putting in a lot of his own time. He managed to track down the realtor who handled the sale of the Taft house."

"Can he tell us who got the money?"

"Yes and no. He's actually down in Florida at a convention at the moment. But his next door neighbor had an emergency number to reach him and he gave it to Larson. The realtor can't remember the name but is certain that it was a man. They only met once and he couldn't give us a description other than average this and average that. He says he'll try to get hold of his secretary and have her open the office and go through the files and get the information for us, but there was no answer when he tried a little while ago."

I had a sinking feeling that tomorrow morning might be too late, but at least we were making progress. "Sounds promising, but I hate waiting around."

"He did remember one other thing. The man was Wendy Taft's father."

I thought back to what I knew about the family. "I thought he had disappeared."

"The family split up in 1980. As far as we know, Wendy Taft had no further contact with her father."

"His name wouldn't be Taft. They reverted to the mother's maiden name after the divorce."

"That's right. So we don't know his name or what he looks like or where he's from, and we can't find out until tomorrow at the earliest and maybe not until the day after. And we're not even sure that there's any connection. Anyway, Larson is trying to track down a neighbor who used to be close to the Tafts. She'd be pretty old by now and is probably in a nursing home, if she's still alive."

I wanted to tell Bullard that I didn't think we had that much time, but even if I could convince her, there wasn't much more that she could do. "No sign of Helen Viele yet? I think she may be in danger."

"We don't know for sure that she's next in line, if there is a line."

That wasn't much consolation. "How about John's laptop? Did that ever show up?"

"No, in fact that's a puzzler. This Staines character who worked for him claims that your friend never carried one, just an Iphone or something."

"Then what was he carrying when he checked in, and where did it go?"

Bullard made an unpleasant noise. "No one's answering my questions so why should they answer yours?"

CHAPTER SIXTEEN

It wasn't hard to track down Mickey Palotto. He was in his office, staring at some paperwork with an expression that suggested it was written in ancient Greek. His door was shut so I knocked and his head came up. Mickey wasn't one of the most guarded people in the world so I identified irritation, dislike, and anxiety as they took turns contorting his face. Mickey had been a typical high school bully, though admittedly he sometimes stood his ground when opposed. He'd won more fights than he'd lost, but the paunch visible through his embossed shirt suggested that he would probably win no more.

He gestured for us to come in, making no effort to conceal his displeasure.

"What do you want, Birch? I'm busy."

"Filling out job applications?" I asked.

His eyes narrowed suspiciously. "What do you mean?"

I realized I was giving in to an adolescent urge to tweak the bully and reproached myself. "Nothing. Can we talk a minute?"

"If we have to." Mickey had ignored Dusty but now he turned toward her. "Please take a seat, Miss." So he had acquired at least a few manners since last we'd met.

Dusty didn't budge, however, and we both stood through what would prove to be a very short interview. "If someone on the staff lost their passkey, would they report it?" I asked.

For a second I didn't think he was going to answer. I had no real authority, after all. But he resolved some hidden internal struggle and shrugged. "Sometimes they do, sometimes they don't. I tried to tighten up the system but Jameson – she's the head of housekeeping – pitched a hissy fit about wasting time and how shorthanded she was already and Drake told me to wait for a better time." He snorted an ugly laugh. "That's Drake's solution to every disagreement. Wait for a better time. Only there never is a better time."

"Is there anyone working here who might have it in for you? The cell phone had to have been embarrassing." His mouth tightened and I quickly added, "it was obviously planted in your office."

He sat back in his chair, which creaked alarmingly. "Pretty much everyone resents me except for my guys. I treat them good and they know it. But no one here has any sense of discipline or order and they all hate changing the way they do things, even when it's obviously going to fix   a problem. So yeah, I have some enemies here – the head of maintenance, the facilities manager, the lazy ass clerks on the front desk, and even a couple of the bellhops. Doesn't bother me at all. I'm not here to be liked. But the cell phone thing – that's no skin off my nose. Sure I was pissed that someone made me look silly, but it wasn't the first time. I'll get over it, and if I find out who it was, I'll get even."

For just a second, I saw a fifteen year old boy looking out through Palotto's eyes. "Has anything unusual been going on in the hotel recently, say, in the last month or so?"

"We had some cash disappear from a couple of rooms. It was one of the room cleaners, but we couldn't prove it. Just told her not to come in no more."

"No new personnel?"

He shook his head. "Not for a long time. Jobs are scarce, in case you hadn't noticed."

This was turning out to be even less productive than I had expected. I was about to thank him and leave when Dusty came up with a question. "Has anyone been acting out of character lately?"

His eyes turned toward her and there was a short silence. "Yeah, as a matter of fact. Drake, the manager, has been taking a lot of time off. It started more than a year ago. There was a death in the family somewhere out west and she took ten days of vacation, and just about a year ago she took a few days for personal reasons. She's been an even bigger pain in the ass since then than she was before, always looking for something to criticize. We don't have enough security cameras but she gets bent out of shape if the shift leaders forget to sign the log when they go off duty." He leaned forward and lowered his voice. "And one of the guys told me he heard her sobbing in her office a couple of weeks back. I think she's cracking up."

I didn't think we'd learned anything useful from Palotto and while I planned to mention Drake to Bullard next time we talked,

I was in no hurry to do so. I felt that I was floundering about in a morass. With the exception of Romeo, all of the people on our list were still suspects, which meant effectively that I had no suspects. I started playing with combinations – Mr. X and Miss Y – and that didn't help at all. If there was a partnership, one half of it almost certainly had to be someone outside the group, and in that scenario, why hadn't the conspirators bothered to provide an alibi for the partner who was known to the police? Or was it someone we had neglected to put on the list right from the start? There were several somewhat familiar faces attending and I could even attach first names to a couple of them, but none had ever been part of what I thought of as the inner circle, the people who had been around for a long time and who generally associated with one another at festivals.

"Do you want to check with Sasha and find out if Helen has turned up?"

I glanced at Dusty and shook my head. "She'd have called, or would have had Helen call us. I think I want to revisit the murder scenes."

"We can't get inside the rooms without keys."

"I don't need to get inside."

We didn't have any trouble catching an elevator at the Driscoll this time. Neither of us spoke as we walked down the corridor, pausing just outside the room where John had died. I waited for inspiration, but it must have been detained elsewhere. "Let's go down the stairs," I said.

There wasn't much changed since the last time I'd been here. There was a delivery van parked just outside the door at ground level and two hefty men were unloading boxes and carrying them toward the loading ramp. Dusty started to open the door but I waved back toward the interior and we followed the corridor past a couple of offices and a pair of restrooms before reaching the lobby.

"This is a waste of time," I said. "Let's go back to the room and sit for awhile. Maybe something will come to me." There was a stirring in the recesses of my mind that I recognized. Sometimes the clues to the solution of a puzzle begin to assemble themselves in my subconscious. Concentrating on them too hard is counterproductive because the elusive connections are still too fragile. If I concentrate too hard, the pattern breaks up. If I leave things to ferment, sometimes inspiration hits me. And sometimes, of course, I'm just fooling myself when I think the answer is within my grasp.

But I had the sudden feeling that I was making things more complex than they really needed to be. The scenarios Dusty and I had constructed fit the facts but they were too elaborate.

We were in the elevator when Bullard called, unfortunately not to tell us that Helen Viele had turned up. "We think we've found the missing passkey from the Biltmore."

"Where was it?"

"It was partway down Plimpton's throat. Someone really didn't like this guy. Anyway, that tells us something."

"The killer doesn't need it anymore," I said.

"Right. And that probably means that he's finished everything that he intended to do."

It was a fair assumption and if true it meant Bullard might have been dealt all the cards she was going to get. "But you still haven't found Helen Viele."

"No, but I have no reason to believe that she's not just shacked up with someone, or over in the mall buying a new wardrobe."

"You don't have the name of Taft's father yet."

"No, and it might be a couple of days before I do. By then he could have flown to Tibet, if it is the father we're looking for." Bullard sounded discouraged.

"I can't think of any other motive."

"That doesn't mean there isn't one. What if the Taft business is just a red herring? What if someone had it in for Plimpton, knew something about the circumstances of his great discovery, and decided to make it look as though that was the motive. The other two deaths might just have been camouflage. Plimpton died hard; the other two never knew what hit them. I think that's important."

This possibility had occurred to me too, but since it didn't lead to any promising lines of inquiry, I had set my doubts aside. Which might be exactly what the killer wanted. It would be as easy to underestimate him as the opposite. And if Daryl was the only real target, then the possibilities multiplied. There were a lot of people who didn't like him, and some of them had pretty good reasons for it. I couldn't think of any off hand that might have justified murder, but then again, most murderers are looking at things from a different angle than the rest of us. And I knew little or nothing about Daryl's private life. He might have had legions of mortal enemies including neighbors, relatives, ex-lovers, business associates, and guys he bumped into in his local bar.

"Daryl wasn't a popular guy," I said.

"So I gathered. If I had had to deal with him regularly, I might have shot him myself." She sighed. "We're going to have to dig into his background with a backhoe. That's going to take time. The others too. Even the sister doesn't know much about what Bates might have been involved in before she moved in with her."

I felt a flash of guilt, as though it was somehow my fault, and wished her luck.

As we entered the Biltmore lobby, I felt a wave of fatigue that was mental and emotional rather than physical. I had lost three friends – no, two friends and an acquaintance – within the past three days and another was missing. I had been tricked into finding John's body and the festival – which I had hoped to enjoy – was ruined for this year at least and possibly for years to come. I had no reason to believe that Dusty or I was in any physical danger, but there was always the chance that Mr. X would take umbrage at our efforts to help the police. I would have tried to send Dusty home if I'd thought that there was any chance in the world that she'd go without me, but there wasn't.

All I wanted to do at that moment was to lie back on the bed in our room – with the door securely chained – and close my eyes for a while. Maybe things would settle into a more useful pattern.

So naturally someone called our names before we were halfway to the elevators.

It was Ray Ricello. He and Tanya were standing near the desk, surrounded by their luggage. Martin, the bellhop, was loading it onto a cart. They were obviously checking out. Suppressing a sigh that was more like a groan, we turned to join them. "Are you leaving us?"

Ray nodded. "I think it's time to get out of town. They're dropping like flies."

"I'm surprised you're not taking notes," said Dusty. "This would make a nifty little movie, don't you think?"

For a moment Ray seemed to be seriously considering it. "Nah. Maybe a television episode but there's not enough action for a movie. Now if someone had been killed by a bomb or disemboweled and thrown out a window..."

Dusty and Tanya both looked mildly shocked. "These were friends of ours," I said in a tight voice.

Ray bobbed his head. "Yeah, sorry. No disrespect intended. Directors tend to take an abstract, distanced view."

"We're not leaving because of the murders," explained Tanya. "But the money people put us on a tight schedule and we have to put together a cast and a production team right away. We're going to be filming in Hawaii."

"What's the title?"

"Haven't decided yet. Just pitched a concept and they liked it."

Ray was looking pleased with himself, so I decided to deflate him a little. "Direct to video, I assume."

His face didn't exactly fall, but it teetered. "That's the wave of the future. The big studios will always dominate the theaters and make the big splashes, but those of us down in the trenches are going to produce the classics that last for generations."

I refrained from mentioning that *Return to Dragstrip Hollow* was unlikely to be numbered among the classic films of the century.

Martin had finished loading and was standing patiently, waiting for a chance to break in. "Should I take these to the garage or do you need a taxi, sir?"

"We need the airport shuttle. Our flight is at eight."

I glanced at my watch as Martin wheeled the cart out through the front door. "Well, have a pleasant flight. Maybe we'll see you next year." I turned to Tanya. "And we might see you on the screen even sooner."

A taxi pulled up to the curb and Martin and the driver started loading the luggage. We shook hands all around – neither Dusty nor Tanya was much of a hugger, at least not in public. As they walked out, I had a sudden flash of memory. Tanya had said something about having a cousin who had sold some memorabilia to John and felt that she'd been cheated. The details didn't match, but for a moment I wondered if Wendy Taft might have had more than one cousin.

A new scenario began assembling itself in my mind. Tanya knew the hotel business and might have been able to figure out how to steal a couple of passkeys. She would certainly know a great deal about the behind the scenes activities of the staff. Both of them were familiar with makeup and costuming and either could have donned a convincing disguise. Although neither had provided a strong alibi for the other, it had not been necessary and they would have had no difficulty anticipating the plans of both Muriel and John. Ray had never liked Daryl and had made no effort to hide it, but now that I thought about it, I couldn't remember any specific incident that could have given rise to his animosity.

"I don't think they killed anyone," said Dusty, and I was rudely pulled out of my thoughts.

"I never said they did."

"But you were thinking about it. I could tell by the way you stared at them."

"It was just a mental exercise." I paused. "But why are you sure they didn't?"

"Ray might do it, if he thought it would give a boost to his career or his reputation. His only goal in life is to be known as a movie director. I think he'd even give up Tanya if he had to. Ray is so caught up in himself that he doesn't really have room for other people. He would never risk it all to exact revenge for someone he hardly knew and I can't think of any other reason why he'd kill John or Muriel. Hell, he wouldn't do it to avenge Tanya."

I had to concede the point. "What about Tanya?"

"I thought about her. She's a smart cookie. She and Helen are a lot alike except that Helen likes variety and Tanya prefers consistency."

"She doesn't set her standards very high."

"Neither of them do. But I'd bet the rent that she's no more emotionally attached to Ray than Helen is to the last six guys she slept with."

"You don't pay any rent," I pointed out.

"That's why it's a safe bet."

And finally we made our way up to our room.

CHAPTER SEVENTEEN

Finally back in our room, I realized that my mood had changed. It took a conscious effort to avoid pacing the room and when I lay down on the bed, I found that I couldn't relax and almost immediately got back up. Dusty was restless as well and announced that she was going for a walk to clear her head. I sat at the desk, turning over the pages of notes we had made, convinced that the solution was there some place, if I only had the wits to find it. I was still troubled by a few details that seemed wrong. We had figured out ways in which the killer could have carried his equipment to and from John's room, but they all seemed risky to me. There were also a couple of different ways he could have found out what room John was in and when he was arriving, but they also struck me as chancy. The person we were looking for was more precise than that, more prepared. He – or she I reminded myself – must have studied both the Driscoll and the Biltmore thoroughly in advance, and that involved the risk that they might be remembered. Could they have used a disguise? If there were two of them working together, could they have split the task to minimize the risk? It occurred to me that Bullard could find out if any of our suspects had traveled to Providence or Boston over the course of the past several months. But that presupposed that the killer was someone on our list.

If the person we were after was not a member of our group, then how had the relationships among Muriel, John, and Daryl been identified? There had been very little contact among them during the year or so since the death of Wendy Taft, and none of it could have been easily observed. If this was some avenger from Frampton – her mysterious father perhaps – then how had he been able to choose his targets so accurately? The only person I could think of who fit the bill was Helen Viele, obviously not Taft's father, but she could have been working with him. Dusty and I had decided early on that there was a strong possibility that two people were involved.

I read through the chronology again, slowly, examining each element and just when I began to think I was wasting my time, one piece fell into place and I remembered a conversation or two that had not seemed important at the time. Finally one jagged piece fit with the next, and a more elegant solution began to emerge. Hastily I drew a vertical line down each page and began filling in a new scenario parallel to the old one. Everything fit, and with surprising ease once I had begun. It all seemed so simple now.

I knew who our killer was. I was positive. There were still a few things that I didn't know, but none of it was crucial. I picked up my cell phone to call Bullard but before I could touch the keypad, it lit up to announce an incoming call. I didn't recognize the number but it was local.

"Yes," I answered somewhat curtly, figuring it was either a robocall or a solicitation.

"I hope I haven't caught you at a bad time." I recognized the voice. It was the person whose name I was about to provide to Bullard.

"No, it's fine."

"You know who this is, don't you?"

"Yes, I do."

"And you know what I've done." It was a statement, not a question.

"I'm not sure that I know what you mean."

The sigh was audible. "I'm rather surprised that you didn't figure it out sooner, but I suppose I should be grateful because if you had done so, I wouldn't have been able to finish. I chose you to find the first body because I wanted to be sure you were involved. I couldn't make it too easy, of course, because Plimpton had to die before you caught on. But there's only one name left on my list and I'd rather like it if you would humor me and be my witness."

I tried to pretend ignorance again but was cut off. "Come now, I've just confessed to killing three people. I know you're not that dense."

"All right. What do you want?"

"I want you to come visit me. There is someone with me, a friend of yours, and she is unharmed so far. I want to explain to you why all of this was necessary. No police, of course. They would insist on making some kind of rescue attempt and we can't

204

have that. You aren't one of the guilty ones and I have no wish to harm you in any way. I assure you that you'll be perfectly safe unless you try to interfere."

"What about the person with you?"

"I haven't decided yet. Why don't you come and try to influence me? I promise I have an open mind on the subject."

There was no choice, of course. Helen's life was at stake. "All right. Where are you?"

"Excellent. But first there are some ground rules. You will not terminate this call until you arrive. I don't want you to call the police. You will take the elevator down to the lobby and leave the Biltmore. I'll give you further instructions as you go so that you can't write a note or anything troublesome like that. And in any case, someone will be watching you from the lobby onward."

I stood up. "I'm leaving now."

"Very good. I promise you an entertaining evening and the answers to your questions."

There was no one in the corridor and the elevator arrived empty. When we reached the lobby, I instinctively glanced around. I doubted very much that there was really someone watching but I couldn't be certain. There were about a dozen people in sight but none of them seemed to be paying any attention to me.

The night had turned cooler than usual. I stood in front of the Biltmore with the phone at my ear. "Now where?"

"Come over to the Driscoll."

I had expected that answer and set off promptly. I hadn't seen anyone I knew since leaving the room and in any case had no idea how I could communicate with someone without tipping off the killer. I was actually less nervous than I should have been. I believed the statement that I was not a target, but I didn't understand why I had been summoned. But Helen was a friend and if I could possibly save her, I needed to try.

"I'm in front of the Driscoll."

"Come up to room 701. You've been very good so far. Please don't spoil things."

Once again the elevator was empty. No one had followed me from the Biltmore so I was confident that I was dealing with a lone wolf, despite the suggestion that there was an accomplice.

I knocked on the door of room 701 and it was opened almost immediately. A handgun was pointed directly at my face. "Hello, Martin," I said as calmly as I could manage.

"Come in, Mr. Birch. I have a great deal to tell you."

It was a room like any other, except that most of them didn't come equipped with bound and gagged hostages. Helen Viele lay on the far bed. She appeared to be undamaged and, based on what I could see of her face, really pissed off. Her eyes flickered back and forth between Martin the bellhop and myself.

"Sit down, please. Make yourself comfortable. I have a lot to tell you."

"You were Wendy Taft's father, weren't you?" I remained standing. "You've been dropping hints all along. You told me that your wife and daughter had left you and that they were both dead." It was all unraveling in my mind by now. "You even told me that you had worked at the Biltmore for a while, just long enough to know how things worked there and how to get around the safeguards."

"The answer is yes to both your questions. I was indeed Wendy's father. Not a very good one, I confess. There were reasons for that, inadequate ones I admit. We'll get to that. And it did amuse me to provide some hints. It may surprise you to know that I have a sense of fair play. However unlikely, you might have figured it out before I had accomplished everything I intended. I cheated of course by telling you things before they were significant. This is the last important thing I will have done in my life and it felt as though it required a certain level of style. I'll answer your questions truthfully, but first I must insist that you sit down and turn your chair toward the wall. I don't want you to feel a sudden rush of heroics and spring from your seat to wrestle me to the ground. My wrestling days are long since over and I might accidentally shoot you in the scuffle. That would be very unfortunate."

I did what he asked. I couldn't think of a viable alternative.

"That's much better." Martin retreated to the other chair and sat facing me. His weapon was still pointed in my direction, but less aggressively. "I have a long story to tell. It starts back before any of us were born, during the 1930s."

"*At the Mountains of Madness*," I said.

"A group of young people decided to make a movie. They didn't have much money but one of them – Joseph Bigelow – was a wizard with special effects. In those days it was mostly modeling and odd perspectives and other camera tricks, but he knew them all and had a few new ones of his own. Adele Stern was the only woman among them, a rather plain girl who had escaped from her fanatically religious family to run off to Hollywood and become a film star. Unfortunately, she only made it as far as Michigan. I don't know how she met the others, but it's really not important. They made the film on a shoestring budget but the war came before they could find someone to promote it and the three male leads were all killed rather tragically if not heroically. Adele, who had been feeling increasingly guilty about her religious lapse, decided that this was a divine punishment. I suspect that one of them was her lover but I don't know which she chose. Her family would not take her back so she moved to the Upper Peninsula, taking with her the only surviving copy of the film, perhaps as a way of reminding herself of her iniquitous ways."

Despite the situation, my latent enthusiasm for film history was stirring.

"Adele married Arthur Taft in 1946. Arthur had lost both legs in France and I suspect that Adele considered the act of caring for him as a kind of penance. I imagine she must have thought about destroying the film more than once, but for whatever reason, she did not. They had a daughter, Mary, who was born in 1947. Like her mother, Mary began to chafe at the restrictions of the church she was forced to attend and left home when she was eighteen. She moved to Providence and found a job as a waitress. There she met Martin Gimbal, yours truly, who was at that time the most junior bellhop at the Driscoll Hotel. Martin was single and poor and had no kitchen facilities where he rented a room, so he spent a lot of time eating in the cheap diner where Mary worked. One day he summoned the courage to ask her out, and she was lonely and unhappy and said yes. Neither of them had ever been on a date before and neither had any real experience with hard liquor. Martin thought it incumbent upon him to pay for several drinks and Mary felt similarly about the need to consume them. The short version of this is that two virgins spent an evening fumbling together in Martin's bed and both were mortified in the morning."

Martin uncrossed and recrossed his legs. I was watching the hand that held the handgun. It didn't move.

"That might have been that, except that Mary turned out to be pregnant. Both parties felt compelled to legitimize the child and they were married, although Mary stayed in her own rooms and Martin kept to his. This rather bizarre arrangement persisted for twelve years, by which time Martin was making enough money to move to an actual apartment, one large enough to also accommodate a wife and a soon to be teenaged daughter. He proposed this alteration in their circumstances to Mary who reacted in a quite unexpected fashion. Like her mother, she had been unable to permanently suppress the urge to lose herself in religious ecstasy. She was simultaneously convinced that Martin had been a temptation sent by the devil to seduce her and that she had sinned irreparably by giving in to the sins of the flesh. Happily, she did not blame Wendy for any of this. But the offer to further legitimize what she wore as a sinful badge of dishonor had pushed her over the edge. She filed for divorce, claiming abandonment since we had not lived together for the decade of our marriage, and Martin, stunned and bewildered, did not contest it. Their union was dissolved. Shortly after that, mother and daughter pulled up stakes and returned to the family home where Adele still held sway. "

He looked away for a second, his face showing pain. "I could have gone to court and fought the move, I suppose, since I had been awarded visitation rights. But I really couldn't afford a lawyer and as it turned out, couldn't really afford to travel out to Michigan to visit. I saved for a while with that purpose in mind – I was very fond of my daughter – but as time passed the need grew less urgent. Mary embargoed my letters and refused to allow Wendy to write to me – I was a wicked seducer after all – and an adolescent girl has more pressing things to worry about than a distant dad who never lived with them in the first place. It just became easier to let things be. I didn't even know that Adele and Mary had died until the lawyer wrote me about Wendy's death."

I didn't interrupt. As long as he was talking, Martin wasn't shooting anyone. Out of the corner of my eye I could see that Helen was straining to loosen the ropes around her wrists. Even if she got them free, she was so hobbled that she wasn't likely to be able to do much to help our situation, but she might distract Martin long enough that I could wrestle the gun away.

He had been silent for almost a full minute, but he picked up the narrative. "My belated trip to Michigan finally happened. The verdict had been accidental death and I accepted that at first. It didn't take long to go through the contents of the house. Adele and Mary both believed that worldly possessions were a drag on the soul, so they kept only what was necessary to their survival. None of it was valuable and I donated almost everything to the Salvation Army. There was no copy of the lost movie, needless to say, no film memorabilia at all. I did know that Adele had once appeared in a movie that had never been released; Mary mentioned it on one of the rare days when we were trying almost successfully to be a family. I put the house up for sale and the only things I took away with me were some photographs and my daughter's diaries."

Something must have shown in my face because Martin nodded. "That's right. She kept detailed diaries from the time she was ten up until the day of her death. I didn't read them right away, and not all at once. I brought them back to Rhode Island and went through them slowly and carefully, trying to gain some secondhand experience of a life I should have participated in. Most of it was trivial, but I relished every word. It was a bittersweet experience, up until the very last volume. Then it just became horrifying."

"Wendy hadn't quite reached the point of rebellion that had gripped her mother and grandmother. She was drifting away from the church but hadn't formally made the break. She was shy like her mother and not fond of confrontation, and rather wary of the outside world. I think that if she'd lived longer, she might have moved away, but then I suppose the embedded guilt would have brought her back just like it did with Mary and Adele. We'll never know. She didn't really start mentioning the attractions of the outside world in her diary until the trip to Chicago where she met Muriel Bates." He glanced toward Helen briefly. "She thought her cousin Helen was basically nice but rather outspoken. She considered Muriel a kindred soul. They talked for a long time about a lot of things. Wendy knew about her grandmother's aborted acting career, but she had never seen the film, didn't even know the title, although she did know that it was on a shelf in the hall closet. When Muriel mentioned her fondness for movies, it was only natural that she'd tell as much of the story as she knew. Muriel was quite interested and Wendy invited her to come visit at the time, although she thought it would never happen. People tend to make grandiose plans like that without every really expecting to follow through."

"That might have been the end of it, except that Muriel was persistent. She wrote Wendy a letter and asked her for the title of the film. Wendy didn't really know but the canister was labeled 'mountains madness' and she wrote back with that information. Muriel wrote again and said that she thought the movie might be valuable, but that was just after Adele and Mary died and Wendy didn't answer until another letter arrived a few weeks later. She was depressed and worried about finances – Adele's social security and her mother's small pension had both stopped – so she put Muriel off. The whole subject disappears from the diary for several months, then there's mention that Muriel had written again. She and a friend were going to be in the area and wondered if they could stop by and visit. There seems to have been no mention of the movie this time, but of course that's what they were really interested in."

"It was one of the Holy Grails of film fans," I explained. "I'm surprised Muriel waited as long as she did."

Martin nodded. "Unfortunately, your friends were in for an unpleasant surprise. The strain of religious mania had asserted itself. Wendy somehow decided that the deaths of Mary and Adele were a punishment because she had strayed from the faith. She had started attending church again – although there was a new pastor who wasn't quite so fire and brimstone as the one she'd remembered, and she found him disappointing. In any case, she couldn't think of a way to dissuade your friends from visiting, and she had liked Muriel. They talked her into letting them see the canister, but there was no projector in the house. The man, Boncoddo, had brought some kind of hand held device that allowed him to examine individual frames and he did so, although Wendy was apparently already beginning to regret having mentioned the existence of the print. She had decided to honor her grandmother's determination that the film never be shown again. She told them so quite clearly even after they mentioned that it might be quite valuable. Apparently Boncoddo began shouting at her and she had to threaten to call the police before he could be convinced to leave."

"They stayed for almost a week," I said.

"Wendy wrote that they called her several times and even showed up on the doorstep once. She wouldn't let them inside. Eventually they went away and Wendy thought it was over with. If it had ended there, the three of us wouldn't be together in this room today. But it didn't end. One or both of them mentioned it to Daryl Plimpton."

"He went out to try his luck."

"He claimed to be representing the estate of Lester Grant, one of the actors. He had a paper that said that Grant was the rightful owner of any and all copies of a movie called *At the Mountains of Madness*. Grant was the chief investor, I understand, so there might even have been some validity to the claim. But Wendy thought the paperwork looked odd."

"Probably forged," I ventured. "Grant had no relatives and left no will. There is no estate."

Martin nodded. "He came to the house twice. The second time she threatened to call the police again. She was very upset when she wrote that entry in her diary, and it was the last entry she ever made. Two weeks later they found her body at the foot of the basement stairs. When I arrived, there was no film canister and it looked to me as though the house had been searched. I kept watch on the internet, but months went by before it turned up."

"Daryl debuted it in Los Angeles," I said quietly.

"Yes. I had decided by then that my daughter did not die accidentally. Someone crushed her skull and threw her down those steps in order to steal the only thing she had of value."

"It might have been an accident. Daryl could have found her dead and might have taken advantage of the opportunity to steal the film."

Martin shook his head. "No. I asked him all about it after I was sure that he was going to tell me the truth. I suppose in a way it was an accident. She was outside when he arrived and she ordered him off the property. He lost his temper and when she started pushing him toward his car, he hit her with the back of his hand. Wendy was a tiny girl, just like her mother. She fell back and hit her head on a stone in the garden. So he carried her inside and staged the accident, then took the canister and made a thorough search for anything else related to the movie. There was nothing except a handful of black and white photographs."

I didn't see anything in this version of events that would contradict my understanding of Daryl's personality. I had never seen him being physically abusive, of course, but that doesn't mean he was incapable of it. "Okay, you had a valid grudge against Daryl. But why John and Muriel? They weren't even in Michigan when your daughter died."

"They had to have known that Wendy wouldn't voluntarily give him the film. They were accessories before and after the fact. If they hadn't told him about her, then he would never have gone to see her and she'd still be alive. When he revealed that he had the film, they must have known that something was wrong and it would not have been hard to find out that Wendy was dead and how she'd died." His voice rose slightly and I could see the tension in his body.

I glanced toward the bed. "What about Helen? She had nothing to do with any of this."

There was a flicker of emotion on his face, gone before I could interpret it. "She started the whole thing by introducing Muriel to Wendy. But we'll go into her part of the story later if you don't mind. I need to finish my preamble. My first inclination was to track down Plimpton and kill him, then pursue the others. I had some money from the sale of the house in Michigan so I could travel and I knew whereabouts he lived. I'd be out of my comfort zone, however, and if I got caught, I'd never be able to track down the other two. I had also been experiencing some health issues. I was struggling with this problem and doing research on all three of them when I discovered that fate was on my side."

"The festival was in Providence this year."

"Exactly! And some of the guests would be at the Driscoll. I started skimming through the reservation lists when they were thrown out, looking for those three names. It was too much to hope for that all three would book rooms in the Driscoll, of course, but Boncoddo is an unusual name and it practically leaped off the printout. That's when I started making plans. This is the point where you have to help a little because I'm curious about how much you were able to figure out. I must admit this has been rather more exciting than anything else in my life. You did say that you already knew I was responsible."

"I figured it out just before you called. I should have realized the truth a lot sooner."

"Surely not? I thought I'd confused the issue quite effectively."

I knew that the longer this conversation lasted, the better the chances that Helen and I would come out of it alive. I settled back in the chair. "There were several ways that someone could have learned that John was staying here. That didn't point in any direction so even when you mentioned the discarded reservation lists, I didn't think it was significant. Discovering which room he was in was somewhat more of a puzzle."

"The simplest answer is sometimes the right one. I occasionally spell people on the night shift. Mona likes to go out for a smoke and I watch the desk for her. I looked up the reservations to find out what room he was in."

"But you moved him?"

He raised an eyebrow. "You noticed that? I'm impressed. Mona came back early and I needed an excuse for having the database open. I told her that Boncoddo had called and requested a room near a stairwell. She actually made the change. Go on."

"Next we considered your paraphernalia. Why the overkill, incidentally? Was it just to confuse the police?"

"Pretty much, but it was a touch of irony as well. I found Boncoddo's review of the movie *Clue*, which he liked immensely. I think he would have appreciated the humor of it if he had been around to watch."

"We figured you had to have been carrying a bag or something, but when you went up with John, you would only have been carrying his luggage. So I'm guessing it was already stashed inside the room."

"Very good. Yes, a bellhop carrying a bag upstairs is almost invisible in a hotel. I even drew the bath water and sprinkled it with salt ahead of time. Then I went downstairs and waited. I'd seen his picture online so it wasn't hard to pick him out and since I'm senior bellhop, I get to choose which guests I handle. So what did I do next?"

"You brought him upstairs, knocked him unconscious, drowned him in the bathtub, which you then drained, and distributed the other misleading items around the room. Oh, and you unpacked some of his clothing and put it in a drawer so we'd think you had left before the attack happened. It was very imperceptive of me not to wonder why John would have taken socks and underwear out of his bag without first hanging up his clean shirts, which were right on top."

"I didn't want to be absent from my post for too long. I had underestimated how long everything would take."

"Then you packed up your paraphernalia in your bag and went back to work. Did you stow it temporarily in an empty room?"

Martin shook his head. "Too risky. We were booked solid. I brought it down to the check room and retrieved it later. I told Darlene that it was for an imaginary guest who had checked out and wanted to do some shopping before leaving the city. I took it home with me later."

"You purloined a master pass key, of course."

"Not necessary. As senior bellman, I have one issued to me." He tapped his pocket. "Miss Drake has forgotten that I have one and I don't remind her."

"What happened to John's laptop?"

"He never had one. I made that up on the spur of the moment. Bad decision that, but I was speaking before I realized what I was going to say. I should have stuck to my plan. Fortunately it didn't matter."

"And the cell phone? Why was it planted in the security office?"

DEATH IN BLACK AND WHITE

"More distraction and frankly Palotto is an officious little prig. I was delighted at the opportunity to cause him some discomfort."

"I was a bit surprised when you seemed so uncertain about whether or not his office was normally locked."

Martin nodded. "I hadn't expected that question so I didn't have a prepared answer. I don't suppose it would have mattered either way."

"John wasn't a bad guy. He didn't deserve to die."

"Neither did my daughter." Martin seemed to gather himself together. "So, what did you figure out about my second foray into capital crime?"

My temper was fraying but I reminded myself that it was important to prolong this conversation for as long as possible. "It wouldn't have been hard to find out what room Muriel and her sister were sharing."

"No. That was a bit of a problem though. I had no idea in advance that her sister was coming with her and it was just luck that I heard them talking when I went over to the Biltmore."

"You said you worked there for a while."

"Yes, and I knew just where to find a uniform and an unguarded service cart. The champagne was in an overnight bag. I had to move quickly because I was afraid someone there might remember me, but it wasn't as hard as it sounds. I stole a master pass card a week ago and left a blank one in its place so no one would realize it was gone. The maintenance people have extras for emergencies. I knew neither of the sisters would recognize me so that wasn't a problem, and I didn't put on the uniform until the last minute. My regular clothes went into the overnight bag, which I stashed in a supply closet."

"You opened the champagne and managed to slip in something to knock them out. Why didn't you just shoot Muriel then?"

"The sister, of course. She hadn't done anything wrong. Delivery people are pretty much invisible so I wasn't worried that she'd be able to recognize me, but she certainly would have noticed if I'd killed her sister. And she would have raised an alarm. I needed time to return the cart, change back into ordinary clothing, and get out of the building. It would have been easier if

I'd known she'd be in the shower where she couldn't see me. But even if I'd had my gun with me, shooting her then would have been too risky."

"So you waited until they were unconscious and then went back."

"The rest was almost too easy. I started to get nervous because everything had gone according to my script. It was the planning, of course. I had tried to think through every possible contingency. But something might have gone wrong. Someone who knew I didn't work there might have spotted me before I could change clothes. You can't anticipate everything that might happen."

"Wasn't it pretty cold blooded, shooting Muriel while her sister lay unconscious in the next bed?"

"Yes it was. I took no joy in it but I felt a paternal duty. I regret any distress I caused the young lady."

I suppressed a temptation to be sarcastic. I wanted Martin to remain sociable and talkative. "So how did you get to Daryl? I know it had something to do with a supposed programming overrun." I actually had a pretty good idea, but I wanted him to keep talking.

"It wasn't difficult. I simply told Patty Burgess that someone had mentioned the program in the Sturgeon room was running more than an hour behind schedule. She placed the call to Plimpton while I was talking to the projectionist, who rightly insisted that he had kept to the timetable. I reported back to Patty that it had been a misunderstanding. Then I went down to the lobby and waited for Plimpton to arrive. I told him that Miss Burgess was using one of the guest rooms while her office was being repainted and took him upstairs to the empty room I'd prepared for him."

For a second or two, Martin looked unhappy. "Our subsequent interview was unpleasant. I held him at gunpoint and threatened to kill him unless he admitted the truth. I'm afraid he didn't hold out for very long. Then I told him that I was going to tie him up while I went for the police, which wasn't a very plausible lie, but he was in no condition to think logically by then. Once he was tied up, I'm afraid all of the anger and grief that I'd been feeling became quite overwhelming. I had planned a simple execution like the others, but I'm afraid I got rather carried away. I regret the loss of control, but he deserved what he endured. And even if he had been convicted of his crime, he would not have been imprisoned for long for involuntary manslaughter."

He leaned forward and raised his weapon. "And that brings us to now. The furious young lady over there is the final link in the chain. I'm afraid I took your name in vain. I told her that you had sent me to look for her and that you were waiting in this room. I'm afraid I told a bit of a fib about you and I being old acquaintances to help put her at ease. And no one ever suspects the bellhop; we're more invisible than butlers. I'm rather sorry about the bump on the back of her head but unlike Plimpton, I don't think she would have readily allowed me to tie her up, gun or no gun."

"There's no reason to kill her. She didn't do anything wrong."

"Oh, I quite agree. I considered the possibility at one point, but there was nothing in the diaries about her after the trip to Chicago. No, her purpose here was insurance. I was determined that you would be the one to whom I told my story, not the vulgar Detective Bullard. She would not have appreciated it. But I couldn't count upon you to come unless there was a strong reason why you should put yourself at risk. I confess that I considered abducting your young lady friend, but she seems very nice and I wouldn't have wanted to hurt her even incidentally."

"All right. I'm here and I've heard your story. What's next? They'll catch you eventually, you know. Bullard is smart and relentless."

Martin's face turned grim and he stood up. I tensed myself, wondering if I could throw myself sideways over the arm of the chair and grab his arm before he shot me more than four or five times.

"The game is over now. Would you please get up, very slowly if you will, and go over to stand by Miss Viele?"

I did as I was told, half expecting to be shot along the way. Martin shifted position so that he could cover us both. "Now untie her."

I removed the gag first. Helen gave me an intense, unfathomable look as she took a deep breath, but she didn't say anything. The knots around her wrists were tight and it took a bit of work to loosen them. The ankles were considerably easier. She sat up, massaging her wrists, and glared, but remained silent.

"I imagine it will take a minute or two before you can stand. Please take your time."

Defiantly, Helen swung her legs over the side of the bed and stood upright. She swayed a bit and I put a hand on her arm to steady her.

"That's it then," said Martin. "Have a nice day."

Helen and I both gaped at him, completely at a loss for words. He laughed, but without humor. "You're free to go. Both of you. I'm sure you're tired of my company by now, and I myself am…just tired."

We didn't wait for a second invitation. I opened the door and followed Helen out into the corridor. Neither of us spoke. We were only halfway to the elevator when we heard the shot from the room we'd just left. No one else seemed to notice. It was quiet after that.

EPILOGUE

At the Mountains of Madness was released about six months later. Dusty picked up a copy but neither of us has watched it yet. Since Daryl apparently acquired the film as the result of a crime, the proceeds are in limbo until and unless another claimant appears. Otherwise, it apparently will go to Helen Viele, Taft's only cousin. Angela Bates and Robert Strossi sent us invitations to their wedding. Romeo Bolduc had a stroke and is in a wheelchair. Ray Riccello is directing *The Horror of Bikini Island*, starring Tanya Gregory, who is the only member of the cast who doesn't have a topless scene. Mickey Palotto was fired after he was caught stealing linens from the Driscoll.

Jimmy Gonsalves opened his theater and hired Terry Wareham as manager. It seems to be doing well. Helen Viele surprised everyone by campaigning for the festival board of trustees and was duly appointed. Jo Parkin won four million dollars playing the lottery. Lynda Harris was arrested for shoplifting.

Sasha Bullard receive a long overdue promotion to Chief of Detectives, which means she won't be on the street as much anymore, but will be working longer hours for not very much more money. She seemed happy about it, but with Sasha it's hard to tell. Martin Gimbal had bone cancer. He had been diagnosed a year earlier and had refused all medications except painkillers. He would not have lived long enough to retire.

Dusty and I haven't decided yet whether or not we'll be attending next year's festival, but we probably will just to show solidarity with the new regime. Daryl, incidentally, surprised everyone by having a will. He left everything to his housekeeper, who turned out to be a naturalized citizen after all. It is ironic that his only known act of generosity required that he die.

The big surprise was that Martin Gimbal also left a will, although his estate only amounted to about fifty thousand dollars. He drew it up himself on the morning of the day he died and had it witnessed by two of his co-workers. All of his worldly possessions are to be conveyed to Angela Bates "to recompense her for the discomfort she endured at my hands."

Angela promptly donated it to her favorite charity.

The End

Paul Birch and Dusty Rhodes will return soon.

www.ingramcontent.com/pod-product-compliance
Lightning Source LLC
Chambersburg PA
CBHW072051170626

46813CB00004B/1306